PAUL BOWN lived with his family in Asia for many years, where he worked as the Bursar of a theological college.

Since 2015, he has entertained and, on occasions, irritated his friends with fanciful stories of dragons, penguins and parrots. He has also self-published three short children's stories.

Treacherous Pursuit is his debut novel.

He lives in Somerset, UK, with his wife and one of his adult children.

TREACHEROUS PURSUIT

Treacherous Pursuit

ISBN: 978-1-7394896-0-1

Typesetting and cover design by The Book Typesetters
hello@thebooktypesetters.com
07422 598 168
www.thebooktypesetters.com

Cover photo by Usama Yasin, unsplash.com

TREACHEROUS PURSUIT

THE *INDUS* SERIES: BOOK ONE

PAUL C BOWN

Dedicated to my wife Kate,
a fellow-traveller in the journey of life…

and to friends in Pakistan,
for their exemplary hospitality, generosity
and compassion.

Dedicated to my wife Kate,
a fellow-traveller in the journey of life,

and to friends in Pakistan,
for their exemplary hospitality, generosity
and compassion.

Map of Pakistan

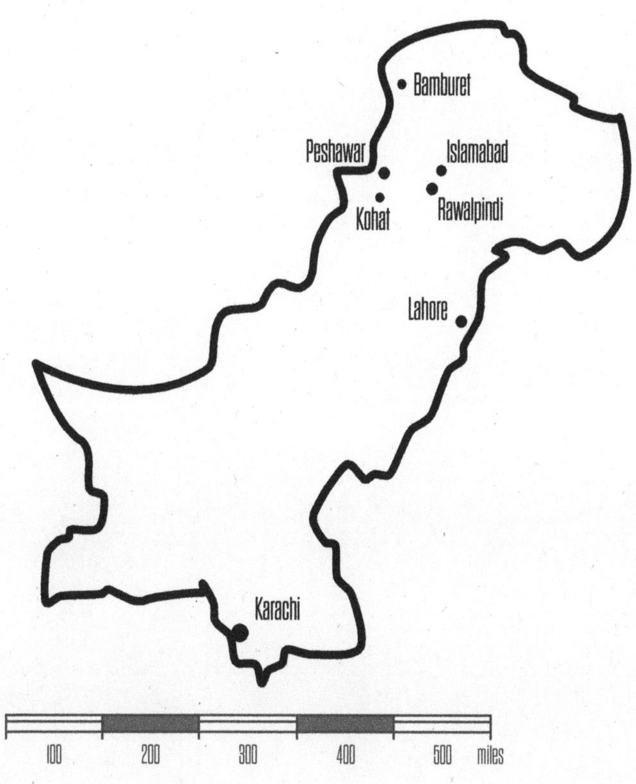

Chapter I

Steven

I exit through the double-plated glass doors of the airport arrival lounge and unbutton my light jacket as beads of perspiration pepper my chest. The kaleidoscope of fluorescent tubes and the cacophony of noise arising from frenetic activity all around me do little to ease a burning sensation above my right eye. I stop still with the onslaught and rub my eyelid to ease the pain. After a long flight, I have arrived in Pakistan – a country I couldn't care a damn about visiting.

'Taxi?' a scruffy man dressed in *shalwar-kameez* asks as he approaches me from behind my left-hand shoulder.

'No, my uncle should be here,' I mutter under my breath as I scan the dense crowd of passengers' relatives and friends waiting for arrivals.

I unashamedly stare at the man as he bustles forward to accost another newly arrived foreigner.

'Need help?' Another lanky fellow with teeth heavily

stained from chewing betel nut grasps the trolley with large, hairy hands and begins to push it.

'No, no help.' I wrestle back control of the trolley and push it in the opposite direction.

'Steven, good to see you.' Uncle Neil forces his way through the throng of greeters. 'How was the flight?'

'Yeah, OK-ish.'

'Good. My driver is waiting in the car over there.' Neil looks towards the huge concrete concourse of the Jinnah International Airport car park, searching for the vehicle. 'He should be here in a few moments.'

We start walking towards the 'pick-up' bays.

Neil grabs the trolley from me. 'I can push my own trolley,' I say, but Neil strides ahead, oblivious to my remonstration. I want to shout, 'leave off…' but relinquish the challenge. I have only just arrived.

I sink uneasily into the faux leather seat.

We emerge from the jostle of the airport complex to the asphalt jungle. Vehicles bear down from all directions in a crazed madness of blaring horns, screeching of tyres and swaying metal. Men hang from a metal cage of a bus like flies latching onto meat. A young motorcyclist with a long, shabby *kameez* leans over the handlebars, with a young girl perched on the petrol tank, and a woman sitting side-saddle as pillion, her *dupatta* wrapped around her lower face.

After a two-kilometre drive towards the city centre, we pull up at the lights. I hear shouting at the side of the road. There's a fracas. In the dim shadows, I make out a Honda Accord parked alongside the carriageway with a shabby, nondescript saloon sitting at seventy degrees in front, blocking any exit. There's a tall man standing at the kerb and two women remonstrating, one in floods of tears. Two young children, wailing in sympathy with their mother, are hiding behind the mother's legs. Three men are busy pulling luggage from the boot.

'What's going on there?'

'Oh, forget it,' Neil says. He squares his jaw and looks firmly ahead in the upper half of the windscreen.

'No, come on, tell me. There's something wrong, isn't there?'

Neil turns to me.

'We don't worry about such things… this is common here. Forget it. We can't help.'

'No, I won't "forget it". Pull over. Women and children are involved.'

'Now look here, Steven. You may be used to your superman community intervention in the UK but here we value pragmatism just to survive. No one gets involved – it's too dangerous. These men will have guns. We're driving on.'

The traffic lights turn from red to green, with amber hardly having a look-in.

Pervaiz engages first gear.

Suddenly, the wreck-like saloon screeches past our vehicle and swings in front. The nearside front passenger thrusts his arm through the window, signalling with a pistol for us to draw up at the side of the road.

I cringe at the string of expletives my uncle mutters.

Pervaiz glances helplessly at Neil – a startled, rabbit-caught-in-the-light look. I notice a slight tremble of the forehead. Neil points to the side of the highway and sinks back into his seat.

Quickly, I reach over the front seat to the steering wheel and press the palm of my sweaty hand on the horn. Pervaiz looks at me in a wondering sort of way. Neil tries to fight my hand off the wheel, but I bear down on the button with all my weight.

'What are you doing? You'll get us killed.'

Moments tick by as the horn blares incessantly like an alphorn beckoning a response from a distant valley. Instinctively, I bear down even harder, willing the decibels to increase.

The man who had signalled us to pull over gets out of the car. He begins a swagger towards us, aiming at me in the front of the car.

Suddenly, he looks over his shoulder towards the other side of the highway. He stuffs his gun in his pocket and runs back towards the vehicle, the engine of which is revving, spewing black smoke from the exhaust. The car speeds off before the passenger had time to close the door.

I look round to see a police pickup doing a U-turn around the traffic lights and accelerating madly in pursuit of the saloon, lights flashing in the dark.

I slump back into the seat, my heart pounding. Neil and Pervaiz sit still. The seconds tick by.

I open the car door and step out into the balmy night, the sky a clouded soup of fumes and dust. A plane is coming into land overhead, engines roaring, oblivious to the theatre below.

'Where are you going now?' my uncle asks.

‘To see if the others are OK.’

I do what I always do, get involved.

The woman who had been crying is now back in the car with the two children, all sitting in the back seat. The other woman is talking with the man at the side of the highway.

I approach the man. ‘Is anyone hurt?’

‘No,’ he replies, forcing a smile. ‘Just money, phones and laptops… gone.’

He takes out a cigarette and points the packet in my direction.

‘No thanks, I don’t smoke.’

‘*Sali* had a long flight from the States with the children.’ He speaks calmly, looking up the highway in the direction of the city, taking drags from the cigarette and blowing streams of blue smoke into the warm air.

‘She’s tired: She’ll be OK when she’s had a rest. These things happen. It’s awful to meet the men of the night on the roads.’

I stand there, not knowing what to say or do. I glance at the car in front of me. I see Neil’s frown in the nearside mirror.

The man eyes me.

‘You were lucky that the police were around. I thought you’d get shot. You have to play ball with these buggers.’

He finishes his smoking and throws the butt of the cigarette into the side of the road.

I sneeze. The air hangs heavy, not just from the carbon monoxide fumes of the diesel trucks, but from the encounter at the roadside.

We slow and swing into a small street, driving past two or three high tower blocks. We come to a ramp and drive into the subterranean car park. An attendant with henna-coloured hair and moustache opens the barrier.

Pervaiz jumps out and hurries to the boot, removing my luggage. I race off after Neil, who is striding towards the lift.

Neil's flat is on the third floor. He opens the outer grill door and the inner door to reveal a lavishly furnished lounge with a marble floor and tapestries hanging from the walls.

'Take a seat,' Neil says. I perch on a stool next to the dining table.

He leaves the room. I can hear the running of water in the bathroom and then activity in the kitchen. Neil returns with a glass and a bottle of whisky.

A Pakistani woman appears from the kitchen with a tray of two glasses and a bottle of cold water.

'Do you have paracetamol?' I ask.

'Hilda, get the paracetamol in the top left drawer, by the water filter.' Hilda leaves.

'Our house help,' Neil mumbles apologetically.

He sits down and pours himself a generous glass of spirit. He looks me in the eye as he swigs the fluid, his face clammy and the glass quivering in the light. He is a bull of a man; stocky with a square jowl and pitted face. The yellow nicotine stains on his hand betray his addiction. He must smoke outside – there's no smell lingering in the flat.

'Let's be clear. While you are here in my home, you won't do further heroics. What you did on the highway was stupid. You don't know how things work here. If you're not careful, you'll get yourself in deep trouble. I don't want to send a body back to your mother.'

I straighten up and meet his eye.

'I'll do what I need to do to get the samples I've come for. And to respond to need. You can't lecture me.'

Neil snorts and bangs down his glass on the coffee table, the bull waiting to charge. Pervaiz taps on the grill door. Neil rises to let him in and shows him to a room down the corridor that I suppose is to be my bedroom.

Neil returns, glowering as he looks down at me.

'You and I will have to come to an understanding. I have a responsible job here. I agreed to accommodate you on certain conditions. You will keep out of trouble, understand?'

I want to walk out there and then. But he's my uncle. I have nowhere else to stay. I don't walk out on people. Rules are rules.

I shift in the chair but can't relax. The incessant noise of traffic, horns blaring, Bollywood music wafting from one of the shops below, and the hum of the air conditioner bear down on me. The pressure around my temple increases. Then the tinnitus kicks in. A piercing, high-pitched whistle that threatens to overwhelm all auditory senses. The air conditioner hum retreats. I relive a childhood sensation of disconnection. I'm observing myself from vantage points – the corner of the room, the ceiling, the door.

Man, what next? My self-talk becomes blue and desperate. Frantically, I rehearse my coping techniques. Distraction, rational thinking, breathing. I press my knuckles into the side of my leg.

'I think I'll lie down.'

Neil, still flushed with anger, shows me to the bedroom.

I wake from the brief siesta. My head feels clearer. I lie on the bed gazing at the black marks on the ceiling fan blade.

I'm startled by a knock on the door.

'Hilda wants to clean the room,' Neil says.

'Fine,… wait a minute.' I pull my suitcase from under the bed, take out my passport and wallet, and then exit the room.

Neil is working at the dining table. He looks up as I sit down and momentarily stops his work.

'Tea?' 'Hilda can make it.'

'Yeah. Cheers.'

'We'll wait until she's finished in your room.'

I muse. Christmas last year. I was working late in the laboratory, up to Christmas Eve. The cleaners came in. I managed to disengage from work long enough to exchange Christmas greetings.

We broke off work to discuss Christmas hell-holes. The laughter became raucous. Kerry said that last year, such was the breakdown in domestic harmony by mid-afternoon Christmas Day, her son had chucked mince pies at her eldest after losing in the newly acquired Mario Carts game. Jacqui snorted. Christmas was not worth the experience. She refused to join the family and drank herself silly, sleeping the whole time. The best experience ever.

One of the cleaners was Asian. I had never spoken to her before. She piped up, cutting into our coarse irreverence by insisting that Christmas was a holy time for family worship and solidarity. The hilarity quietened. We listened. I could see Kerry smirking behind Parveen's back. But it was brave of her to confront our flippant disdain of the season.

Kerry and Jacqui went off to clean the other offices. Intrigued, I engaged with the Asian traditionalist. She confided in me about her background. A Pakistani Christian, she had many warm memories of the Christmas season. But now things had changed. Her city and community were caught in a cycle of violence.

I was concerned. I didn't know there were many Christians in Pakistan. We talked more. Her extended family was in trouble. Unemployment, illness and a run-in with the police. She and her husband were sending all disposable income to prop up their relatives in the homeland. Christmas would be bleak.

Parveen turned away. Her shoulders sagged as she lifted the vacuum cleaner. She swept back her long, dark hair. I couldn't help noticing the large gold earrings dancing in the fluorescent light. Her *dupatta* seemed an extraneous encumbrance – she would stop periodically to wrestle it back into position.

I considered Parveen's determined challenge to my carnal Christmas activities. I looked up from the computer as she started dusting.

'So, how do you celebrate Christmas in Pakistan?'

Parveen stopped and looked in my direction. Not so much at me, but through me, as though speaking to an audience behind.

'We buy new suit of clothing for all family. We go to

midnight mass and then the Christmas Day service. We cook for all family. They all come.'

Parveen looked away. I detected a nostalgic longing for the life that was in the distant past, but no longer.

'Oh.'

Words have the habit of failing me when I'm in unfamiliar territory.

I returned to my computer.

'Is work busy these days?'

Neil looks up. 'Yeah, pretty much. I'll go in shortly – on my own. You stay here.'

He continues with his work.

I pick up the Times magazine on the corner of the dining table and thumb through it.

'Hilda, *chai*,' Neil calls out, as Hilda exits my room, bucket and mop in hand.

'She understands English?'

'Yes, she's from the Christian area. She understands more than she speaks. You'll get used to her.'

Now that I had my uncle's attention, I continue.

'What arrangements have you made for my trip? You didn't mention much in the email.'

Neil looks away. 'I didn't have time to reply to your latest email. I was preparing for a meeting. Anyway, I thought it would be better to speak with you face-to-face.

'The trip isn't straightforward. We've booked the flight to Islamabad. That's the simple part. But it's the onward flight to Chitral that's the problem. They don't fly unless conditions are right. If there's low cloud, they ground the planes.

So, you could be stuck in Islamabad for several days. You could stay in a guest house there, but as you only have two weeks, it's touch-and-go whether you would have enough time to get to the clinic.'

'OK, but what about going by road? Are there other options?'

'Yes, there are, but it's a long, tiring trip by bus. And you don't know the language. Then there's the question of safety. There are frequent landslides and buses sometimes end up going over the edge of cliffs.'

'Smart!' I say.

'I'm trying to arrange for someone to accompany you who knows the lie of the land and can help with translation. Patras' nephew said he would go, but his father has been taken ill suddenly and is in hospital, so I need to check that he's still available. I'll check later this morning when I get into the office.'

'OK.'

'So tomorrow I suggest you have a look around the city. Take a taxi to the old Metropole and do the tourist thing...'

'And when's the flight to Islamabad booked?'

'This coming Thursday, the 5th.' It should give us some time to find a replacement if Patras' nephew isn't available.

'Meanwhile, make yourself at home. Watch the TV. It's cable. There are some reasonable channels – CNN, sport, some of the American soaps...'

'OK. Where's Claire?' I ask, as innocently as possible.

'She's at some kind of ladies' function connected with the Deputy British High Commission – a writing club, I think. She won't be back for a while yet.'

I get up from the table and collapse into a wicker chair, sinking near to the floor. It is lower than I expected. I rummage through the pile of magazines on the coffee table for something to take my mind off the earlier conflict. There's a local newspaper in English, dated yesterday. I'm interested in reading what makes front-page news. Suddenly there's a brilliant burst of light from the window. I glance across to the neighbouring block of flats. A man is hurriedly closing his window blinds, a pair of binoculars in his hand.

Chapter 2

I search for a further glimpse of the binocular-wielding snooper. He has disappeared behind the blinds. Glancing down at the alleyway between the two buildings, I see people coming and going as usual. I shiver.

'I'm off to the office now,' Neil says, standing by the grill door. 'If you need anything, ask Hilda. She'll be around until 3pm or so.'

'Have you got wifi here?'

Neil points to a black box by the phone. 'It's on the back of the router.' He turns abruptly and, grabbing his briefcase, leaves the flat. Hilda secures the door. She looks up at me and smiles timidly, then returns to the bathroom.

I go to my room. I press out the correct size of SIM card from the cardboard wallet on my bed and slot it into my phone, snapping the phone shut. No one in the UK has this number.

There's a particular person I don't want to hear from. Rachel.

I first met Rachel on a hot May afternoon. I was standing outside the Ashmolean Museum in Oxford to meet my brother, who was around for the day.

Suddenly a young woman who was chatting to an older friend near where I was standing fainted and collapsed on the pavement. I could see the companion panicking as she tried to revive her friend, shaking her vigorously and shouting at her. Curious pedestrians crowded around to gawk, whilst others crossed to the other side of Beaumont Street.

I walked over to the scene. 'Here, let's get her on her back,' I said, as I crouched close to the prone body. 'Give me your handbag to put under her head.'

The young woman's friend looked at me cautiously. Reluctantly, she passed the bag to me. As the two of us rolled the woman, I steadied her head and then looked closely at her condition. She wasn't fitting. Good. Her delicate mouth was slightly open, and her brown hair swept untidily across her petite but distinguished face. She wore a tiny hearing aid at the back of one ear.

'Does she have any medical condition – I mean, that you know of?'

'No, this is the first time I've known Rachel to faint,' she said. 'She seemed a bit lethargic this morning. I'm not sure she's been drinking enough water in this heat. I hope she's going to be all right.'

'Bring her feet up to raise her legs,' I said.

'What's happened?' Rachel opened her eyes and looked around. She felt her side.

'You fainted. This man helped me to get you comfortable.'

Rachel sat up with her head between her hands.

'How do you feel now?' I asked.

'A bit groggy, but OK, I suppose. My ribs hurt on my left side. Does anyone have water?'

I took the bottle of water from my rucksack and gave it to Rachel. She took several sips.

'Let me ask the Museum about a chair for you,' I said. I climbed the steps and entered the Museum foyer. A reception staff member found a wheelchair. I wheeled it out through the wide access door and down the slope to where Rachel was sitting. Rachel's friend helped her into the chair.

'It's probably helpful to find a soft drink,' I said. 'I don't have one myself.'

Just then, my brother Reuben arrived. He approached cautiously, a nervous tilt of the head as he interpreted the scene.

'Reuben, good to see you. Journey OK?'

'Yeah, long, the traffic was heavy.' He looked quizzically at the two ladies at my side.

'Rachel fainted, but she's OK now,' I said. 'You wouldn't have a soft drink on you?'

Reuben produced a bottle of Sprite from a Boots carrier bag. 'Sorry, it's not cold.'

'Are you going to be OK to get home?' I asked. 'Should I call a taxi?'

'We'll be OK,' Rachel answered. 'I'm feeling OK now, apart from this dull pain in the ribs. I can take a bus.'

'Thanks,' Rachel's friend said. 'Are you local?'

'Yeah, I work at one of the research laboratories at the Uni.'

'Oh, I'm in a laboratory also,' Rachel said. 'Third year MSc Bio-Chemistry by research. I don't think I've seen you there.'

'We probably don't keep the same hours,' I said. 'I don't socialise very much outside of my particular area.'

'Well, thanks again. What's your name, just in case I do bump into you again?'

'Steven'.

Reuben and I watched the two ladies walk away. 'Do you want to look around the Museum first?' I asked.

Reuben seemed unusually quiet and withdrawn. I knew he was floundering in a relationship, but wasn't aware of any recent developments. His poor mental health and emotional difficulties were ongoing. From early childhood, he had struggled with low self-esteem and depression. After graduating from Bath University, he had found it difficult to get a job. The last I knew, he was working as an IT support staff member at a firm of architects, but I had seen from his social media posts that he was bored with the work. Then he had met Sandra. His posts were all about the fun time they were having and the future they were building together. It seemed Reuben and Sandra were spending money big time – an expensive engagement ring, a holiday in the Caribbean, a deposit on a flat. But something must have gone wrong as more recent posts were far more subdued. I picked up that there were tensions in the relationship. Sandra had moved out. Reuben was finding it difficult to keep up with the mortgage payments on the flat and had gone to Uncle Neil and Claire for emotional and financial support. He had been disappointed.

'How's work going?' I asked. Reuben was unusually silent.

'It's not what I expected. A lot of trouble-shooting to keep old devices and software running, when management should be investing in upgrades. My department head had a run-in with one of the senior managers. Since then, the atmosphere's been heavy. I used to enjoy the work, but now it's a bind. I'm looking for another job.'

We rounded the corner and entered the Money Gallery. 'Are you still in the flat?' I asked.

Reuben's face darkened. 'I'm just about managing the payments, but Sandra has demanded her share of the deposit back. Damn the girl… I thought we could work something out, but she's adamant. What am I supposed to do? How can I get that sort of money? I'll have to sell and then I'll be back to renting.'

Reuben looked enquiringly at me. But there was nothing I could offer. I wasn't in a position to put up the money for Sandra's share of the deposit.

'Is there anyone who could help?' I knew Reuben had a very restricted social circle of friends. He wouldn't listen to me as his brother – he never would.

We moved into the 'The Hans and Märit Rausing Gallery'.

'It's all right for you,' Reuben said. He stood to the side of the gallery, staring at me mournfully. 'You've got a career. You've got your own flat.'

'Self-funded research isn't much of a career. But I know where I'm heading. Why not spend some time with Mother? Get away to think. Meet some new friends. Things may seem different if you can step out of the pressure for a while.'

'It all takes money. We're under pressure at work. They've trimmed down the IT support staff. It was difficult to get today off to come to see you. I won't be popular if I take any more time off before the summer.'

I could see that Reuben's interest in the Museum artefacts was waning. We made our way to the café. He slumped into the soft bench seat adjacent to the serving area while I bought the coffee. I glanced over at him while queuing. He was hunched over, his head between his hands. I didn't know how to help. I only hoped he would not do anything stupid.

A few weeks later, on a Friday evening, I went to the Turf to enjoy a pint. Michael was leaving the department and had invited friends for a farewell drink. Students crammed all available space. I could tell from the raucous laughter that many were in high spirits. I was struggling to hear Michael as we chatted. He had a quiet voice and mumbled.

A young woman passed by and almost stumbled into my lap. Her glassy eyes looked through me as she struggled to regain her balance. She smiled, her head swaying slightly. Taking off her high heel shoes, she stumbled on a few metres.

Then she curled and vomited.

I whisked a paper napkin from the table and desperately covered my mouth and nose as the stench wafted in my direction. My senses span in a vortex of disgust and horror, igniting a vivid scene from two years past.

The images were still distinct: Reuben, shouting in the distance as I ran to the high barred gate at the back of the pub. His soiled trousers and untucked shirt; his arms steadying his limp body against the wall of the damp alleyway, and his vile cursing, while two men rifled through his clothing for his valuables. I hollered as I bore down on the men. They stopped and straightened. One stumbled. The other picked up a glass lying in the gutter, broke it and leered at me with his bloodshot eyes, challenging me to approach. I slowed. Reuben looked at me helplessly, like a schoolboy caught with his trousers down. The adrenalin peaked. I charged at the men, knocking the glass-brandishing arm so forcefully that the man swung around and collapsed in a heap. Then I lay into both of them. As suspected, they were both drunk. They hit back, but I was getting the better of them, dodging most of their blows. I eased off when a member of the door staff entered the alleyway. I shouted through my bloodied lip. The men ran off.

Reuben was snivelling. I wrestled control of my shaking body to lift him to his feet and support him to the car. His wallet had gone. I hated his naivety and his predisposition to attract profligates as friends.

'It's Steven, isn't it?' I looked up. Rachel smiled. She looked at the woman, who was now staggering towards her group of friends. She was standing up-wind of the vomit.

'Yeah. Great to see you again. How are things going?'

'Fine.' Rachel reddened.

'Are you with friends?' I asked.

'They've left. It's become busy in here. I was on my way out and then I noticed you here.'

'Rachel, this is Michael,' I said.

'Hi,' Michael said. 'There's no point in long introductions as I'm leaving this fair city. I've been looking at new treatments for Duchenne muscular dystrophy, but I've finished my work. I have an offer of another research post in London.' Michael took a sip from his beer glass. He placed the glass on the table and lounged back into the chair. 'This is my favourite pub. I've spent many an hour here during my time in Oxford. It's a hidden gem.'

Rachel nodded. I could tell from the taut facial muscles that she didn't catch all that Michael had said. I remembered the hearing aid I had seen behind her left ear.

'Why not move outside to the quieter tables? 'We could talk more there.'

Rachel hesitated. 'I was on my way home. I don't want to break up your conversation.'

At that point, Rick arrived with his drink and greeting Michael, sat at the table. Rachel stood rooted to her spot.

'I'll leave you to catch up with Rick,' I said. I left the table and beckoned Rachel to follow me outside to the enclosed garden area.

I took a deep breath of the sultry air and found two chairs. Rachel sat and looked at me awkwardly.

'Sorry, I should have asked you if you wanted a drink while we were inside.'

'No, I've had enough to drink tonight,' she said in a thin voice. She fumbled with her hands, drawing her right hand down her left arm as she momentarily shivered.

'Are you OK?'

'Actually, no.' Rachel shifted position in her chair and moved closer to me.

'I have a jilted boyfriend here,' she whispered. 'He's over there, checking on us.' She directed my gaze with a point of her chin to a young man sitting at a table across the paved area. 'We fell out several weeks ago. It was messy. He was becoming very possessive and unreasonable. Since then, he's been stalking me and calling out threats. I didn't notice him when I arrived earlier with friends, but when they left and I tried to leave, he followed and grabbed me. That's a bit much, init? I fought him off and ran back to the pub. So, I'm here, wondering what to do and how I'll get home safely. It's a bit silly.'

Rachel looked despairingly at me. Tears glistened in her eyes.

I looked away, sat back in my chair, and pondered. Was this true? Or did Rachel merely want me to walk her home?

'So would you like me to walk you home?'

'Yeah,' Rachel said, in a quiet voice.

'OK, I've just about finished here anyway,' I said. 'Let's go back to the bar so that I can tell Michael I'm leaving.'

We got up and returned to the lower bar area. I found Michael and Rick and told them I was walking Rachel home. Rachel looked away, embarrassed. Michael and Rick smiled.

We left from the front entrance, through St Helens Passage to New College Lane. The young man came after us. As he drew near, I turned around, my body tensing for a fight. He was a few centimetres below my height, of moderate build. He looked a decent fellow with a sallow complexion. He staggered towards us with an unnatural gait.

'What d'*ya* do with my girl? She's mine. You're stealing her… taking her away. I won't have it.' His voice reverberated off the low arch of the building.

'Robin, you know that it's over,' Rachel said quietly. 'We've talked it through. We agreed that it's not working. Why are you hassling me?'

'You won't listen,' Robin called out. 'Listen to me. We need to talk again. It's not over. What the…?' Robin cursed and spat on the ground in front of him.

'I'm taking Rachel home. Rachel's made her own decision. She has the right to be left alone. You're upset, but you need to respect that right. OK? Otherwise, we'll call the police.'

'So, you're going home with your new lover-boy, are you? Robin called out. 'Best of luck to you…'

I turned and put my arm around Rachel. She looked at me in surprise. I marched her off with onlookers smarting at the coarse language Robin was using as he continued to rant and rave. After we arrived at the bus stop on Catte Street, we turned to see Robin lurching back in the direction of the pub.

'Are you OK?'

'O what… oh yeah.' I knew it was going to be

unpleasant.' Rachel paused. 'Thanks for doing this. I'm taking liberties, but when you came to my rescue outside the Museum, I knew I could trust you.

'Robin's not that bad, really,' she said. 'He's just very upset. I'm also cut up about it. But I'm moving on – he doesn't want to. It's not as though there was anything physical…'

'Well, there have to be boundaries. Is he also a student at Uni?'

'Yes, in his first year. I think he's found life difficult.'

'So, which way is home?' I drew a deep breath as I looked out onto the street.

'My home or your home?' Rachel answered mischievously.

'You know where we're going.' A smile crept over my face. 'As soon as we arrive at your flat, I'll leave you to hit the sack and sleep this off.'

Rachel reached out and caught my hand. 'It's not too late,' she said. 'The bus should be here soon.'

She leaned gently against the bus stop pole and looked at me, her eyes twinkling in the rays of the setting sun. A gentle warmth pulsated through me. I was intrigued by this young woman. She exuded a child-like simplicity, weakness and vulnerability but inner strength at the same time. I was determined to get to know her more.

I spent much time with Rachel over the next few weeks. We met at the side of Hereford College at Folly Bridge. Our favourite activity was an evening walk along the canal. We would set out down the track towards Sandford Lock, at a relaxed pace, pausing to remark on the architecture and the wildlife we came across. I discovered that Rachel was an expert on wildfowl and would point out any unusual species on the water. I pointed out the cruiser I would buy if I had the money, and described the European ports I would visit. In jest, Rachel chided me for coveting. I feigned repentance.

I told Rachel as little as possible about the content of the research. She knew better than to pry. In turn, I asked only general questions about her research and let her fill me in on the details as she felt comfortable.

One evening we met at the usual rendezvous and set out, Rachel's shoulder-length hair blowing gently in the breeze as we ambled along the water's edge. I held out my hand for Rachel to grasp. Our relationship had developed over the three or four weeks we had been seeing each other. We had not defined this development – it had been organic, a result of sharing our life stories, passions and hopes for the future. We were both taking our time to see where the relationship would take us, treading slowly and carefully, enjoying the present and holding onto the future lightly.

We sat on a bench, and I reached into my rucksack for the chilled beer and plastic glasses. I put my arm around Rachel's shoulder as I poured the beer. She glanced at me pensively.

'There's something wrong, isn't there?'

'What do you mean?'

'You're not as relaxed as usual. I could tell as soon as we met. You're preoccupied with something.'

'Well, it's a family matter... it's not a big deal,' I said. I turned and looked in the direction of the city.

‘Family is a big deal. I worry about my siblings sometimes. What’s up?’

‘Nothing. It’s not worth discussing.’

Rachel moved away from me, dumping my arm on the bench. She turned and glared.

‘Where is our relationship going if you aren’t going to share family news with me? Am I some passerby? Don’t you think that I care for those in your life? What do you take me for?’

‘I didn’t think you would want to know, that’s all. There’s nothing you can do about it. It’s a difficult situation.’

‘Well, at least give me the dignity to try,’ Rachel said, standing and facing me. ‘Don’t bottle it all up. Trust me.’

‘But why now? Why can’t we talk about it later?’

‘Because you’re making me upset with stupid excuses not to share. You don’t trust me,’ Rachel shouted.

I looked around. People were looking in our direction.

‘That’s not fair – I do trust you. But sometimes people don’t want to share.’

‘You’re hiding something from me. That’s a lack of trust. Why don’t you trust me?’

‘I do trust you,’ I shouted. But it’s an intensely personal issue. Why are you so interested in my family? It’s none of your business.’

‘What do you mean, “None of your business”? Am I some kind of call girl you hire for pleasure? A tart you take out and pay off at the end of the night? Is that the sum of our relationship, Mr Grant? If it is, you can stuff it…’

Rachel threw the remains of her beer into my face and marched off in the direction of the city.

I stood, shaking with anger. Why were women so unreasonable? Why did they make things so difficult? Why did they always want things on their own terms?

The next evening, I stood outside the laboratory block on South Parks Road where Rachel was working. I knew the hours she spent at the laboratory and planned to catch her as she exited. The previous evening's fracas on top of the difficult family news had left me numb.

I waited for half an hour, but Rachel didn't appear. I avoided entering the building, the 'hallowed ground' of her research arena. Whether Rachel was watching for me or not I didn't find out, but after an hour she opened the door and strode off across the courtyard, scowling when she caught sight of me.

I set off in pursuit and caught up with her when we arrived outside the university complex.

'Can we talk about our misunderstanding last night?' I called out, racing to keep up with her. Rachel ignored me and kept on walking towards the bus stop.

'Look, I'm sorry. I was insensitive yesterday. I was hurting and didn't want to share. I realise it was a problem, that you saw my not wanting to share as mistrust. But it really wasn't. I'm just not good at sharing very personal things about my family.'

We had reached the bus stop. I saw Rachel's bus coming down the street. She turned to me, indecisive.

'OK, we'll talk about this. Come with me on the bus. We'll have coffee in my flat.'

On the bus, Rachel looked out of the window with a grim expression. 'We're not talking here,' she whispered, 'not after the commotion you caused yesterday.'

'Look, I'm sorry for any embarrassment yesterday, but even lovers have tiffs, sometimes in public.'

Rachel's eyes widened: her facial muscles suddenly relaxed. She swivelled round on the padded bus seat.

'You've never used that word before. Is that how you see our relationship?'

I forced a smile. 'Well, we have grown close over the weeks. I hated myself last night for upsetting you. You're very special to me…' I choked the words out.

Rachel moved closer to me and reached out her hand. I took it and looked up at her angelic face. The dimples in her cheeks deepened with her broad smile.

At the flat, I settled onto the sofa in the sitting room while Rachel fussed in the kitchen. I had been to her flat on a few occasions. It was untidy. On a previous visit when I had stolen a glance into her bedroom (she was in the garden at the time), I saw clothes on the floor, the bed un-made and books strewn across the bed. The bathroom was tidier, but the kitchen was a mess. A half-cut loaf of bread on the breadboard, jars of spices and chutneys on the worktop, and unwashed dishes on the draining board, haphazardly stacked together. The cooker looked reasonably clean. Glancing around the sitting room, I saw magazines dropped at the side of the chairs, and a watermark on the glass coffee table-top, presumably from an overfilled drinking glass.

Rachel came in with the drinks and biscuits on a tray. She looked at me intently.

'Yesterday I received news that my brother, Reuben, the one who was there when you fainted, had been admitted to a psychiatric hospital.'

'Oh, I'm sorry,' Rachel said. She sat straight.

'He and his girlfriend had split up. That hit him badly. They had been living together in a house they were sharing. She demanded the return of the money she had put into the deposit. He had to sell the house. His work wasn't going anywhere. It all got to him as one evening a party-goer found him in a disused shop doorway, drunk, with one of his wrists slashed. They rushed him to hospital and stemmed the bleeding before he bled to death. But he was in a bad way emotionally. He's been sectioned.

'Then, on top of this, I received a letter the day before yesterday. It was an anonymous threat to do with the research I'm doing. It said that there would be serious consequences if I carried on with it.'

'Why such a determined threat? What is it about this research?

'I've already told you. The effect of a rogue chemical compound on DNA. You know that I can't share in detail. But I'm also curious that someone would write a letter. It's probably someone who thinks their personal interests would be affected – shares in the food packaging industry or something.'

Rachel sat in stunned silence. She looked confused and anxious.

'Have you shown the letter to the police?'

'I showed it to my research supervisor. He was undecided whether to take it to the police or not. I need to find out what's happened with this. He's probably shown it to the vice-chancellor. He said he didn't want to go to the police this early, but if I receive any more letters, he'll take it further.'

'Steven, you need to be careful, particularly when you are off the university premises. Is your flat secure?'

'Secure in what way? I have a good lock on the front door and it's on the third floor, so it would be difficult for anyone to get through a window. But I'm not going to pussyfoot around just because someone is threatened by the research I'm doing. I've got a life to live.

'You can see why with the letter and with the news about my brother, I was less than relaxed last night.'

'Yeah, but you could have told me these things last night,' Rachel said. 'Then we could have been spared the argument. Anyway, that's water under the bridge.'

'Will Reuben be OK?' Rachel asked.

'Mother visits regularly. I need to visit when I can. He's having counselling. I think he's on medical leave from work, so he still has work he could return to. My uncle Neil may help bridge the gap with a loan for advance rent on a flat. He refused before, but no doubt he would reconsider in the circumstances.

'Obviously, we can't do anything about the emotional fallout from the breakup with his girlfriend. He has to work through this. If he got his life together, he could be quite eligible. Only he's suffered from depression since early childhood. I think he's been on medication. Perhaps they will need to increase the dose once his condition stabilises.'

'Oh, I'm so sorry, Steven,' Rachel said. She then leaned forward and gave me a peck on the cheek.

'So, is all forgiven?'

'Yeah, but keep me informed about these things. I care about you – and your family.'

I put my arm around Rachel and we cuddled.

The telephone rang. While Rachel was answering it, I took the opportunity to look at the time.

'Sorry about that,' Rachel said, returning to the sofa from the hallway. It was the leader of the book club I belong to.'

'I remember your saying that you're into books. What's your favourite genre?'

'Historical fiction. I love to enjoy a good plot and improve my knowledge of history at the same time.'

'Well, I need to be getting back to my pad. I have a call with some Uni friends. We connect once a month or so to catch up with news.'

'Will I see you tomorrow night after work?' Rachel asked, a twinkle in her eyes.

'Yeah, but that will be the last evening for a few weeks. I have to go to Australia in connection with my research and will be stopping off in Pakistan on the way. My uncle has repeatedly asked me to visit, and there's the opportunity to get samples from a remote tribal group. It's all been cleared with my department. They've worked on connections with local clinics to get the samples, but I want to be there to find out more about the tribal groups and make sure the work is done properly.'

Rachel momentarily froze. She turned and walked

towards the window, standing with her back to me.

'Have I said anything wrong?'

'Why the heck didn't you tell me you were going away? Again, you've kept this back from me. Why? Why don't you tell me what's going on?' She turned to face me.

'I have told you, just now. What am I supposed to do? Share my diary with you? This is a work trip. I'll only be gone for two to three weeks.'

'How can you still go after receiving that letter?'

'What letter?' I asked.

'You know, that threatening letter. Surely the university won't allow you to go to such a volatile country as Pakistan after you've received that threat? Someone could be waiting for you there. It would be easy to silence you. I've heard about the law-and-order situation. It's not safe. Why can't someone else get the samples?'

I stood there, bemused at Rachel's reasoning. It had not occurred to me that I would be vulnerable in Pakistan.

'OK. Yeah, others could get the samples. But I really want to meet the tribal people. Then there's the longstanding invitation from my uncle. It's a great opportunity. I really don't think there's any danger. My department head and others in responsibility obviously do not give the letter too much credence, certainly not enough to dissuade me from international travel. As of this afternoon, the trip was on, with their blessing.'

'But you can't go,' Rachel said. 'I would be too worried about you.' She sat on the sofa and stared at me, challenging me to give a satisfactory reply.

'Look, I'm sorry this has upset you. But this is a work

trip. I want to be there to oversee the sample collection. I need to ensure that standard procedures are followed. I can't just abandon the trip because my girlfriend has some kind of anxiety problem about my being overseas.'

'So that's it, is it? You go, leaving me worrying about you for the duration you're away?'

'OK, Rachel, I'll do this. Tomorrow, I'll talk with my supervisor again. I'll tell him that someone thinks this could be dangerous. He and I will talk about it. If we reconsider you will be the first to know.'

'Go,' Rachel said, tears forming in her eyes. 'You've upset me again this evening. Earlier I thought we had sussed things out…'

I gently walked to the front door, turned to look at Rachel, and then closed the door behind me. Talk about a claustrophobic relationship...

I did mention this concern of a close friend to my supervisor. He agreed with me that there was no evidence of increased threat while travelling to Pakistan or Australia. He asked me to make the final decision. I did. The trip was on.

CHAPTER 3

Later that afternoon, Claire returns to the flat.

'Oh, you've arrived then,' she says, finding me still in the lounge. 'Good flight, was it?'

'Not too bad. There was a small child that wouldn't settle during the night, but apart from that I managed to get some rest.'

Claire heads off for a drink and then emerges from the kitchen. 'Has Neil explained where everything is?' She pours herself a glass of cold water and gulps it down.

'Yes, the bathroom, the room I'm using.'

'I hope he told you that the kitchen is off-limits,' Claire says, screwing her nose as she speaks. 'If you need a drink, ask Hilda. We'll make sure you have enough water. There's no other reason for you to go into the kitchen.'

'I think I'll take a stroll in the *bazaar*,' I say.

'Hilda, close the door behind Steven.'

The heat and humidity are worse than when I first

arrived. The musty smell of decaying animal matter is overpowering. I was recently reminded in the lab that minute particles of all substances we smell lodge in the nasal passage. I dismiss the thought quickly. Concentrate on something else, Steven. It's not going to kill you.

When I reach the stairwell, there is a slight breeze. I look through the gaps in the concrete walls over the city. It is noisy and chaotic, but colourful and vibrant. There are people everywhere: In cars, on motorbikes, walking, hanging out of the buses, and talking or arguing with each other on the street or in shop doorways.

I don't have any Pakistani rupees, so I walk, observe, and browse shops. I also listen carefully to the rhythm and intonation of the speech. I read about the Urdu language before leaving the UK and am confident that I can begin to communicate in the several days I'm in the country. I come across a travel agent with the green and white advertisement of Pakistan International Airlines in the window. I enter the shop.

'*Asalam-a-lequm.*'

The man sitting behind the wooden desk smiles, returning the greeting. He has thick, greasy hair, a flabby face, and is chewing betel nut. A thin bead of red drool forms a rivulet down his chin, splaying into the stubble and hair. He chases the back of his right hand across his face, leaving red smears. He appears not to care.

'I'd like to visit Chitral. When are there flights from Islamabad?'

'When do you plan travel?'

'I'll be in Islamabad on the 5th, this coming Thursday.'

He sits down behind the computer monitor. 'They only fly Fridays,' he says. 'There are seats available on Friday. Do you want to book now?'

'When does the flight leave Islamabad?'

'11:00 hrs.'

I shift the weight on my feet. The palms of my hands moisten. I stare at the travel agent. What's Neil playing at? Why hasn't he booked this flight?

'Sorry, no money,' I say. 'I'll get some money and come back.'

The man gives a toss of his head as he relaxes back into his chair. He looks at me quizzically. I leave the shop, striding back to the flat.

Neil returns at around 6:30pm. He nods to me as he passes through the lounge and heads for the kitchen, where I hear him pouring a drink. After twenty minutes, he sits down in a wicker chair opposite me.

'I took a walk around the block,' I say. 'I need to get some local currency.'

'Yeah, if you go to the city centre tomorrow, there are plenty of money changers.' Neil is distracted as he thumbs his way through Newsweek.

'There are flights from Islamabad to Chitral on Friday,' I say.

Neil looks up. His eyes narrow.

'I went to a travel agent. He said that there are seats on the flight. Why haven't you booked me a seat? We exchanged emails about this before I came. I have a limited window of time here in this country – you know that I'm flying to Australia and have to be back in the UK by the end of the month…'

Neil puts down the magazine and glares. 'Wait a minute. Before the accusations start flying. I couldn't find someone to accompany you, what with Patras' nephew being unavailable. I delayed for your sake. It seems you don't trust my judgement.'

'I'm a grown man. I don't need to be "accompanied". This is my work, my research. I have to get on that flight. If you won't book it then I will.'

Neil eyeballs me. 'This is Pakistan. Travelling into the northern areas is dangerous. You go at your own risk, young man. Anyway, why can't the local doctor at the clinic up there do the work for you? He will be getting the samples. Why do you need to go?'

I stand, a nerve twinging in my leg and shooting dull pain to my right foot. 'We've been through this in our emails. Why go over it again? I said in my emails that I need to supervise. I need to make sure that the samples are genuine. Haven't you read my emails?'

Claire comes into the lounge and raises an eyebrow. She sits primly at the chair by the table and announces the evening meal.

I join Neil in laying the table from the cutlery drawer opposite the table. He glowers at me.

'Chicken korma tonight,' Claire says. She places the dish on the table and goes to the kitchen to bring the rice. 'I hope you like curries, otherwise you're going to find it difficult here.'

We start the meal. My taste buds sent appreciative

signals to the brain. Boy, I'm hungry.

'Does Hilda cook most of the time?'

'Yes, I never seem to get the time,' Claire says. 'I have too much to do at the Deputy High Commission.'

We eat the meal in relative silence. Claire tells us about her time with the creative writing group. They meet every two weeks. Most work on poetry. A few write short stories. One or two journal. It is one of the high points for the women during the fortnight. Few venture out of their air conditioned flats, certainly not during the daytime.

'When you go to the city centre, you can call into my office,' Neil says. 'There's a good view of the city from my window.' He gets up from the dining table and makes his way towards the wicker chairs.

I take a taxi to the city centre. I have avoided the rush hour, but the traffic is still chaotic. Car horns blare as we make our way along the Shahrah-e-Faisal. The taxi driver drops me by the shell of the old Metropole Hotel building. I pull out the notes and coins Neil has lent me and pay the driver.

The taxi pulls away with a black belch of smoke from the old diesel engine. My priority is to find a money changer. On my uncle's advice, I have brought cash from the UK.

I enter 'Glaxy Exchange'. An electronic chime sounds in the background. The sweet scent of incense sticks burning on the counter evokes memories of a visit to an Asian university student friend at his home in Southall.

The security guard glances in my direction, his face remaining grim. He's clad in what looks like a blue boiler suit with a motif, 'M&I Security', sewn onto the front. A holster with a pistol hangs loosely from the belt on his hips. I'm reminded that I'm in unfamiliar territory.

On the wall at the end of the shop is an electronic screen displaying current rates against the major hard currencies. The digits beyond the decimal point flicker and change every few minutes. One display of digits against the Bahraini dinar has fused.

I step up to the woman assistant at the counter.

'I'd like to buy Pakistani rupees.' I push £100 in £20 notes towards her. The assistant takes the notes and begins counting. She reads out from the computer screen. '21,987 rupees.' She hands me a printed receipt and then gestures with a flick of the head that I am to take a seat while my notes are checked and the money counted out.

The padded bench that runs along the side of the shop, opposite the counter, gives a good view of the bustling street outside. I look closely at a man standing outside the leather garment shop adjacent to the money changer. He resembles a tall, bearded man who tracked me with his piercing eyes at the airport when I first arrived. He is fumbling with a leather jacket – with no obvious intention to buy, looking in the direction of the shop. I look away.

A number pops up on the LCD screen suspended from the ceiling. I check my receipt and walk back to the counter. The woman takes my receipt and shoves a wad of notes through the small glass window. I count the cash. It all looks OK. Some of the notes have seen better days and one has a small amount of Sellotape on the corner, but I guess it will pass.

I make my way towards the door and am just halfway

through when *bang, bang*. I see a motorcyclist with a pillion rider pull away quickly and a man writhing on the pavement. Someone has been shot.

I spring back into the shop. The security guard activates the metal security grill. It lowers to within fifteen centimetres of the floor. The shop grows much darker, lit only by the flickering fluorescent tube lights on the walls. The women assistants sit patiently behind the counter and begin to chat with each other. The other customers strain to look through the grill to see what was happening.

'A foreigner... shot,' a man says to me. 'He exchanged money here.' He turns his face back to the grill.

The police arrive.

'How serious?' I ask.

The man watches as the police haul the victim to his feet.

'Not bad. They shot him in the leg. He... bleeding badly.'

I move towards the grill to see if I recognise the man, but only get a glimpse. A crowd has gathered, and the police are waving their rifles to disburse the spectators. After a few minutes, an Edhi Ambulance arrives. The man is supported by two men into the back of the vehicle.

The ambulance drives off with its sirens blaring. The security guard moves forward to raise the grill and one by one, we leave the shop.

I shudder: What if I was the target, but someone mistakenly attacked the other foreigner after having used the same money changer? I look carefully up and down the street before leaving the relative safety of the shop precinct and walk briskly in the direction of N.T. Enterprises (Pvt) Ltd on

Abdullah Haroon Road, the complex where Neil's office is located.

The steps up to the first floor of the building are dark and unwelcoming. I walk hesitatingly, stumbling on one of the steps. Have I drunk enough fluids? I really must get more water on the go. Why didn't I bring a water bottle? I think of Rachel when I first came across her prone body on the hot day in Oxford. The humiliation of fainting. Avoid at all costs.

'I've come to see Neil Grant,' I say to the receptionist. She smiles at me, asks me to take a seat, and uses the intercom. Within a few minutes, Neil appears, grinning and looking pleased with himself.

'So, you exchanged the pounds for rupees?'

'Yes, but one customer was not so lucky.' I tell Neil about the man who was shot. The receptionist stops her work and looks up.

'Get on with your work, Shazia,' Neil says, glaring at the woman.

Neil shows me into his office and, with a flourish of his hand, indicates a chair by his desk. It is a monster piece of mahogany brown furniture in a medium-sized room, like a bear in a small cave. I can tell by running my eye over the lip that it is veneer over MDF. The smell of the new polyester carpet that I later learn was laid the previous week, reminds me of new builds in the UK.

'You get a good view of the city from the window,' Neil says, lowering himself into his faux leather swivel seat. 'I enjoy the cityscape.'

'Would you like some tea or anything?'

'Water would be appreciated.'

Neil gets onto the intercom and orders Shazia to bring in water and then later, a cup of tea.

'I have some business to discuss with you,' Neil says.

I'm all ears. 'Business?'

'Yeah. I've wanted to discuss this with you for a long time, but when you emailed me to say that you were visiting, I thought it best to wait until you were here in person.'

Shazia knocks on the door and walks in with a tray of cold water and glasses. She places them on the desk near me and hurries out.

Neil takes off his spectacles and picks up a pen to fidget with.

'Look, I want you to work for me here. Business is expanding. I need more help. I know your experience isn't in logistic software design, but I need help with marketing and public relations. I could hire a local, but a foreigner makes a better impression here.'

Neil gets up and walks to the window.

'I can make you rich in a relatively short period. You can have your own flat and driver. Sure, there's no nightlife here to speak of, but from what I know about you, that's not important. I can get you a subscription to the Marriot Hotel leisure facilities. It would be a far better use of your time than sitting behind a desk at that university. What d'you say?'

'How do you have the gall to speak to me like that? The research I'm doing at Oxford is significant. I would rather oversee a hundred research projects than stay here and work for your company. And as for staying in this city – not on your life. When I've collected the samples, I'll be off.'

'You're a cock-sure bastard,' Neil says, walking back to his desk. He sits down and leans over the brown expanse, thrusting his bull-like head and shoulders forward to face me off. 'I've made an offer to you as I want you to have a future. You're wasting your time. You don't have friends or family in Oxford. At least you would be with members of the family here.'

'You have no idea about the friends I may or may not have in Oxford,' I say. 'It's my life, and I will choose what friends I have and where. As for family, Mum is only a train ride away from Oxford. I don't have close family here.'

'You're making a mistake,' Neil says, pointing a finger at me. 'You don't fully know the family situation.'

Neil sits back in his chair and leers at me, his bloodshot eyes adding further menace to his contempt.

'What on earth do you mean… I don't fully know the family situation? I know all that there is to know.' Neil cocks his head to challenge the veracity of that statement.

'You can leave now,' Neil says, pointing towards the door. 'We'll talk more about this some other time.'

'I don't know what you are alluding to, but I'm not interested,' I say, standing up from the chair. 'I know what I'm doing.'

'Do you, now?'

I leave the office in a hurry before the surge of anger gets the better of me and slam the office door behind me. Shazia looks up with concern. I ignore her and am out of the office building in a moment, racing down the steps.

What a prig. As if anyone would want to join him and Clare in their self-made, colonialist-rendered worlds. What card is he playing about the family? Is he bluffing? Or what?

I lie in bed processing the events of the day. I examine and play over in my mind my response to Neil's offer in the office. Neil was making a generous offer, in his own eyes at least. I shouldn't have overreacted. Typical Steven arrogant outburst. It gets you nowhere. You loser.

I turn over in the bed and shake off my self-doubt, as though a change in posture could rid me of this insidious vice. I relive Neil's retort in the office, round and round in my head, and kick off the covering sheet as my heart rate increases and my skin becomes clammy. My anxious thoughts latch onto the next bogey-man: What does he mean by a 'family situation' I know nothing of? Despite internal brainstorming, I'm left with a blank. Damn.

I'm drifting into sleep when images of the Glaxy Exchange attack victim etched deep in my mind, begin to surface. I wake with the vividness of the scene: The man's face, twisted in agony; the police, appearing to help but reluctant to mess up with a foreigner; the crowds, eager to see an entertaining spectacle. I sit up as I rehearse the 'what if it was meant for me?' question. The letter at the university and now this. Coincidence? Or a sustained attempt to put me out of action? I can't decide. I get up and sit on the edge of the bed. After thirty minutes, I'm back under the sheet. I look at the cheap alarm clock. I fall into a deep slumber sometime after midnight.

Sunday arrives. It seems like any other day. The incessant background rumble from the highway and sounding of the car and bus horns continue to penetrate through the single-glazed windows.

'We're off to church this morning,' Neil says over breakfast. 'You're welcome to come. You may meet some interesting folks there. There's quite a gathering.'

Claire looks up from her tea and smiles innocently.

Why do they go to church? Is it part of the illusion? Hypocrisy to the nth degree. How can they not see it? Why don't they squirm?

'Sorry, that's not my scene,' I reply. 'I'm surprised it's yours…'

'Take it or leave it. Pervaiz is coming at 10:30am.'

By the time Pervaiz arrives, I have changed my mind. I am getting desperately bored in the flat and know no one outside of the four walls with whom to socialise. I have a vague interest in the architecture of the colonial past and had earlier planned to explore the ecclesiastical buildings during my trip to the city centre. I'll give the service a miss and look around. Neil can explain a profligate nephew.

Once in the car, I am pleasantly surprised that the traffic is noticeably lighter than on a weekday. It takes very little time to get to the compound and to draw up outside the large, Gothic structure.

I'm at the far side of the compound examining the Cathedral edifice when I see the worshippers file out to the courtyard in front of the church onto the rough tarmac. I stride over to the throng. The regulars gather in their cliques, leaving me standing beside my uncle under the shade of a gnarled *peepul* tree. We greet. We make small talk. We laugh.

We stand there in the sun. I am desperately bored. And hot. And tired.

A young woman comes out of the crowd from somewhere and strolls over to me. I notice her dark hair cascading across her shoulders and a frond curling above her right eye. She has a relaxed gait and an enquiring, intelligent expression.

'Ah, Esther,' Neil remarks. 'This is my nephew, Steven, from England. He's visiting me on the way to Australia.'

Esther's pensive expression breaks into a smile. She offers a delicate, dainty hand that I am almost too frightened to take as we shake hands.

Where did she come from? She's all right. What's she doing here?

My thoughts immediately return to Lydia, from my college days. I shudder with the memory of my indiscretion, which is kept a secret to this day.

'It's good have you here,' she says, releasing her hand shyly. 'We enjoy visitors.'

A Sindh sparrow begins its high-pitched chirping *chup* call in the upper branches of a tree. House crows from all over the compound join in with their strident *kaaw-kaaws.*

'I'm here on business. I'm just passing through. But it's good to meet some of the locals.'

Esther smiles as she looked shyly into my face. Her eyes gleam and she fixes me with a studious gaze.

'Esther is the accountant in her father's finance company,' Neil says. 'She's been here for how many years?'

'Ten', Esther says, with almost a chuckle.

'She's a regular attender here. She knows the city well.'

A figure stands aside from the crowd and beckons to Esther. She glances around and steps back.

'Sorry, I must go. Today we leave early – a lunch invitation at Pearl Continental. Will see you again.'

She turns and heads back to the group several metres away.

'That's the Li family,' Neil says. 'Esther's sister isn't here today – she usually follows her around.'

I turn from watching Esther to see a Pakistani man approach Neil – smartly dressed in *shalwar-kameez.* He is tall, head and shoulders above Neil, and four or five centimetres above my height. I look closely at his Poirot-manicured moustache. Is it real? The close-cut beard fails to hide an honest, open face.

'Nadeem, this is my nephew, Steven, from the UK.'

The man thrusts out his hand to greet me. 'Good to meet you, Steven. I hope you are enjoying your time here.' His head jerks as he speaks, but in a pleasant, harmless way, like the nodding dog toys in the back of cars.

'Nadeem is a pastor of another church,' Neil says, his voice trailing off at the end of the sentence. It is obvious Neil is hazy on the details. Spiritual life and Neil don't mix.

'Yes, I have a church in a *busti* area that meets Sunday evenings, so I come here in the morning. The bishop and I have a good understanding…

'So, what brings you to Pakistan, Steven?'

'Research. I need to get some samples from the north of the country…' I am wary of saying too much to casual acquaintances.

'I worked in research myself many years ago,' Nadeem says.

'Where was that?'

'In Lahore. I worked for a large pharmaceutical company. I found the work interesting, but needed a change. That is why I now help people in the community – it is far more challenging but more rewarding. My excellent wife joined me in the *busti* with all its problems and joys.'

'Do you have a family?' I ask. I remember that this is an important question in Pakistan.

'No, we are still waiting. I cannot pretend that it is easy, particularly for my wife. But it helps us to come alongside other couples that are in the same situation.

'What do you enjoy reading in your spare time?'

I am taken aback – I haven't expected anyone in Pakistan to ask me such an intelligent question.

'Generally, I read technical journals around my research interest. Occasionally I dip into modern history, though the politics can get complicated. Otherwise, crime thrillers. I enjoy audio books.'

'And you?'

Nadeem laughs. 'If I had the chance… I used to belong to a reading group organised by the Parsi community. We studied the classics: Dickens, Hardy, Mark Twain, and Tolkien. I enjoyed it. But life is too busy these days.'

'So don't you get any time to relax?'

'A good film, when I can. I enjoy watching different genres.'

I look over to where Neil is standing. Claire has joined

him from another part of the gathering, and they are ready to leave.

'Are you available to come round to my uncle's flat sometime this week?' I ask. 'We could talk some more.'

'Tomorrow afternoon? Where is your uncle's flat?'

I stroll over to where Neil is standing. Nadeem follows me. Claire is fidgeting at his side, uncomfortable in the increasing heat and humidity, dabbing her mascara with a handkerchief before it makes a more serious mess of her face.

'Is it OK with you if Nadeem comes to the flat for a chat?' If so, what's your address?'

Neil feigns a hospitable spirit.

'Sure. Ittefaq Terrace, opposite Rizwan Bakery, Nursery *Bazaar*. We're on the third floor, turn left out of the lift, third flat along, number 43.'

'I know Ittefaq Terrace. My sister and brother-in-law live in the block next to it.' Nadeem says.

'Is 2pm OK?'

'Yes, that's good.' Nadeem pulls out his mobile phone and makes an entry. 'I'll see you tomorrow.'

That evening after the meal, I return to my bedroom and lie on the bed. Images of Esther flash through my mind: the twinkle of her eyes, her confident, light flirt as she played with her hair as we spoke, the slight wrinkle of her nose as she laughed. I have a weakness for Asian women. It brought me trouble at college. But I am now mature.

Perhaps I would be truly happy with a Chinese young woman, particularly of the westernised variety. Perhaps the difficulties between Rachel and me in our relationship are inevitable. We are too similar in disposition. I would be better off marrying someone with a gentle, Asian spirit that could absorb some of the knocks from my rough edges. 'Opposites attract,' so they say. And yet I don't even know if Esther is available. I will have to find out. What a find.

I open my laptop to check my emails – only personal emails at this time of night. I read a quick email from Mum and a few from friends. I look at the string of emails from Rachel. Some I have opened, but the later messages I have not touched. Rachel has grown more and more unreasonable. She sounds angry and upset. She wants me to phone. Heck, woman, why don't you give me space? It's only a week or two. Why do you want to control all the time?

Chapter 4

Nadeem arrives twenty minutes late. I greet him at the door. Hilda rushes to get a bottle of cold water from the kitchen. It seems she recognises him.

I pour a drink. He takes it gratefully. He shifts his backside on the hard, cotton cushions as he sits.

'How are you and your wife?'

'We are fine.'

'I'm trying to find things to do to bide time. I'm impatient to get to the north to get the samples. There's a flight booked to Islamabad on Thursday.'

'Are you travelling on your own?' Nadeem asks. His eyebrows rise, accentuating his facial stretch marks.

'Yes. I can manage – I've travelled a lot.

'Do you know anyone who could help me practise Urdu? I enjoy languages and I've been studying what I can from the web, but I need someone who knows the language well.'

'Well, that's not me!' Nadeem says with a laugh. Punjabi influences my Urdu. But I know someone who may be able to help. He is from the Muhajir community, those who migrated from India in 1947. His family members are native Urdu speakers. I will find out if he is available.'

'The more time he can give, the better. I haven't got much else to do here. I keep in touch with my department and answer emails, but there's nothing else to keep me occupied.'

I try something. 'Do you know Esther, the woman who attended church on Sunday?'

'Yes.' He looks at me curiously. 'Her family is well known at the church. Her father is a lay reader.'

'Are there many Chinese in the city?'

'Yes, I am not sure how many thousands. Chinese started coming to the country in the 1940s, so many are now second-generation citizens of Pakistan. There were others, construction workers or engineers who were involved in developing roads and other basic infrastructure under the China Pakistan Economic Corridor scheme. I know that some worked at the Gwadar port. I have some good Chinese friends myself.'

'And Esther's family?'

'They have been here for some time. Esther came across from China when her parents settled here. Her father runs some kind of equity financing operation in the city. She is an excellent accountant.'

Nadeem smiles. 'I think you will find that Esther is a big fish to land. Her parents, especially her father, have high hopes for her.'

Just then Hilda arrives with a tray of Pakistani tea and biscuits. I am glad for the interlude. Nadeem has quickly picked up on my romantic interest. It came across as immature. He must be thinking about where this puerile foreigner came from. I change the subject.

'What do you know about the more remote tribal groups in the country? For instance, the Kalash? Have you ever had dealings with them?'

Nadeem laughs. 'Few of us have ever come across the Kalash. They don't travel much. Some are Muslim, but others follow their own religious practices.'

'I read that their language and customs have intrigued anthropologists.'

'Yes, but there are other interesting people groups in the country. Take the Burusho, for instance. I was at school with a student who spoke Burushaski. That is also a distinct language.'

Nadeem looks at me steadily.

'Tell me about yourself,' I say. 'What brought you to the *busti* area? You said that it's more rewarding than working in industry.'

'I had a difficult childhood. We lived among my father's extended family. As you know, marriages are arranged in Pakistan so the family chose my father's wife. Everything was OK, to begin with. But then Mother became depressed and emotionally unstable. I was young at the time but I heard that she often escaped the house and went wandering the neighbourhood. My father was understanding and tried to help her, but she became an embarrassment to the extended family. One day she was so depressed she wandered around partly unclothed. The community threatened the family that if they didn't do something about it, they would call the police. So, to save being shamed, one day they fixed the paraffin cooking stove to explode when she was preparing the evening meal. She died.

'There was no enquiry – the extended family paid off the police, so no one was brought to justice. My father was really upset but the family put pressure on him to marry again.

'I wasn't aware of all these things as a child, but when I grew up and found out, I wanted to help others who had suffered cruelty. Some of my work is as a human rights activist, helping victims of cruelty and abuse. I'm friends with some good lawyers who will take on cases pro bono. There are plenty of thoroughly corrupt lawyers as well who get in the way.'

'So, you work in an office for some of the week?'

'In my lounge. Our house is not large. It can be difficult, but it saves unnecessary expenses. The drawback is that I am easily contactable and often get interrupted. There are many needs in our community. Unfortunately, there is a lot of poverty and deprivation.'

I sit back in the chair and feel an uncomfortable jab as the sharp corner of the rattan wickerwork rubs against the underside of my left leg. I have never visited a Christian *busti*. But his story challenges and intrigues me. I want to see his community.

We chat for another hour or so, and then Nadeem asks to be excused. He has some work to catch up on and members of his church to visit – including one who is sick.

Hilda returns to the coffee table to take the tray and empty cups.

'I have to leave now,' she says. Please tell Mrs Neil that I haven't had time to clean the balcony area as there was much laundry today. I will clean the balcony tomorrow. If I do not leave now, I will not be able to go to my other job.'

'OK. You have two jobs?' I look up, surprised.

'I cook,' she says. 'In *memsahiba*'s house, Clifton. I cook for Mr Li and the family for over five years.'

'So, you go from here and then have to start cooking again?'

'Yes, Mr Steven. My husband works as a *chowkidar* and does not earn much money. I need to work to pay our bills. We have three small children and we need to buy their uniforms and books.'

'How old are the children?'

'They are in classes five, three and one. The youngest is late. He died at six weeks.'

I can tell that Hilda wants to leave promptly, so I discontinue my idle chat and return to an interesting article in Newsweek.

Hilda stops at the door. 'Mr Steven, don't mind. I need money. I am behind with the school fees. I need three thousand rupees. The school says Neela won't be able to sit exam without payment. The exams start next week.'

Hilda looks away at a 45-degree angle, fixing her eyes on a cupboard against the wall. I guess I'm still in her field of vision. She slouches with an uncomfortable resignation, but with head erect and a face set firm.

What the heck do I do now? Even the house help begs. Don't they pay her enough? I suppose she feels entitled to make this ask of a rich foreigner she considers being from her own faith background.

'I can't give. I don't know your family. I'm only a visitor. Ask Mr or Mrs Neil. They may give.'

'They don't give. I don't ask. Mr Neil is an angry man. Please don't mind. I need to pay the school fees, otherwise, Neela won't be able to take exams.'

Is she telling the truth?

I think back to Parveen, the office cleaner. These families have it tough. She probably really needs this extra cash.

'OK, wait a moment. I'll see what I can do.'

I count out three thousand from my wallet. I try to reconcile opposing self-talk: Am I a gullible fool or a compassionate philanthropist?

'Thank you, Mr Steven. You must meet my family.'

'No time for that. I'm off to Islamabad soon.'

'But you must. Tomorrow is my son's birthday. We are having a small gathering. You must come.'

'I can't get there,' I say. 'I don't know how to get around here.'

'You come with me. I take you. Tomorrow.'

I try to think of other excuses. I could lie about another appointment, but Hilda would see me here in the flat. I can't really be bothered. But this woman is insistent. At least it would be more exposure to the culture and language – an excuse to get out. I may even enjoy it.

'Yes, perhaps tomorrow,' I say.

Hilda opens the bar of the grill door with a smile and exits down the corridor.

The following afternoon I'm ready at 4:30pm for when Hilda finishes her cleaning after a late morning stroll in the *bazaar* to find a birthday gift for the boy and a cake for the family.

I have arranged to travel with Hilda to Mr Li's house and wait while she cooks, then accompany her to the party. She assures me that the Li family will not mind my being there while she cooks: they are hospitable and won't fuss. Ordinarily, she travels by bus, but I offer to pay for a taxi. She is chuffed.

I am looking forward to meeting Esther at her parents' home – an unexpected bonus in the arrangement.

We walk to the service road where many of the taxis wait for passengers. I keep in the background whilst Hilda does the negotiating.

The taxi driver is a middle-aged man with a thin moustache and thick black hair swept across a balding patch on his forehead. He stares through the car windscreen during the negotiation. I get into the front of the vehicle and Hilda in the back. The driver ignores me during the journey. On occasions, Hilda breaks the silence to give directions.

I fumble in my pocket for my handkerchief to stem the beads of perspiration creeping down my neck. The smell of diesel fumes is overwhelming, but I keep the windows wound down to get the benefit of a breeze. The taxi doesn't appear to have an air conditioner.

The traffic is heavy as it is rush hour, so it takes a full thirty minutes to arrive at a smart bungalow in Defence Phase II. Hilda pays the driver from an envelope of cash I have given her earlier, and then we stride up to the front of the bungalow and ring the bell.

A Pakistani young man comes to the door and, seeing Hilda, smiles. When he catches a glimpse of me, he quickly retreats and calls out in Urdu.

The entrance opens out into a large reception room. It is sparsely furnished but with a few small rugs close to the chairs at one end of the room. Colourful Chinese hangings with Mandarin script detract from the bare walls. The marble floor glistens. I sniff the air. There is a strong smell of fish.

We take off our sandals and Hilda points with a nod of her chin towards a pair of smart light-weight slippers reserved for guests. A Chinese woman appears from the back of the room and makes her way towards us.

'I am happy welcome you into my home,' Mrs Li says. She turns towards Hilda. 'Hilda had told me you wait while she does cooking. You are welcome to sit here and read. Mr Li home soon.'

Mrs Li turns and walks away. Hilda trudges dutifully after her. I sit at the table. It is pleasant to be in an air-conditioned house after the taxi ride.

With earphones in my ear, I begin searching through my playlist.

Twenty minutes later I hear a car draw up. After the slamming of car doors and the noise of footsteps, two people enter the house.

Mr Li quickly comes over to me and, with a smile and a slight bow, welcomes me to his home.

Esther stays behind her father and smiles awkwardly.

Once the greetings are completed, Mr Li and Esther disappear farther into the house. I hear muffled voices as Mr Li speaks with his wife. After several minutes, Esther comes out with a cup of weak, jasmine tea.

'I am very much happy to see you again,' Esther begins, looking away and smiling to herself.

'I didn't realise Hilda cooks for your family.' I straighten myself in the seat. 'I'm on my way to a birthday party in her home. She suggested that I wait here and then travel with her.'

'Yes, you find it difficult to find her house. You are welcome to rest here.'

'So, you've just returned from the office?'

'We work until 6pm at least. There is much to do. I have small team of Pakistani accountants under me. Sometimes they do not work hard and I have to cover for their mistakes.'

'Oh,' I said. 'It must be difficult to enforce discipline.

'How do you unwind when you return from the office?'

Esther looks puzzled.

'I mean, to relax after your day of work.'

Esther lowers herself into the seat at the opposite corner of the table from where I am sitting, smoothing her slim, light-yellow dress under her as she sits.

'I study for higher qualifications. This takes much time. When I am free, I watch movies and write poetry.'

'And you?'

'I'm into competitive running. 1000 metres is my distance. But these days I don't get to run much. I can't keep up the training. So, I spend time playing the piano and chilling out.'

Esther looks into my eyes with a sense of awe and mystery. I look away, acutely embarrassed.

'Don't feel that you need to keep me company if you have other things you need to do,' I say.

'No, I have time.

'How is the business that you are here to do?'

'I'm taking a flight to Islamabad on Thursday, then onward to Chitral on Friday, as long as the weather is OK. I have some work to do at a clinic near the city. It will only take a few hours. I'll then return to Karachi and fly on to Australia where I have some similar work. I hope to be back in the UK within two weeks.'

'Where in UK do you live?'

'Oxford. It's well known because of the university. I work in one of the laboratories. I like the city – it has a rich culture. It's an interesting place.'

'Have you ever visited the UK?'

'Yes, but just London,' Esther says. 'I went there for study course, but I didn't see much of the city.'

'And how you like Karachi?' Esther asks. Her eyes sparkle with interest.

'I haven't seen much of it. I probably won't get the opportunity to experience much of life here during this work visit. But I could come back at some point for a holiday if I felt it was worthwhile.' I leave my words hanging temptingly in the air.

'You bring your family,' Esther says. 'Your parents or your wife.' Esther looks searchingly into my face.

'My mother would not come. She would not be interested.

I'm not married. I would have to come alone.'

The door opens and Mr Li comes out. Esther gets up. 'Your mother needs your help,' he says. 'I am sure Mr Grant will understand if you leave him now.'

Esther looks at me apologetically and follows her father into the family area of the house. I pull out my phone and navigate back to the playlist.

As I listen, I muse. How could I get to spend more time with Esther? Is she as interested in me as I am in her? Was I fooling myself or could this be the beginning of a beautiful relationship?

I have been sitting for an hour. Hilda appears, wiping her wet hands on her *dupatta*.

'Have you finished the cooking?' I ask.

'Yes, Mrs Li was kind. She know... my son's birthday party and so they only asked me to cook one dish this evening. I go earlier than usual.'

I pick up the parcels I have brought and we walk towards the door. Mr Li comes out to speak to us.

'It has been a pleasure to have you under my roof,' he says, 'though you came at a time when I was not able to entertain you. You must come back again. I will arrange something and speak with your uncle.'

Mr Li closes the door behind us. We re-enter the sultry humidity of early-evening Karachi.

Hilda finds another taxi and, like before, negotiates the fare. I tag along as a foreign visitor.

After twenty minutes, we arrive in the *bazaar* near Hilda's home. Hilda stops the taxi, and after paying the fare, tells me that we are walking the remainder of the distance so that she can buy some *jalebis* for the party. Hilda leads the way. I keep a respectable distance behind her. I am conscious of people staring at me.

We arrive at 'Rehman Sweets' – a small shop down an alleyway off the main street. Outside the shop is a large cooking utensil that looks like a Chinese wok, with a burner underneath. Peering into the wok-like utensil, I can see bright orange *jalebis*, swimming in thick syrup. Hilda buys a kilo of the mixture. We then walk on for a further five minutes until we come to some narrow lanes. I follow Hilda closely as we navigate into the heart of the *busti*. Eventually, we arrive at a small house. Hilda raps on the small metal gate. I hear excited voices from inside.

'*Mama ji!*' I hear someone call out. The door opens and two boys and a girl swarm around Hilda, clutching at her *shalwar*.

We enter the small courtyard. To one side is a pump next to what looks like a drain. I later find out that this is the water pump that fills the tank for the family's needs. The smell from the damp cement floor reminds me of dank cellars at home. Towards the back of the courtyard is a door ajar.

I am directed towards a small room. It is simply furnished with a double bed and two small beds at the side. I can see the figure of a man straightening his *shalwar-kameez*. After a few moments, he walks slowly towards me. He is considerably older than Hilda, with a long, drawn face and large, rough hands. He gestures that I should sit on the double bed.

There are seven excited children in the room, so I guess that some of the children from nearby relatives have joined the party.

Hilda walks off towards a paraffin stove in a partition off the main room. I can hear the clank of utensils and the jingle of cutlery. A strong smell of biryani wafts into the room.

The children are rushing around within the confines of the room. They don't seem to be playing anything in particular. From time to time, a child looks up and stares at me, and then continues with the activity.

'Childs enjoy… Happy time,' Hilda's husband says.

I reply as civilly as possible.

Samuel's sister comes to the centre of the room with a thick sheet. She shoos away the children from the area next to the beds and lays the sheet on the floor. Hilda brings the *degcha* of biryani whilst the young girl sets out spoons and melamine plates, the plastic jugs of water and the metal drinkware.

Hilda calls out to the children to be quiet. They come and sit at the edge of the spread. She introduces me to each child, alternating between English and Punjabi. The children giggle. Eric calls out to them and they stop laughing. I can hear a pin drop.

'Mr Steven will say grace for us,' Hilda says. She and her daughter wrap their *dupattas* around their heads in preparation for the prayer.

I am taken off guard. I have never said grace before a meal.

'For this food and all good things, we give you thanks, Amen.'

'*Amin*.' I look up quickly. The rest of the family are looking at me to see if this was the full extent of my prayer. After a few moments, Hilda begins to spoon the food onto the plates.

The biryani is spicy, hot and oily. I enjoy hot food and the spice distracted from the lack of meat.

'We are happy that you join us for this party,' Hilda says. Samuel looks at me shyly and smiles.

I bring out the cake. 'This is for the celebration.'

'We will eat this with the *chai* and *jalebis*,' Hilda says.

Samuel's sister, Neela, brings the dessert from the kitchen. The children mostly eat the *jalebis*. I try some. I wince at the intense sugary sweetness and oil. I opt for the cake. While I am still eating, the *chai* arrives. The hot fluid helps to neutralise the oily taste in the mouth.

'I have a present for Samuel.'

Hilda calls Samuel and explains. Samuel extends both hands to receive the present.

I see gnarled tree trunks of wrists, thick and deformed. Samuel moves his hands awkwardly. He is conscious of my stare and whips the gift from under my nose.

I wait for a few moments to see if Samuel opens his present, but he puts it to one side.

'Samuel's wrists seem unusual,' I say to Hilda. 'Do you think he should be checked by a children's doctor?'

'I see this. Perhaps we will take him soon,' Hilda says. She looks towards her husband, who returns a stern stare.

'It's getting late,' I say. 'I need to be leaving now.'

'Have some more *chai*,' Hilda says. 'My husband will find a taxi for you soon.'

Why the wait? The event is over. Let me go, woman.

After a further ten minutes, Eric slips out of the room. He returns shortly afterwards and speaks to Hilda in Urdu.

'I've enjoyed the party and meeting your family.' I make my way to the door to retrieve my sandals. Eric steps in front to take the lead.

The taxi ride back to Neil and Claire's flat is uneventful. Eric tells me the fare that he negotiated, in his usual broken English. During the journey, I try out a few phrases I have picked up with the taxi driver, but he then launches into long, involved sentences that quickly have me lost.

Back at the flat, I settle into my usual wicker chair to let the heavy food digest. Claire has gone to bed. Neil is still up doing some work on his laptop. He asks me some perfunctory questions about the evening but doesn't seem particularly interested.

I take out my phone. I received some messages during the evening but have not had time to look at them.

'Why are you doing this to me???' Somehow Rachel has found out my Pakistani number. The text blazes from the brightly lit screen.

I tap the number to return the call, knowing that the credit on the phone would limit the length of the conversation.

'It's Steven. How are you doing?'

'What the hell are you doing? Why have you changed phones? I had to beg your mother for this number. And why haven't you contacted me since arriving? You know I'm concerned about your safety after you received that threatening letter. Don't you care for me anymore? This is a cool way to show your care. I thought we were in a relationship. Doesn't that mean regular two-way communication?'

'I needed some space,' I say. 'I thought you were angry that I had decided to go ahead with these trips. I didn't want to further upset you. I'm not prepared to have shouting matches down the phone, just like we're having now.'

I'm speaking too loudly. I hope the background sounds of the air conditioner and the noise from the street cloak the conversation.

'Perhaps with you, it's "out of sight, out of mind", but not with me,' Rachel says. 'I just can't understand how you can block me out of your life. Was all that we experienced before a sham? Doesn't it mean anything to you?'

'Of course, it means a lot to me. But I just need…'

A robotic voice speaking Urdu makes an announcement and the telephone cuts.

I fume. Why is Rachel so possessive? Why is she so insecure?

Neil returns to the lounge and sits in a wicker chair, drinking a glass of fruit juice.

'Nadeem phoned while you were out. Tomorrow, his church is having some kind of retreat for those who are free. He said his friend Tahir would be coming and suggested that you also tag along. He'll call at the flat at 10am to collect you.'

I don't have anything in my diary, so I nod assent. At least it will get me out of the flat for a while.

I make my way to my room. Neil isn't company I care to keep.

Lying on my bed, I am assailed by vivid images of Esther

flashing through my mind. I try to distract myself by planning the DNA data collection in the north, but my thoughts keep returning to this Asian woman. Why was I so captivated by the diminutive, delicate nature of the Chinese?

Immediately, I see the image of a younger Chinese girl, Lydia, from college days. She is standing by the basketball courts, beckoning me with a sly expression.

'She started it.' I spit out my frustration. I think back to the shameful incident of my college years with a rueful disquiet.

Chapter 5

Eleven years earlier

I got off the bus opposite 'The Crown Inn', retrieving my suitcase from the bag stand. It was heavy with books and sports equipment. I headed off to Apple Mead, the case wheels trundling along the tarmac.

Rounding the corner by the village post office, I saw my mother waiting on the doorstep. Realising that she would have heard the bus, I shuddered involuntarily – it was embarrassing to have Mum waiting for me so keenly in full view of the village. I glanced around, hoping that Dan from Old Manor Cottage and my other peers were not watching.

Mum knew better than to make a fuss of me at the doorstep, so she simply closed the door behind me, smiling intently.

'Was it a pleasant trip?'

'Yeah, long as usual. I wish there were quicker routes. I missed the 8:10 from Castle Knoll and had to wait for the

8:45 that went via Stoke-St-Hartwell. It was slow.'

'Never mind, you're here now. I'll go and make a cup of tea.'

I walked into the familiar lounge and slumped down into the threadbare armchair opposite the TV. I looked around. Not much had changed – a few new photos of my young cousins, an Easter card, a cushion cover I didn't recognise from before.

Mum entered the room with a mug of tea and a box of biscuits on a tray. I had noticed at first glance how much mother had aged since the Easter break. Nothing too dramatic, but the telltale flecks of grey hair, the deepening crow's feet around the eyes, the very slight stoop. I thought of how badly she had been affected by the death of my father, Ryan, just one year ago. I had been able to compensate by busyness, trying not to think of Dad and the events that led to his death. I had read that this was not a healthy way to process the bereavement and had seen some sort of counsellor at school, but I would admit this to no one. Mother did not have the luxury of such distractions. It often occurred to me she had few ways to occupy her time living in such a remote area, particularly as she couldn't drive and only worked part-time at the village community shop.

'How are Glyn and Madeline?'

'They're fine.' I picked up a magazine from the table and began to flick through the pages.

'And how are you, Mum?'

'Oh, my usual self. The shop is busy. I've been making meals for Michael and Lyn after the birth of their first baby

– they're so busy. I'm not sure how they will manage once Lyn has to go back to work. There is always sorting to do – I never seem to get to the end of it.'

I put down the magazine and looked out of the window. The weather forecast had predicted rain for the afternoon, but there was no sign of clouds.

'I think I'll take the suitcase up,' I said, scooping up several bourbon creams into my hand. 'I messaged Mike on the train. He's available this afternoon. Could I have an early lunch at around twelve?'

Mike had his motorbike on the centre stand as I approached the farm. He was kneeling at the side of the bike on the concrete driveway. He looked up as I approached.

'This is new – when did you get it?'

'It was my 17th a couple of weeks ago. The old man put up the cash for it so that I can get to the One Stop at Stoke-St-Hartwell. I'll pay it back in instalments. You heard I got a part-time job at One Stop?'

'When was that? I can't remember anyone mentioning it. Anyway, I'm glad you've found something.'

'Yeah, it's only to raise money for my gap year programme. I wouldn't want to remain in retail.'

Mike stood up and looked down the drive in the direction of the farmhouse.

'Do you want to come in?'

'No, we might as well stay out here,' I said. I took a closer look at the bike. I had a rudimentary knowledge of engines and frames as I had thought of getting a bike some while ago. It looked sturdy enough.

'I didn't know you were into motorbikes.'

'My father used to ride a bike years ago. He takes it out himself when he wants to go somewhere local. He put up the money for the insurance. It's a cheap way to get around.'

Mike leaned over the handlebars and started the engine.

'I'll just ride it to the shed,' Mike said. He mounted the bike.

'Get on the back if you like. We're using the small tool shed by the barn.'

I clambered onto the pillion seat. The bike sagged noticeably with my weight. Mike steadied himself to keep balance and then, engaging first gear, let the clutch out.

The bike lurched forward and then began to pick up pace, the small engine struggling with the weight of the two of us sturdy teenagers. The engine was soon racing in 1st gear so as we hit the dirt track at the back of the farmhouse, Mike lifted his left foot to change up.

Suddenly, a chicken ran out from the corner of the yard in front of us. Mike jammed on the front brake. The front tyre skidded on the loose gravel at the side of the track and we were both thrown to the ground. The chicken ran off, squawking and flapping wings in panic.

'Are you OK?' Mike picked himself up from the ground and hit the engine 'kill' button.

'Yeah, the brambles made some impression.' I rose to my feet, tearing my sweater from the thorns, and dusted myself down. My hand stung. I looked at it and saw that it was bleeding slightly from the impact with the verge.

Mike picked the bike up and took a close look at it. 'I can't see any damage. The indicators escaped – they usually break first. It's a good job the ground is soft here. I'll ride it to the shed and then we can go indoors.'

Mike mounted the bike and tried to restart the engine. After several seconds, it roared into life. He gingerly put it in gear and again set off. I trudged down the track behind him.

I heard a knock on my bedroom door.

'What?'

Mum peered around the door. I was sitting on my bed, my head propped up on a pillow, reading.

She looked around the room. I had begun to unpack, but the half-emptied suitcase was still lying open in the corner of the room. I had taken out the books and had stacked them neatly on top of the bookcase. My shaver and toiletries bag were on the bedside cabinet while a spare T-shirt was hanging on the back of the chair. I had already put up a poster of a wrestler on the wall above my bed, one that a friend had passed onto me, protruding Blu Tack visible at the poster corners.

'Is everything OK? I noticed you had done something to your hand.'

'It's only scratches. I jumped on the back of Mike's motorbike as he was putting it away. We had a slow-speed near collision with a chicken – no one was hurt.'

Mum walked further into the room and sat at the bottom of the bed. I looked up with a mixture of curiosity and contempt.

'We didn't finish the conversation about college,' Mum said.

'What? There's no need to go on about this. You've said that it's where you would like me to go.'

'Your uncle Neil and I have looked into it. It's a really good college – it comes high on the league table. We think you will be happy there. Besides, there are few options. There's nothing close to Castle Knoll that is suitable, and nothing within miles of here.'

'Boarding school hasn't got the best press,' I said. 'In any case, it's going to be expensive. I know Uncle Neil and Pat have said that they will pay most of it, but I don't want to be sponging off them. How much will it cost over the two years?'

Mum looked at me closely. I flung the book onto the bed. I felt my forehead tighten.

'I can't remember the figures, but the family has enough. We received money from your dad's life assurance policy. And Neil is doing well at work. I know it's what your father would have wanted for you. Otherwise, I wouldn't suggest it.'

I continued my stare at Mum and then picked up my book and began to read.

'I'll make a supper drink at ten. Do you still like hot chocolate?'

'Fine.'

At 6pm on a weekday, the Michael Haw College dining hall was noisy. Six weeks into the College term I had got used to the clatter and din, but I still resented the immature antics of some of the other students. I usually arrived early as serving began and sat at the edge of the room, leaving as soon as I had downed the food. Occasionally, some of the other quiet and serious students would join me, speaking sparingly during the meal and leaving quickly, without any need for an excuse. Genuine conversation took place during the morning lesson break when, armed with a coffee from the kiosk, students could gather in groups at a location conducive to thoughtful discussion.

The only exception to this rule was when Monique joined me at the dining table.

I found Monique interesting – nothing more than that. I had only once visited her country across the channel when I was too young to explore and connect with the culture. So, I didn't object on occasions when Monique placed her tray down on the table and pulled up a chair. We would eat in silence for a while, and then the conversation would begin. I enjoyed practising my French. My conversational ability was far beyond that of the average GCSE student. I would ask so many questions. Monique discovered we could cover serious ground in the language, though I admitted to having my limits. She told me on more than one occasion my fluency and the absence of an English accent amazed her. For my part, it intrigued me why for so many centuries, the enmity between our two countries provoked such disdain for these people and their customs, and for the French to consider the English as their most 'dear enemies'.

It was a Thursday. I was looking forward to the end of the week. I had been preparing for a half-term physics exam, working late into the evenings. Earlier in the year, Mum had questioned the wisdom of attempting four 'A' Levels, but I had insisted. I enjoyed the challenge. I only satiated my thirst for knowledge when my mind was coursing through textbook theories and grammatical structures. I could happily bury myself away in my books night by night – some of my friends accused me of being anti-social. By the weekend my body began to protest, so on a Saturday I would concentrate on sport and physical exercise, leaving Sundays for social occasions, unless I was competing in races.

Monique came to the table with her tray and sat down next to me. I was in my usual distracted state.

'Salut,' Monique said. 'Comment tu vas?'

'Bien'. I looked up to see Monique smiling at me.

Ben, a student who lived in the room opposite me, approached and, turning the chair around 180 degrees, straddled it, one of his feet swinging in the air.

'What's up?' Ben asked. I ignored him and continued with my meal.

'Have you heard about the ball on Saturday night? It's in the Moore Hall. I'm helping with the sound.'

'Why are they having a ball at this point? It's near half-term. It doesn't make sense.'

'It's Lydia's birthday. Apparently, it's her 16th. She's organised it and footed the bill. I didn't realise she's so young. Anyway, the student committee agreed and got permission.'

'So do we need to get a ticket or just turn up?'

'You have to sign up – I think something to do with

health and safety. I've got the list here.' Ben produced a clipboard with a typed form from his rucksack.

'Put my name down,' Monique said. 'Are you coming, Steven?'

I stared straight ahead and thought for a moment. It didn't appeal to me. I had a smart jacket-and-trousers that matched but I didn't particularly enjoy dressing up. I would be on the track Saturday afternoon, practising the 1000 metres. It would be a struggle to change momentum and frame of mind to be sociable after a physically active day.

'I'll see. Will the sign-up list be around tomorrow night?'

'Sure, I'll have it with me.'

'I'll see then.'

I could hear the thump of the music from my room. I closed the door behind me and locked it, then headed for the stairwell. I walked stiffly, the cuffs of my white starched shirt protruding from the sleeves of the jacket. The jacket itself felt too long, almost flapping against my legs as I descended the steps. I felt like a penguin heading towards the water. I would have been far more comfortable in casual dress.

No one seemed to notice me as I slipped into the hall. I headed for the refreshments table and helped myself to a plate of crisps, sausage rolls, pork pie and salad. I didn't expect to see alcohol and wasn't bothered to pour a soft drink. I'd return for water later.

Standing to the side of the table, I surveyed the scene. Ben was trying to chat with Sarah at the far side of the hall

– it was obvious that he was struggling to communicate over the volume of the music. Michael and another student, whose name I couldn't quite remember, were cavorting in the middle of the building, surrounded by thirty or so other students who had joined the dance floor, jigging, jiving and twisting with few inhibitions. Monique sat at a table talking with Dave. One of the teachers was sitting at another table, keeping an eye on the proceedings, and sipping his soft drink with a bored expression.

From out of nowhere, Lydia appeared.

'Happy birthday!'

'Well, thanks. Glad that you could come.' Lydia smiled.

'It's a good turn-out.'

'Yes, I wanted to do something special for my 16th. I know that most of you have already crossed sixteen. My family wanted me to celebrate.'

Lydia put her left hand to her mouth and bit the corner of a fingernail. Realising what she had done, she thrust her hand down and looked up into my face. She had a child-like innocence, but was very pretty. Her cherub face contrasted with her strong black hair, neatly cut to shoulder length. The modest, fitted dress accentuated her slim lines.

'So where do you come from?' I asked, partly to break the spell she seemed to be holding me under.

'London, West End – not very exotic. Obviously, my parents came over from Hong Kong after the second world war. They're in the hospitality trade.'

'So, why Michael Haw College? Aren't there closer colleges to where you live?'

'My sister, Eunice, came here and enjoyed it – she did

well. My parents visited and liked the place. I wanted a bit of distance from my parents, so they agreed that I could study here. They are able to afford it.'

'What are you studying?'

'Oh, English Literature, History and Art. And you?'

'Biology, Physics, French and Music.'

'I'm interested in going into teaching,' Lydia said. 'My aunt's a teacher. It's hard work but rewarding. She got me to do a presentation in class at her school. It was cool.

'Well, I'd better go and see some of the other students. Angela has just walked in. I think she's finding being away from home difficult…'

Lydia looked intently into my face, smiled, and walked off.

The following Monday at the mid-morning break, I looked out for Lydia. I hadn't noticed her prior to the ball – she had been just one of the younger students – part of the crowd. Since Saturday evening, she had been in my thoughts.

I found her sitting under an oak tree behind the main buildings with two fellow students, Kevin and Ralph. The three were laughing hysterically. I strolled nonchalantly up to the group.

'Hi Steven,' Ralph called out. 'We don't usually see you mixing with the crowd. What's up?'

I forced a smile. 'I was wondering what all the laughter was all about. After all, it is Monday morning.'

'Kevin here was telling me about some of the student pranks his brother and friends got up to when they were at college,' Ralph said. 'It sounds hilarious. We could do with having more fun around here.'

Lydia laughed. 'Your brother sounds like a real dude. Most of us just want to get good grades and then move on. My family puts the pressure on.'

'But what's the problem with a bit of spontaneity' Kevin said.

'I've got an idea for a prank,' Ralph said. 'You know Keith. He's a real nerd. He hardly comes out of his room except for meals. I don't know what's wrong with him, but he's awkward and clumsy with it. He can't feed himself breakfast without getting the cereals all over the table. He hardly says anything to anyone. What if we use the polystyrene cups on the floor, "the impossible maze" idea, to get him to communicate? I'm sure he would start talking pretty quickly if he was faced with cups filled with water all over his floor.'

'Yeah, why not? It wouldn't hurt him. It may bring him out of his shell,' Kevin said.

'I'm not sure this is a good idea. Anyway, you'd never pull this off,' Lydia said. 'How would you get the cups into his room and fill them with water? He hardly leaves his room.'

'He goes for dinner. He doesn't stay in the dining room for long, but perhaps you could start talking with him, Lydia? You could delay him while Kevin and I get to work in his room.'

'What about our meal?' Kevin asked. 'I get hungry in the evenings.'

'If we are organised and work quickly, we could do this in twenty minutes. We only need to put cups inside the door, over a wide enough area that he wouldn't be able to climb over. We'll still make it for a quick bite.'

The friends smiled.

Ralph looked at his watch. He set off towards the academic block with the other two with him.

I strolled away, mulling over the discussion. I hadn't been included. I was still an outsider. Yet I was in no way inferior. I stood as tall as any student and had respect among the student community due to my athleticism. But I had no hope of getting to know Lydia. I was not part of their clique and I didn't know what to do to join.

Later that evening, I was in my room studying when I heard a shriek down the corridor, followed by cursing, shouting and then laughing. I got up from my study table and made my way to the source of the outburst.

Keith was standing in his room, his hands behind his head, shaking with anger. I could see that he had knocked over several cups. Small pools of water were lying on the carpet. Keith had used his bath towel to mop up the water, but it was seeping around the edge of the towel. Ralph and Kevin were standing at a distance down the corridor, laughing loudly. Sam, Keith's neighbour, entered the room and started to help Keith with the clean-up operation. Keith sat down on his bed and let Sam carry on with the task. Hearing more sniggers from outside, Sam gently closed the door. I could hear Keith's rants and threats against the perpetrators of this practical joke. I knew that they were empty. Keith couldn't and wouldn't do a thing. It was just part of boarding school life. Part of what you had to get used to.

The following Wednesday evening, I left the dining room after spending a challenging half an hour conversing with Monique. I was in a hurry to get back to my room. The submission date for my biology assignment was approaching fast, and I realised that I had to knuckle down to it.

As I rounded the corner of the dining block, I met Lydia, walking towards the women's hostel. Lydia slowed, smiled disarmingly, and looked up into my face, her large brown eyes sparkling with interest.

'Haven't seen you for a while,' she said.

'I've been busy,' I said, trying to appear disinterested.

'Haven't seen you on the track either.'

'I don't get to the track much during the week. It's getting dark too early. Saturdays are my day for practice.'

'What do you get up to after classes?'

'Well, what are we supposed to be doing?' I said, lifting my right foot to rest on the quoin of the wall and flexing my calf muscles.

Lydia raised her eyebrows.

'There's a new game on the net called 'Spice' that I've found. I play and listen to the classics.'

'We hang out at the far side of the track by the green benches. We're usually there around 4pm,' Lydia said. 'Ralph does his keep-fit routine there – it's hilarious. Why not come and join us one afternoon?'

Lydia winked mischievously.

'I might pass by someday, depending on how things are going. Keep-fit is a fad. It's better to do serious sport.'

I found the three of them the following Friday afternoon

at the benches. True to Lydia's word, Ralph was stretching ready for his keep-fit regime. Kevin was sitting on the bench chatting with Lydia with a cup of coffee in his hand. He watched me out of the corner of his eye as I approached.

'Do you come in peace?' he asked, with a grin on his face.

'Just taking up an invitation,' I said, looking squarely at Lydia.

The two of them continued to chat while I sat on the corner of the bench watching Ralph's exaggerated movements. Lydia glanced in my direction from time to time, her eyes drilling into me. I tried to read her. Did she want me to intervene? Perhaps she was bored. Why couldn't she just leave the bore and walk off with me? Was she so insecure that she needed a male to rescue her?

'What did you think of the prank?' Kevin spoke unexpectedly and caught me off guard in my thoughts.

'Cool, but not so cool for Keith. He was upset.'

'I think it did him good. He and Sam are now good buddies. It was harmless fun.'

'How about another?'

'Another what?' I asked.

'Poke'.

I waited for Kevin to continue.

'I sometimes watch the rugby training on a Sunday morning. There's a guy called "Patrick", the hooker. He's hilarious. He must be all of 1.5 metres tall. He can't throw the ball straight and he runs like a chicken. The others make fun of him, but the coach keeps him on the team, all in the name of "inclusion". Martin and Gary complain about his play, that he's a liability to the team. I say that we encourage him to give up on the game by collapsing the scrum and piling on him.'

'How are you going to do that?' I asked. 'You don't play rugby yourself.'

'They are always looking for extra boys for the practice sessions. I'll volunteer. If I organise it with Martin and Gary, they'll speak with the other boys. We'll bear into Patrick then collapse the scrum on top of him – enough to give him a scare.'

Lydia sniggered. Kevin looked adoringly into her face. I felt a pang of jealousy.

'Are you in on it?' Kevin asked.

'Well, I'm not playing rugby on Sunday morning,' I replied. 'It's not part of my routine. But I'll be around, anyway. I'll see how the game is going. I could do some extra running practice later in the morning.'

'So, I expect to see you there,' Kevin said. 'Give some moral support to your friends…'

Sunday morning, the weather was dank. Autumn had arrived in the West Country. I propped myself up in bed and drank a strong cup of coffee to get me out of the warm sheets. I smeared the condensation on the inside of the window with my finger as I finished my drink, thinking of the dreariness of winter and of the number of weeks still to go before the Christmas break.

Once I was outside, I realised it was not that bad. There were gaps in the clouds, with some signs of the sun trying to break through. I quickened my pace towards the playing field, breathing deeply of the musty, raw smell of mud and foliage.

Lydia was there, standing a few metres from the touchline. She was cradling a steaming cup of hot chocolate in her hands. She looked up from her drink and smiled when I stood next to her.

'What's happened?' I asked.

'Nothing yet. Just drills so far. They're warming up. It will be a while before they start play.'

'Does Kevin still have it in mind to pile on Patrick?' I asked, looking closely at the players to find the small, lean player that Kevin treated with such contempt.

'Yes, I think so. Martin and Gary are there.'

'Do you speak with your family over the weekends?'

'Yes, Saturday nights we speak over the internet,' Lydia said, turning from watching the boys. 'I catch up with my young sister – often my parents don't have much to talk about.'

In the corner of my eye, I caught sight of an oriental-looking girl arriving at the benches behind us in a wheelchair. She stopped the chair on the steep slope next to the bench and put the brake on. She then slowly twisted her body out of the chair onto the bench, making use of an aluminum walking stick to take the weight of her body on the left side. She settled onto the bench and wrapped a snug blanket around her body.

She had a thin face leading to a pointed chin, and dark, wispy hair. Though she was by no means pretty, her demeanour was of a confident, determined young woman.

‘Who’s that? Is she one of your friends?’

‘That’s Rita. She’s from Liverpool – you’ll hear that if you ever speak with her. She’s in the upper sixth. I don’t know her very well.’

At that point, a whistle blew. Lydia and I turned to see the large group of boys dividing into two teams. Kevin shot Lydia a glance and leered at her. I felt a shiver run down my spine.

The first fifteen minutes of play were regular. The sports teacher, Allen McKenzie, acting as coach and then referee for the practice match, was busy shouting instructions, warnings and encouragement to the players. The game was messy but civilised. Then Martin gave a forward pass to Gary, and the referee blew his whistle to call for a scrum.

The players took their places. Gary and Martin made sure that they were props.

The referee called ‘crouch, bind, set’. The ball was ready to be thrown into the tunnel when the scrum began to turn and then slowly collapsed, Martin and Gary ensuring that they ended up on top of Patrick.

The referee blew his whistle and came over to the action, shouting for the players to get off the hooker. Patrick was moaning in pain. Martin and Gary picked themselves up from the writhing body and slunk across to where the other players were standing.

Allen reached down with his hand to haul Patrick up from the ground. Patrick cried out in pain.

‘Get up, laddie,’ Allen called. ‘You can’t be hurt that much.’

‘It’s my arm. I think they’ve broken it,’ Patrick wailed.

'Let's have a look,' Allen said. He knelt by Patrick and had him move his arm, Patrick crying out with discomfort.

'It's not broken, but your elbow's badly bruised,' Allen said. 'You'd better go off and find some ice. Take a break from rugby for a while until it's more comfortable.' Allen helped Patrick to his feet.

While Allen had his back to the other players, Kevin, Martin and Gary were punching the air with their fists. The other boys looked on, some sniggering, others alarmed. Lydia lifted her chin in acknowledgement of Kevin's successful follow-through of his plan. Positions were reallocated, and the game recommenced. Lydia sat down and watched.

'Did you enjoy that?' Kevin asked Lydia as he sauntered up to her, following the end of the game.

'Yeah, but I hope Patrick's all right. He may be a pain for the rugby team but he doesn't deserve to be damaged.'

'You're too sensitive,' Kevin said. 'The other boys were happy to see him go. They said so just now as the match ended. Patrick should concentrate on chess or whatever – not a man's game.'

Kevin stood surveying the muddy field. Allen was still on the field, chatting with two of the team members.

'You won't get in trouble for this?' Lydia asked, her gentle face taut with a frown.

Kevin looked across to the college building. 'Who cares?'

Ralph came across to the group. 'Our side won,' he said. 'I'm going to shower and change.' He trudged off towards the shower block.

'What prank are you going to stage?' Kevin asked me.

'I'm thinking.'

'Don't think for too long,' Kevin replied, putting a muddy arm around Lydia's shoulders.

Lydia removed the arm with a look of disgust. 'Go, get showered and changed', she said. Kevin laughed and headed off.

Lydia followed Kevin's progress to the shower block with her eyes. She turned to me.

'Those two are immature, but they're cool to hang about with. They're generous in the cafeteria. There's not much going on around here apart from the study to occupy my time – I do get bored. I thought that college social life would be better than this. Anyway, I'm looking forward to your contribution to our fun,' Lydia said, with a mischievous stroke of my hand.

I caught her hand. It was very delicate, but warm and inviting.

'I won't let you down,' I said, looking into her beautiful, amused face.

There was another practice session the following Saturday. Allen had warned the team of the dangers of indiscipline. He had insisted that they get serious about things – there was a match coming up with a college nearby whose team was a formidable force. He wanted the team to be up to scratch. In previous years, Michael Haw College had nailed the match. They needed to defend their title.

As I approached the playing field, I saw Lydia standing near the benches, with the familiar cup of hot chocolate in her hands. Kevin and Ralph were standing opposite her, chatting about something.

I looked on the field to see if Patrick was back. I scanned the players. He was nowhere to be seen. It looked as though Patrick was still suffering or that he had decided to take the hint.

'Hi,' Lydia said as I came close. 'What's up?'

I smiled. 'I've been arranging some fun for this morning,' I said. I drew close to Lydia, who looked at me and then at my opponent. Kevin had turned to speak to a player heading off to the field and had not seen my strategic move towards his girlfriend.

'Oh, what is it?' Ralph asked.

'You will see in time,' I said, a sardonic smile creeping across my face.

'I hope it's good.'

'Just wait and see.'

Kevin turned back to where Lydia was standing. His body tensed as he made his way towards the two of us.

Lydia looked at Kevin reproachingly. Kevin slowed his pace. I saw the oncoming threat and moved away.

'The coach is calling us to the field,' Ralph said, trying to diffuse the tension.

Kevin shot me a warning glance and then made his way with Ralph to the centre of the field.

Lydia enjoyed being the centre of such rivalry. Her eyes shone as she inched her way closer to me and touched my hand.

Meanwhile, far up in the row of benches, Rita arrived in her wheelchair. I looked round to see her manoeuvring out of the contraption onto the bench, her usual stick in one hand. Lydia followed my gaze.

Rita had hardly sat on the bench when the wheelchair began to roll down the steep cement ramp that led from the embankment to the service road. She cried out in alarm and struggled to get up from the bench to catch the chair, brandishing the walking stick as best she could. A student sitting on the bench turned round and saw the chair careering down the ramp. He took off after it. Others began tittering. The practice session on the field paused at the sound of the commotion. Thirty plus boys stood watching the drama unfold. I looked at Lydia, smiled, and raised my eyebrows.

Rita was now halfway down the steep slope, struggling to maintain balance. She fell and knocked her head on the concrete. She lay there, unconscious. Two students raced towards her and turned her to the recovery position. One removed her coat and covered Rita. The other ran off to fetch the duty nurse on call.

The wheelchair trundled across the car park at the foot of the ramp and smashed into a car.

I felt my shoulders drop as I turned away from the carnage. I was shaken.

'What have you done?' Lydia asked.

'It was supposed to be a practical joke. I slackened the wheelchair brake last night when Rita was in the dining room. She parked the chair next to my table. How was I supposed to know that it would turn out like this?'

The duty nurse arrived. Rita had gained consciousness but when she went to move, her arm hurt. The nurse and students gently helped her to her feet and supported her as she walked towards the student block.

Allen blew his whistle, and the practice session continued. Lydia looked at me in disgust and walked away.

The headteacher called a general meeting for all staff and students. He explained that someone had tampered with Rita's wheelchair brake and had caused the incident. Rita had suffered a broken arm and had to have pins in the bone. She was now in her room. Her academic study would be affected by the injury. The wheelchair was not badly damaged but the impact of the collision with Mr McKenzie's car had caused a sizeable dent. Mr McKenzie would be claiming from the insurance.

If this was a practical joke, it was in extremely bad taste. Rita was a vulnerable student. Everyone had a duty to look out for such students.

If anyone knew who had tampered with the wheelchair, they were to speak to a member of staff. The College would not tolerate such malicious vandalism.

The students poured out of the hall. I caught sight of Kevin. He returned the gaze with a slight nod of the head. I knew that Kevin, Ralph and Lydia would not grass on me, but my friendship with Lydia was now over. She had made it very clear that I had overstepped the bounds of decency in setting up this prank. She wanted nothing more to do with me.

I felt devastated. I kept playing the choices over and over in my mind. Should I do the honourable thing and admit my culpability? If I did, I would be expelled from the

College and could face criminal charges. The headteacher would force me to explain to Rita and perhaps to Rita's parents. My head swam with the implications. But how could I stay silent? What kind of man would that make me? How would I be able to live with my conscience?

The only way I could begin to resolve the dilemma was to promise myself never again to take advantage of a vulnerable fellow human being. Instead, I would look out for the vulnerable, the marginalised, and the hurting.

'Let this be a warning to me to never repeat this again,' I wrote in my journal.

Chapter 6

The retreat is at a local theological seminary. The first part is purely recreational. That's fine by me. We change into our swimwear using the bathrooms and enjoy a relaxing lounge at the side of the large pools in the seminary grounds, in the shade of the leathery foliage of the Babur trees. A kite rises from an aerial protruding from the roof of a nearby house and swoops over our gathering as if to warn us against too much frivolity.

We then shower, change, and make our way to a hall for *chai* and refreshments.

Nadeem approaches me with a young man following close behind. 'Steven, this is Tahir. He's the man I mentioned who could help you with your Urdu study.'

I look into the face of a tall, stocky man with square shoulders and a thick-set jaw. I guess he is in his early twenties. He reminds me of a wrestler I idolised in my early teenage years. You're a bear of a man. What have they been feeding you?

'Good to meet you, Tahir.'

'Nadeem told me about you. He said you want to learn Urdu. But he also said that you are going up north soon to Chitral. How will you learn Urdu in such a short time?'

I laugh. 'I enjoy languages. I want to practise a few phrases and discuss some of the grammatical points I read on the internet – that's all. Yeah, I don't have much time for serious study.'

'Well, when are you free?' Tahir asks. 'I'm usually free during the daytime.'

'Actually, I only have tomorrow morning. In the afternoon, I'm taking the flight to Islamabad and then onto Chitral on Friday.'

'I will come at around 10am.'

'Fine. Nadeem knows where the flat is. He can give directions better than I could.'

Nadeem turns from talking to another church member. 'Tahir is an Urdu teacher. He used to teach at the British Deputy High Commission.'

'Language is such an integral part of identity,' Tahir says. 'My family came to Pakistan from Lucknow at the time of partition. My uncle is a lecturer in the Urdu department at Karachi University. We have a long history of the language and culture.'

'Cool, I'll look forward to seeing you tomorrow morning.' Tahir nods and turns away to talk to an older man. I catch Nadeem's attention and signal for him to join me at the far side of the room where we could talk.

'Nadeem, I hope you don't mind me mentioning it,' I begin. 'I visited Hilda's family last night. During the evening, I gave Samuel a birthday gift and caught sight of his wrists. They were malformed. I'm pretty sure it's rickets. I mentioned it to Hilda, but she didn't seem too concerned. I don't know why they are delaying taking him to the doctor. If something isn't done soon, his wrists could be permanently deformed.'

Nadeem frowns – his head hangs awkwardly. The nodding dog syndrome.

'Yes, I heard about this. Some time ago, they took him to the local clinic in the *busti*. The clinic doctor gave them a few pills and said that they should refer him to a specialist, but they don't have the money to do this. I wasn't aware that the wrists are still causing problems.'

'Well, is there anything we can do about it? We can't just leave the situation. If nothing is being done because of a lack of money, I could help. Surely it wouldn't cost too much for Samuel to see a pediatrician and to get proper treatment?'

'I will talk with Hilda myself,' Nadeem says. 'Sometimes it's an issue of honour. The family may not want to accept money for this. Leave it to me and I'll see what I can do.'

Nadeem leaves me and makes his way to the table in the centre of the refectory to gather the group for the spiritual reflection. I hope to get out of this part, but I can't see how. Reluctantly, I follow the group to a room off the courtyard where the act of worship was to take place.

Later that morning, my phone rings.

'You must have made a good impression with Mr Li,' Neil says. 'He's inviting you to join them tonight for the evening meal at 7pm. He says you could travel again with Hilda and then stay for the meal. His driver will take you home. He hopes you can come.'

'Yeah, I don't have anything booked for tonight,' I reply nonchalantly. I might as well get out while I have the opportunity.'

The call ends. Nadeem approaches me.

'Is everything OK?' he asks.

'Very OK.'

Nadeem drops me back at the flat mid-afternoon. I'm feeling sleepy – I still find it difficult to get off to sleep before 2am or so most nights, and the hot, humid weather saps my energy. I trudge up the steps to the third floor, still reluctant to use the lift. A rap on the metal door brings Hilda running to open it.

'I'm going to rest,' I say to Hilda and make my way to my room. Hilda dutifully brings me a glass of water, knocking on the door before entering.

'This evening I will be travelling with you again to Mr Li's house. They have invited me to stay for the meal.'

Hilda steps back and smiles. 'Yes, that is fine.'

Yes, it would be fine with you, woman – a free ride in the comfort of a taxi instead of the cattle wagon. You know when your bread is buttered.

Hilda leaves me with my thoughts and dreams of meeting my exotic woman.

I set my alarm for 4pm just in case I fall asleep. I lie on the bed, the ceiling fan rotating slowly above me to create a slight breeze. I doze off thinking of the beautiful Esther, her feminine figure and delicate facial features. In my mind's eye, I visit her alluring eyes and exquisite lips. I dream of a life together in the UK, of warmth and companionship.

I slowly stir to hear a loud tapping on my door. 'Mr Steven, I leave in ten minutes. Are you ready?'

I curse myself for falling asleep. I promised myself a shower before setting out. I rush into the ensuite bathroom and yank at the stainless steel tap impatiently. Fifteen minutes later, I emerge hastily dressed and smelling sweet. Hilda looks at me suspiciously. If she knows what's going on, she disguises it well.

'We will take a taxi again,' I say. Hilda feigns relief.

I watch the traffic as we retrace our steps to the Li family home. I asked Hilda to find a taxi that had an air conditioner. The negotiated fare is higher than the previous day, but I want to arrive less dishevelled and smelling sweet, rather than carrying the odour of sweat and diesel fumes. The air conditioner is barely making a difference even in the front of the cab. I am tempted to wind down the window again. Suddenly, a thought flashes through my mind.

'Hilda, should I be taking a gift to the family?'

'Sometimes we do this, sir. It is part of our culture.'

I think rapidly. 'Is there a good bakery near Mr Li's home?'

'Yes, the "Treats Bakery" is close.'

'Ask the taxi driver to stop there for five minutes.'

The taxi draws up outside the bakery. I run into the shop, locate the dessert section, and buy one of the most expensive desserts on display. I hope it tastes as good as it looks.

I run back to the waiting taxi. When we arrive at the house, Hilda instructs me to pay fifty rupees more than what we have initially agreed. The driver takes the money greedily.

We knock on the door, but this time Mrs Li is standing with the Pakistani young man as we enter. Unlike the previous evening, I am immediately shown into the Li family lounge and a comfortable chair. The boy brings a tray with cold water and a glass.

'I am happy welcome you to our home,' Mrs Li says. Obviously, during the previous day's visit, I had only been welcomed to the outer court of the home.

The room I am sitting in is larger than the reception area. There are still many Chinese hangings with Mandarin script on the walls. Carpets cover much of the floor. There are many comfortable chairs and plants in large pots. I notice family photographs set out on the tops of cabinets. The cabinets themselves are of teak rather than the cheap, heavy veneered furniture of the local *bazaar*. The potent smell of fish is still there but is mixed with incense.

What if our future home smells like this? It stinks. Could I get used to it? Could I mask the smell?

Mrs Li lowers herself into a chair and smiles at me benevolently. Hilda walks through to the kitchen area.

'I so sorry there is little to entertain you until Mr Li and my daughters return home,' she says. 'I have magazines you read. The boy will bring tea in a few minutes.'

I know little about Chinese customs, so I refrain from

asking Mrs Li questions for which I urgently seek an answer. Instead, I wait for her to initiate the conversation.

'My daughter says you do research in Oxford.' Mrs Li begins. 'What kind of research?'

'Unfortunately, I can't tell you exactly what the research is about. It's sensitive. It has to do with types of plastics used in food packaging.'

Mrs Li nods, as though she fully understands the gravity of what I have shared. She probably is none the wiser. But we play the game.

'This research bring you to Pakistan?'

'Yes, there are several people groups in this country that have limited exposure to plastics. I'm collecting samples to analyse the DNA of these people.'

'You are a clever person.'

I blush and look away.

Woman, if only you knew. Oxford is full of the intelligentsia, and I'm no darling.

'Do you have your house in Oxford?'

'I have a flat,' I say matter-of-factly. 'It is all I need. Housing in Oxford is very expensive.'

'Do your parents live there?'

'My father died when I was fourteen. My mother lives in the countryside in south west England. It's where I grew up. I visit my mother as often as I can.'

At that moment, the Pakistani boy comes into the lounge and speaks to Mrs Li in broken English. They need her in the kitchen. She excuses herself and leaves. I am glad to be spared further interrogation.

A few minutes later, the young man returns with tea. He

leaves me to browse the coffee table magazines.

I hear footsteps outside, and the door of the reception area opens. The steps follow across the room and a slightly younger but heavier version of Esther steps into the lounge. I gather this is Esther's sister. She smiles and says, 'Hallo', but then walks straight past through to what I am to learn later is the bedroom area.

Then I hear the car pull up, more footsteps, and two people talking. Their voices become louder until they enter the room.

'Mr Grant, I am so happy you come to share our meal this evening,' Mr Li says. 'My daughter tell me you will be leaving Karachi soon. I want to give you pleasure of dining with local businessman's family before you leave.'

I stand and shake Mr Li's hand. Should I bow? I avoid looking in Esther's direction.

'Please accept this as a small token of appreciation for your kind invitation,' I say. The rehearsed sentence flows out smoothly.

Mr Li passes the dessert to Esther, who takes it to the kitchen area.

'Please excuse me for a while,' Mr Li says. He heads off to the bedroom area, presumably to change for dinner.

Esther returns to the lounge. She sits a distance from me and sips chilled water. She seems embarrassed but eager at the same time.

'I hope you not waiting for too long,' she says. 'My father and I leave the office early today.'

'I came with Hilda – I'm not sure I would be able to give directions to the taxi driver in Urdu yet.'

'Are you still planning to leave Pakistan soon?'

'Yeah,' I reply. 'I have to keep to my original itinerary. But there seem to be reasons why I should return to Karachi soon.'

Esther's face glows. She looks down at her glass and runs her forefinger around the top rim distractedly.

'Have you been busy today?' I ask, trying to make conversation.

'Yes, usual work. I do take breaks and talk to friends. Over lunch period, I was in contact with lawyer friend who is working with bonded labourers to bring case against their employer.'

I look up. I never knew that Esther's interests included social justice issues.

'It is very sad,' Esther continues. 'Here feudal landlord and brick kiln owners use their political connections to use forced labour. The family my friend know had been removed from exploitation, but some police helped one of the brick kiln owners to kidnap the family and bring them back into same situation they were in previous.'

'I never knew this happened so much here,' I said. 'I've read about modern slavery in the UK. We're trained to look out for it there.'

'Yes, much happens here. Police offered bribes to ignore prostitution crimes, including sex trafficking, and some say that border officials help those involved in human trafficking.'

Esther looks away.

'Oh, I'm sorry.'

Esther turns back to look at me, her eyes widening and

her facial muscles relaxing once again.

'We see progress, even though it is too slow coming. There are positive signs.

'Have you been in touch with your mother and friends after arriving here?'

I push thoughts of Rachel and her accusations to the back of my mind and force a smile.

'Yes, I've spoken to my friends one or two times on the phone,' I reply. 'I regularly talk with my mother.' Esther nods.

'What do they think about you in Pakistan? Are they anxious?'

'Unfortunately, Pakistan doesn't generally have a good press in the UK. People think that travelling to India is OK. But when you mention you're taking a trip to Pakistan, people are much more concerned. I guess it just comes down to image, that's all.'

'Do you think of coming to live in Pakistan in the future?' Esther asks.

I look quizzically at her. Has Neil mentioned something to her? Was this a plot to get me here? I decide to feign indifference.

'In the short term, I need to finish the research I'm doing in the UK. In the longer term, I'm happy to go where life takes me. That could be Pakistan, Australia, the US – who knows?'

Esther shifts uneasily in her seat.

'Do you return to China to see your relatives?'

'I go back several times since moving to Karachi,' Esther says. 'We have strong family connections there. I have new niece I would like to see soon. Family is very important for our community.'

Our conversation continues for a further hour. We exchange opinions, views, and preferences on all manner of topics. We pussyfoot around the issue of where we would like to be in the future. If I get too close to the subject, Esther clams up, embarrassed.

Mr Li comes into the room and announces the evening meal is ready. I am shown into the dining room and seated at a place reserved for me at the large, ornate table. The meal begins with grace said by Esther's father. Then we eat. There is little conversation during the meal itself – everyone seems content to enjoy the food. Then I follow the family back into the lounge, where we sit and talk. The interrogation begun by Mrs Li is recommenced, this time led by Mr Li. 'What was my father's profession when he was alive? What was my childhood like? How many siblings do I have? How many uncles and aunts? What was my mother planning for my marriage? Is my income adequate for living away from home?'

9:30pm arrives. I announce my intention to return to the flat. The driver is called, and I am whisked away in the family saloon back along the city's major artery, the Shahrah-e-Faisal. When I arrive, both Neil and Claire are up, watching CNN. Neil grins as I walk past on my way to the bedroom. I spy a tumbler and a small bottle of whisky on the glass-top coffee table. He has been drinking.

'How'd you get on?' he calls out.

'Good. I had a pleasant evening with the family.'

'When you are ready, come and sit here – I want to talk,' Neil says.

I look at Claire. She gazes non-committedly into the distance. If she knows what the topic of conversation is to be, she isn't giving it away.

I freshen up in the bathroom and change into a *shalwar-kameez* suit that I use to sleep in. I take a glass of water to the wicker chair.

Neil stares into my face. I can smell the spirit on his breath.

'Have you thought any more about our conversation in the office on Monday?' he says.

'No, and I'm not interested. It's not a proposition that I take seriously.'

'Not even if the Li family responds positively to your interest in Esther?' Neil adds with a smirk.

'That's my business, not yours. Esther is her own woman. Anyway, all of this is presumptuous. It may all come to nothing.'

Neil pours himself another half-tumbler of whisky and swigs it down. His eyes burrow into mine. I can see a slight tremor on his face.

'You know that you are really my son, don't you?'

I jolt up, turning over the coffee table with all its contents onto the floor. Claire gets up and quickly makes her way to the bedroom. I despise the cowardly retreat.

'What baseless crap are you speaking? Where's your respect for your brother, my father? What would my mother say if she could hear you saying this? Don't you have any shame?' I can feel my heart rate accelerating fast.

Neil leers and cocks his head provocatively. 'But it's true. I'm your father. Your mother and I had something going on...'

'I couldn't care a damn if you are my biological father,' I shout back at Neil. 'It makes no difference to my future plans. I'm not staying here and will never join you. You and I are finished. I'll leave in the morning.'

I turn to leave the lounge, afraid of the path my anger is taking me.

'Obviously, I can check with Mum what you've said. If it's true, there will be a reason why she didn't tell me. No doubt you've gone behind my mother's back.'

Once in the bedroom, I begin to pack, throwing my clothes haphazardly into my suitcase. Leaving first thing in the morning isn't practical – Tahir is coming early for the Urdu lesson. Then I am leaving for Islamabad in the afternoon. I will need to move after the language class and before leaving for Islamabad. I don't want to take my large suitcase up north – the smaller cabin bag will do for the few nights I was away. Where could I store it if I can't find anywhere to stay?

I am still seething with anger when I pick up my phone to call Mum. My hand is shaking as I navigate to the contacts screen to call the number. I stop myself. Neil is probably telling the truth – he wouldn't dare make up a story like that, even if he was worse for the drink. I need to process this news and then phone Mum when I am in a better emotional state, or better still, wait until I can speak to her face-to-face.

I slump down on the bed. I can hear Neil and Claire

arguing in their room. I gulp some water and try to relax. I am in no mood to sleep.

I have been checking the time ever since the early hours of the morning. Eventually, 7:30am arrives. I groan and curse under my breath as I get out of bed and shower. I dress quickly and make my way to the flat door. Out of principle, I'm not going to eat another meal under this roof – I'll look for breakfast in the *bazaar*.

The street seems less busy than usual, but a few of the shops are open. I find what would resemble a transport café in the UK, with workmen sipping *chai* from saucers and greedily bolting down greasy curry with *chapati*. I enjoy the aromatic smell of curry, though I couldn't stomach it myself so early in the morning. I sit on a bench and order *chai* and cake. The other men stare at me, but the café owner serves me.

I watch this part of Karachi go by and ruminate on the events of last night. I still can't bring myself to believe that Neil could be my biological father. Mum has some explaining to do. How would this affect my suitability as a future partner for Esther if Mr and Mrs Li get to hear about it?

I am still musing about this as I meander through the *bazaar* back towards the flat. I enter the service road, leaving the shops behind me. The gate of 'Suleman Media Consultants' is already open. I glance across at the open office door. These men start work early. A security guard stands by his booth, pistol in his holster.

A car races along the Shahrah-e-Faisal. Shots ring out. The assailants seem to be targeting the office complex. The armed guard takes cover and returns fire. A bullet hits the wall behind me just a few centimetres from my face, leaving a deep pockmark. I throw myself onto the road, prostrate. Another bullet ricochets off the road ahead of me, ripping up dust and loose grit. Looking up from the road, I see workmen further down the street cowering into gaps in the wall. Some have taken shelter behind a few straggly trees. A few bystanders further away gawk. The car drives on. In a few moments, it is all over.

I slowly get up from the road. No one else moves. The security guard looks out from behind the wall but shows no inclination to help me.

I feel my body shaking. Despite a sense of dizziness from the shock, I walk as best as I can at a brisk pace towards the flat, aware that I'm lurching as I walk. Someone is keen to eliminate me.

Chapter 7

Neil

'Hi, Brad. An update. Yeah, I know it's early. Time zones are a bind to work with. OK, grab a coffee. Don't wake Christine.

'Listen, the son-of-a-bitch still isn't budging. I made the offer. He wasn't interested. I can't think of any more leverage. He's my son, but he's not willing to play the line. He's no one to me. I've already screwed his family.

'What, another attempt. Where? Not here? A few minutes ago? What happened? Come on, you agreed you'd keep the attempts away from here. It's messy if it happens too close to our flat. Even in this country, there could be complications. Claire would get emotional. Cut the action around here, understand?

'He's gone sweet on the girl. It seems to be working out. Yeah, the director's daughter. But it's going too slowly. We don't have much leeway. He's planning to be back in the UK soon. We have to think of something else.'

'You're the one with the ideas. There must be something we can do. OK, I hadn't thought of that. Would it work here? Run it by your contacts. They have experience.'

'I have to go. Keep me informed. I'll do likewise. Ciao.'

I return to the bedroom.

'Who were you phoning?' Claire asks.

'Yaqoob at the office. I need him to get things ready for a client visiting today. Shazia's not in. We need someone on reception.'

'Was that Steven who went out earlier?'

'Must have been.'

Claire tucks her head into her pillow and turns away from me.

'You're a beast. Look at how you went about last night. No wonder Steven reacted. You drink too much.'

I clamber over the bed and yank Claire 180 degrees to face me.

'Ow.'

'Woman, I'll remind you that you're living a pampered life here because of my business. And that my son's research publication could put an end to that.

'But we don't know. I don't understand his research.'

I climb into bed and prop myself up to face Claire. 'But I do. I've done the homework. It's not going to work.'

Claire rolls over on her side and turns to me. 'If it's not going to work, what will you do?'

'It's got to work. We've put too much into this. I'll think of something. I'll pull strings. I'll find a way around it.'

'Is our Malaysia trip still on? Claire says. I need a break.

We got a good deal on the hotel. We're still going, aren't we?'

It was five years ago. I met Brad and Christine on a Royal Caribbean International cruise – a round-trip exploration of the Arabian Gulf. Brad was the loud one, particularly after imbibing large quantities of alcohol following the evening meal. He could always out-drink me. Christine and Claire got on well, though they were as different as chalk to cheese. Christine the socialite, vivacious, sophisticated and informed. Claire the self-conscious fawner, the ardent social climber. I used to laugh at Claire's anxious dissection of the evening's conversation late at night in the cabin, picking through the recounted dialogue for scraps of affirmation and validation. Man, she's so insecure.

Brad and I would wander the deck late evening, leaning against the rails and looking out to sea. The content of our conversation was not for women. Nor were our antics.

Men talk about work. We were no exception. I mentioned my upper-managerial position in a London-based company. Brad spoke of his burgeoning business in the US. He had found ways to improvise, to do it cheaper, to outsmart the competition. There was a growing market in the developing world, particularly Asia. There was a goldmine to be harvested. He needed entrepreneurs of high calibre to set up and rake in the profit.

I have always been business astute. I took serious notice and began negotiations. Claire was oblivious to the agreements I was signing off on.

I left it until we were back in the UK before I started

selling the proposal to my wife. Claire remonstrated. She didn't want to live in a tropical country. She wouldn't like the food. What about social life? Where would she fit?

Brad put up the cash for an exploratory trip. We made good connections. I did some digging and got Claire a visit with the wife of a Deputy British High Commission official. She saw it could work. She wouldn't need to mix with the plebs. Let others do that. We had no dependents, so it was straightforward.

I gave some concessions to sweeten the pill. We could return to the UK during the hottest months. We would have a comfortable home, fully air conditioned and secure. We'd have a driver. We would use our new location as a springboard to travel farther east. At least two trips a year. She would be the wife of a high-flying businessman, travelling frequently in first-class cabins.

I'm still surprised she swallowed the pill. I knew it wouldn't be a picnic in the park. Claire soon discovered the day-to-day reality of living in a country trying to keep its head above water. Six months into our new life, she upped and left. She was gone for seven weeks. I made some changes and convinced her to return. Since her arrival back, she's been onboard, but a skittish passenger.

It was four years six months ago I first clapped eyes on the concrete edifice in the Sindh Industrial and Trading Estate. Brad had pulled strings with the manager of another of his subsidiaries in Karachi, and they had loaned me the driver for the day. The car was shabby and road-weary. Rafiq was an aggressive driver who took chances. That was my style. I had no patience for courtesy in

Pakistan. It wasn't my vehicle, and we weren't doing any speed, so there was no great danger to life or limb.

'This is it, sir,' Rafiq said, as we pulled up alongside the unit. I got out of the car as a pickup roared past on the off-side, down the sandy track.

'Sir, you OK?'

'Damn, yeah'. Rafiq passed me a cloth. My shoes turned from dirty yellow back to black as I rubbed.

Rafiq spoke to the watchman at the gate. He let us through, staring as we walked up to the factory building alongside spindly plants in pots dotted along the path.

Rafiq opened the main gate into the building, his arms peppering with sweat as he strained with the weight of the heavy metal.

The unit was cavernous but derelict. The previous occupiers had not cleaned up on departure. After five minutes of meandering around, peering at rough wooden benches and rubbish strewn in the corners, my shirt was soaked.

'Why so much concrete? Don't they know how to build in any other material? I pity the bastards working here.'

'How do the workers get here?'

'Sir, buses and pickups. They come. They will work,' Rafiq replied, a wry smile lightening the furrows of his creased and pox-holed face.

The phone rang. It was Brad. I pushed past Rafiq to a dwarf palm tree and stood in the shade.

'Yeah, I've looked around. It's a concrete shack. It's usable, if that's all we've got. How do I get fitted up? Who's your contact? He's here? Why didn't you get him to meet us? Ask your contact to get him around to us. We'll wait.'

'We're going back to the car,' I said to Rafiq. 'You get the car cooled. I'll come.'

A long thirty minutes later, a smartly dressed man arrived in a Suzuki saloon. He got out and marched over to me, introducing himself as Akhtar Qureshi. I lead him to the unit. He didn't seem too interested in seeing inside. He had seen it all before.

He could source the machines. He worked with another local unit that kitted out units. What production capacity were we planning? He winced. A big operation. Yes, the unit was large enough. We would have to check on the basic infrastructure on site.

What pellets were we using? He hadn't heard of the US company. His technical team would work with us. They would need the exact specification of the material before his team could source the equipment.

Rafiq drove me back into the city centre. We passed endless concrete edifices rising from the sandy soil, bleak cathedrals of Karachi-style capitalism. Worn tyres and litter abandoned at the side of the road did little to ease the heaviness. A stray dog ran in front of the vehicle, causing Rafiq to slam on the brakes. What the heck, I'm not coming out here too often.

The following weeks were a blur. Brad introduced me to a myriad of his connections, who advised on every part of the operations. I was constantly travelling, in the heat, dust, and noise. I took flights to other cities. I hopped over to the Emirates. Early mornings, late nights, and strange food at ridiculous hours. Always appearing professional and business-like.

I hated it. The time spent in formalities. The polite conversation. The clamour for respect and prestige. What a obscene waste of time. Give me the UK anytime.

I learned how to do business in this environment. Budgets had to allow for backhanders, payoffs and financial inducements. Men scratched my back and expected payback. The competition had to be obliterated. I experimented with moles in other companies, to get the edge on quality and productivity. Marketing was cut-throat. I provided incentives to the middlemen to drop other products and to use mine. It wasn't difficult.

Two years into production, I was called early in the morning to the factory complex. Armed men had stormed the building at night, shooting the watchman and damaging some of the machines.

The stand-in watchman, a young man in his late twenties, saluted me on arrival. I cursed under my breath. What kind of insolence was this? Bilal, the Production Manager, gestured to the supervisor. Out of the corner of my eye, I saw Fareed walk over to the concrete hut at the gate and lay into the worker. Later, when I emerged, he was gone.

The gate to the factory unit was open. A small group of men parted to the right and left as Bilal and I approached. The early morning sun glared off the white distempered breeze blocks, leaving floaters dancing in my vision. I made a mental note to replace the sunglasses I kept in the car that disintegrated yesterday and which I tossed to the side of the road. Cheap, sub-standard rubbish.

An older man with henna-coloured hair jabbered away to Bilal in Urdu as we walked around. I stopped to caress the warm metal casing of one of the specialist pieces of equipment that had been spared the attackers' fury, scarred with dirt and grime. This was my capital. Money I had worked for.

'I want to see a list of the affected machines,' I said to Bilal. I followed him to his office. The other men accompanying us on our tour lingered outside the hallowed room.

'You have the supplier's contact numbers. Get onto them. I want the damaged equipment replaced immediately.'

Bilal nodded.

'What do the police say?'

Bilal looked up from the documents strewn across his heavy metal desk. 'I know Station House Officer. I will meet him later today. I will see what can be done.'

I put Bilal on the spot. 'Any ideas who could be responsible?'

'Sir, we are making enquiries. It is too early to say. I will personally inform you as soon as we know.'

'Good man.'

'OK. Sir, what about Wahid?'

'Who's he?'

'The *chowkidar* who was shot. He's at the government hospital in Liaquatabad.'

'Oh. So, he's alive?'

'Yes, Sir. They shoot him in the leg. Will you visit?'

'Why not you represent me? Tell him how sorry I am. Take something with you. Here…' I fished out a five hundred rupee note from my wallet and slapped it into Bilal's palm.

Chapter 8

Steven

I rap quietly on the grill door. When Hilda lets me in, I brush past her into the lounge and then to my room.

'Mr Steven, what is wrong?' she calls out.

'Nothing. I need to rest.'

I slump back onto the bed, my head against the headboard. Looking up, the room spins before me. Reaching for the drinking water on the bedside cabinet, I pour three straight glasses and gulp them. I stand and pace the floor. I have to think straight and fast.

I'm definitely the target. I know the 'why' but not the 'who'. I need to know. Yeah, I'm going to find out. They don't put Steven off so easily...

So, what to do? I keep to the itinerary. I'll meet them at some point. They'll be waiting. But I'll be waiting too.

I need a plan. Come on, think.

Plan part 1: Welcome Tahir to the flat and keep composed. Have a shortened language lesson with him. Then tell him I need to take a rest – after all, I have an afternoon flight to catch. When he leaves...

Part 2: Phone Nadeem. Explain the argument with Neil, but don't give details. Ask him if he knows somewhere I could stay on the pretext that I am estranged from my uncle. Then later share with him the attempt on my life. Ask him whether to go to the police or to stay quiet.

Part 3: Move out by 1pm, either to someone's home or an inexpensive hotel. No, a hotel wouldn't be any good – it would be easy for an assassin to gain entrance. It would have to be someone's home. From there, I travel to the airport and take the flight to Islamabad.

It is not yet 9am. I have time for a brief rest and another shower before Tahir arrives.

The tapping on my door grows louder.

'Mr Steven, a man, Tahir is here to see you.' I shake myself from sleep.

'OK, I'm coming.' I tidy my clothes and splash my face with water. After a few minutes of grooming, I feel just about presentable.

'Tahir, great to see you.' I walk towards my guest seated in the lounge and shake his hand.

'How is your family?'

'They are well,' Tahir says. 'You know I live with my parents and brothers?'

'No, I can't remember Nadeem telling me,' I say. 'How does it work out? In the UK we try to leave home as soon as possible after university.'

'We have the family system in Pakistan. We don't send our parents to homes or hospitals to be looked after. It is a matter of honour that we repay our parents by looking after them in old age.'

Tahir's manner comes across as abrasive. My heckles rise. Yet as I talk with him further, it's obvious that he is direct and honest. I admire that in him.

'You can tell how important family is for us as we have different words in Urdu for our relations. In English, you just have "aunt" and "uncle". In Urdu, we have various words that describe whether it's the paternal or maternal aunt or uncle. We have different words to describe where the uncle or aunt fit in their family in relation to their siblings. Even the in-laws have different familial names. It is very developed.'

Tahir smiles smugly.

'I've noticed as I've listened that even within the immediate family there seem to be different names for the siblings based on their seniority.'

'Yes.' Tahir smiles. 'We hold our siblings close to our hearts.'

'No family squabbles, then?'

'Of course, but we respect our parents and they, or elders, sort things out.'

I sense we are getting down to business.

'Can I ask you about grammar?' I ask. 'I'm having difficulties understanding how to conjugate verbs in the past tense. Do some verbs have a gender?'

'Yes, they do. The verb "to marry", for instance, is feminine, so has to be followed by the feminine form in the past tense. Other verbs also have a gender. Remember that when the verb is transitive, the ergative marker 'ne' breaks the relationship between the object and the subject in the past tense…

'What's wrong? Why aren't you listening to me?'

My eyelids droop during Tahir's explanation. I momentarily enjoy the sensation of blurred vision as I fight to stay focused. Recent events have taken their toll.

'Nothing. Sorry, I must have lost concentration,' I say.

'The other tenses are more straightforward. Obviously, you must look for the gender of the subject. The verb agrees with the subject, not the object.'

Tahir stops speaking. 'Why are you sleeping? You must be unwell. But you are travelling this afternoon? You need to see a doctor before you travel.'

'I'll be OK, Tahir. I will rest as soon as I can.'

'It's foolish to me to travel up north if you are not well,' Tahir says. 'You probably need to see a doctor first. I will take you on the back of my motorbike. I know a good clinic in my area.'

'I'm not ill. I didn't sleep well last night.'

'Well, get some rest before you travel.'

The language lesson finishes at 11:15am. I am glad to see Tahir leave. Normally I would have enjoyed his company, but I am on edge since the attempt on my life and want to move from the flat and get settled somewhere before making my way to the airport. I phone Nadeem and explain that Neil and I had a big argument the previous night and that I need to move out. Nadeem graciously offers to accommodate me in his home. He will take the bus to the flat and then we will travel together back to his house in a taxi. I insist on paying for the taxi fare.

He arrives at 12:15pm and by 1:15pm, I am settled at

his small home. His wife serves lunch – a simple lentil curry with *chapati*. Nadeem eats with me, but his wife and children eat separately.

'You do not look well,' Nadeem tells me after the meal. 'I suggest you delay your trip to Islamabad. You will have no one to help you if you are unwell there.'

'It's not just tiredness,' I say. 'I'm concerned about something that happened this morning. I think someone was trying to kill me.'

Nadeem lowers his drinking glass and stares at me.

'What happened? Why didn't you tell me?'

'I wanted to wait until I could explain properly.'

I tell Nadeem about the attack as I walked past the Suleman Media Consultants' office complex, and how the bullets seemed directed at me, though I couldn't be sure.

Nadeem thinks for a while. 'These incidents happen here. Sometimes robbers target banks, petrol pumps, or institutions, and bystanders get caught in the crossfire. But as you say, it may have been a direct attempt on your life.'

'Should we go to the police?'

'No. It's best not to get them involved. They will insist you leave the country.

'You should cancel this trip to Islamabad and Chitral. It's not safe, particularly if you go on your own. Get someone else to do it. I will help you reschedule your flight back to the UK.'

'I can't get someone else to do this,' I say. 'I need to be there to make sure the samples are taken properly. This is the reason I've come to Pakistan.

'The clinic is arranged, and people have been contacted

to come. It's all ready. My laboratory supervisor has been pulling strings from the UK. I can't back out now.'

There is a rap on the gate. Nadeem leaves the room. I hear him talking with someone and then he and the guest enter the room. It is Tahir.

'What happened this morning?' Tahir asks, in his gruff, coarse voice. 'I came to tell Nadeem how worried I was about your health. He says someone targeted you. Why didn't you tell me when I visited earlier on? I could have helped.'

'I didn't want to cause alarm. There's nothing you could do. I've told Nadeem, as I thought someone should know.'

'So, you don't consider me a friend?' Tahir asks. He looks at me with steely eyes.

'No, it's not that.'

'Steven was uncertain what to do,' Nadeem says. 'We need to think clearly about what should happen next.'

'He can't go up north on his own.' Tahir turns to me. 'You don't know the language or the culture. You could get in trouble. You need to cancel the trip.'

'I've said to Nadeem that this isn't possible. Everything is in place. I need to go for my research. This is my job.'

'Stupid man,' Tahir says, shaking his head.

'My flight is at 5:30pm. I will need to be at the airport by 4pm. I'm happy to take a taxi.'

The phone rings. I eye the number suspiciously, but take the call – it's a UK number.

'Steven, it's Kate. I'm sorry to have to disturb you, but I have some bad news for you. Your mother has had a serious heart attack. She's in the cardiology unit at the Exeter hospital. She's stable, but the doctors are saying she could have another heart attack at any moment.'

Aunt Kate is generally a relaxed, easy-going character. On this occasion, her voice is tense.

'Is she conscious? Is there any way I can talk with her?'

'The doctors have sedated her. She won't be conscious for a day or two, possibly longer.'

I speak the question of which I dread the answer: 'Do I need to come back?'

'Yes. You do. As soon as possible.'

'Thanks for letting me know,' I say feebly.

Tahir and Nadeem stare at me.

'I have to go back to the UK. I don't know how much you heard: My mother has had a serious heart attack.'

'I'm sorry to hear that,' Nadeem says.

'How do I change my return flight?'

'Give me the ticket. I'll work on it.'

I arrive at London Heathrow at 12:55pm, sleep-deprived and anxious to see my mother. Kate is waiting for me as I exit into the arrivals area. The place is abuzz with passengers hauling suitcases and friends, family members, and others waiting for their loved ones. A small child pulling a toy carry-on bag stumbles in my way. I halt myself while the mother shouts to the girl and whispers a brief apology.

'I won't ask about the flight,' Kate says as she approaches. 'I can see that you didn't get much sleep. At least it was on time.'

Kate is ten years younger than Mum. She has a splendid figure and rich auburn hair. I have never figured out why she has not married, particularly as she has a good job as a palliative nurse. Perhaps she's not the marrying type.

'I'll take you straight to the hospital,' Kate says, as we walk towards the short-term car park. 'You can crash on the back seat.'

'Is there any update on Mum's condition?' I squint into the sun as we pull out of the car park.

'No, she continues to be sedated.

'Reuben is at her bedside. He's accompanied by someone from the unit. He seems a little better. He's only there for the day.'

I am looking forward to seeing Reuben again. I had felt powerless to stop his slide into a financial and personal crisis. At least he was getting some help. We would have a small family gathering.

I sink back into the back seat to make myself comfortable as we pull onto the motorway. I notice a motorcyclist on a powerful black and gold bike overtake in the outside lane, head down into the wind. His turn of speed reminds me of my pursuit to get results from the samples in Chitral. I muse on who is taking the most risk, this motorcyclist or I in my ignoring of the attempts on my life. At least the driving is ordered in the UK and so road travel is safer. I doze for a few moments.

'How have things gone in Pakistan?' Kate asks.

'I hadn't got the samples done before I left. It's been problematic trying to arrange the trip to Chitral. I'll need to return and get on with the trip as soon as I can.'

'That's a nuisance. It's a good job you enjoy travel. It must be tiring.

'Have you spoken to Rachel recently? She'll be glad to know you're back.'

I bristle with a pang of guilt and anger. My pulse rate begins to quicken.

'We chatted a few days ago, but not since then. I've had other things on my mind.'

'I forgot to ask you whether you're hungry,' Kate says. 'I'd planned to stop at a service station around Bristol, but we could stop before then if you need something.'

'No, I'm fine. We had plenty of food during the flight. I'll just snooze for a while… you can wake me when we turn off for the services.'

We arrive outside the hospital by early evening. I enjoyed a strong coffee at the services and feel more myself despite a prick of a headache. It is a sight for sore eyes to see the green foliage outside the modern, well-apportioned building after the grey and brown of the Karachi metropolis.

We enter the building through the door next to Oncology Outpatients and head towards Level 2. In area C we find the Coronary Care Unit and make our way to the desk. A harried nurse with wispy grey hair and a pale face looks up at us. She recognises Kate from earlier visits.

'We've come to see Linnet Grant,' Kate says.

'That's OK. You remember where she is?' The nurse speaks to Kate, hardly looking up from her typing.

'Yeah. Are my nephew and his attendant still here?'

'No, they left. Mrs Grant gained consciousness early afternoon – I think they were able to chat with her. Mr

Grant said something about needing to get back to where he's staying.'

'Thanks.'

Kate takes off at full speed towards her sister's bed. I walk briskly behind her.

Mum is propped up in bed, dozing. Various wires snake from her chest to nearby monitoring equipment. She has a deathly pallor, the pinch of her forehead indicating that she is not out of pain. I look at the green electrocardiogram lines charting the waves and spikes of the heartbeat cycle. It all seems regular, from what I can tell.

We settle into chairs next to Mum's bed. The plastic of the rough seat chides against the back of my leg. Kate leans over and gently smoothes Mum's hand. Mum slowly stirs and opens her eyes.

'I didn't hear you come,' she says. 'Have you just arrived?'

'Yeah, only just now.'

'Have you come from your trip?' she asks.

'I only heard yesterday. Friends helped me to get a flight. I came as soon as I could.'

'I know you did… I'm sorry I've disrupted your schedule. Did you finish the work in… what was the country?'

'Pakistan. Unfortunately, no. I'll have to go back. But it doesn't matter.'

'Trust me to fall seriously ill when you're away,' Mum says, raising her head from the pillow. Kate continues to caress her hand.

'So, how are you feeling now?'

'I feel like I've been hit by a double-decker bus. The

pain's better now. If I lie here quietly, it's OK. If I try to do anything, I get short of breath.'

'You shouldn't be trying to do anything,' Kate says, smiling endearingly at her older sister and talking louder than I thought was necessary. 'Just rest.'

'Do you know what brought this on?'

'I'm not sure. I did some heavy gardening in the morning... the patch at the bottom of the garden, behind the greenhouse. The ground needed turning – it was full of dandelion weeds and couch grass. The seeds were spreading in the wind. Usually, it doesn't affect me. I felt really tired after all the digging. Then early evening I went to see Mrs Skipper next door to borrow a mousetrap. It came on then. Eileen phoned for the ambulance.'

'Well, you'll just have to take it slower in the future,' Kate says. 'Get Bill to turn the ground – he won't mind.'

'But I'm not yet sixty. I need to be able to do these things myself.'

Mum sinks her head back into the pillow. 'I need to rest – sorry.'

'We'll go to the waiting area,' Kate says in a whisper. She rises and I follow her out.

'I'll go home now,' Kate says. 'What are your plans?'

'I'll go for a walk around the hospital grounds and come back after an hour or so. I'll stay here overnight and then see what the situation is tomorrow.'

'You're welcome to stay with me. You know where I am. I have the small guest room you can use.'

'I've forgotten your house number. I'll text you before coming.'

Kate strides out from the unit, smiling at the duty nurse at the desk as she passes.

I return to the ward at 6:30pm, making sure that I am clear of the evening mealtime. Mum is sitting higher in the bed and has a bit more colour in her cheeks. I take a chair and draw it up to the bed. Mum looks at me with concern, her eyebrows deepening into a furrow. Her voice is laboured, her expression grave.

'Neil phoned me. He told me he had explained the situation to you.'

'Are you sure you want to talk about it now?' I ask. 'Would it be better to leave it until you are better?'

'No, I need to get it off my chest. Stress has been a contributing factor to this heart attack. I suspected Neil would tell you while you were staying with him. It's not a part of my life I am proud of, but there it is.

'Your dad was working away for Celebra Beverages, up north, somewhere in Northampton. For six months after we were married, he was away during the week, returning two weekends a month. We had just moved into the flat near to the village – you wouldn't remember it. I didn't know anyone in the village and became lonely. It was not too difficult during the daytime, as I was working at the Chestnut Drive Tea Rooms, but the nights were hard.

'Your Uncle Neil and his wife used to visit regularly. They were good to me. Pat was such a caring person. Neil used to do the 'man' jobs around the house. When they couldn't visit, they used to phone.

'Then Neil and Pat had a falling out. I can't remember

what it was about. The phone calls stopped.

'I didn't hear from either of them until one night Neil turned up on my doorstep. He was drunk and very upset. He had driven to the village – I'm not sure how he avoided an accident. I couldn't turn him away. He slept that night but stayed the next day – and evening. I was as much to blame as he was. In the morning, he left. He knew he had to make up with Pat. They got back together again, and we both kept the incident quiet.

'Your father came back the following weekend. After some days, I found out that I was pregnant. I wasn't sure who the father was, but it was assumed that it was Ryan. Nothing was said and so we all continued as normal.'

'So, Neil may not be my biological father, after all?'

'Recently he's started to talk about it again with me. He's suggested getting DNA tests done to find out, but I told him straight you would never agree to it.

'The problem is that, as you know, Neil and Pat were never able to have children. Neil wants a son, so he's convinced himself that you are that son.'

'Well, I'm convinced that he will never be my father,' I say. 'I couldn't imagine having such a despicable person as a father.'

'Don't be too quick to judge. He was once a good man. Business pressure has changed him. There's still some good in him, though it's hard to see these days.'

'Did he tell you he had asked me to work with him in Karachi?'

'Yes, he mentioned it. I think he's lonely.'

'Well, he had better return to the UK then.'

Mum repositions herself on the bed and reaches out for my hand.

'Don't make an enemy of Neil,' she says. 'You and Reuben are mentioned in his will.'

The all-too-familiar anger stirs me to an outburst. 'Mum, I'm not going to sidle up to someone whom I despise just to benefit from a legacy!'

'OK but remember that Reuben is vulnerable. You have a good job and good prospects. Reuben has always struggled. Where will he be in ten years? It may fall to you to lend him a hand in the future.'

'So, I can be the bad boy and Reuben can inherit it all,' I say, aware that I was talking far too loudly for the ward.

Mum closes her eyes and withdraws her hand. I realise she needs more rest.

'I'll leave now. I'll be back tomorrow. Kate has offered to have me at her place for the night. I can phone for a taxi.'

Mum smiles feebly. 'I'm sorry to burden you with this,' she says. 'It would have been better if Neil had kept it to himself.'

I rise slowly and rush towards the door. I need time to think. The taxi to Kate's can wait until later.

The following morning, I return to the ward on my own. Kate needs to work and says she would visit in the evening. This time, there is a pretty, petite Asian woman at the desk. While I watch, she flits from one task to another like a busy sparrow, unaware that I am waiting to check in with her. She finally looks up.

'I've come to see Linnet Grant.'

'Do you know where she is?'

'Yeah, I came yesterday.'

'Go straight in, sir. I think she already has two visitors.'

As I approach the bed, I see Reuben and another man, who I presume to be his attendant, at the bedside. Reuben looks up with a sense of embarrassment. His face is remarkably relaxed for the ordeal of being sectioned. I wonder what drugs he is on.

'Good to see you,' I say. 'You look well.'

'Thanks... things are slowly improving. This is Jon. He's my escort.'

Jon gives a cursory wave and a smile, then settles back into the book he is reading.

'Mum is feeling brighter today,' Reuben says, looking towards the figure propped up in bed.

'Yes, I had a reasonable night of sleep. The nurse said they may transfer me to the general ward today, after the doctor visits.'

'Are you up to reading? Do you have things to do to pass the time?'

'Plenty,' Mum says, and waves towards a pile of magazines and a few books stacked on the top shelf of the bedside cabinet.

'Would you like to use the TV?'

'I'm not up to it at the moment. Kate will look after that. I hope to be back at home within a few days.'

Reuben stands and walks over to me. 'I need to talk with you... something that's been on my mind. Can we walk in the grounds?'

Jon looks up. I search his face for his reaction. Mum tenses.

'As a patient escort, I'm here to make sure that Reuben keeps and feels safe. I can sit in the waiting area while you walk, but Reuben should return to me here in the ward.'

'No problem.'

I follow Reuben out of the ward into the corridor, and then through the corridors to the exit. Reuben walks with an unnaturally floppy gait – further proof that he is on strong sedatives. Once outside, Reuben's pace slows to a saunter. I come alongside and fall in with his pace.

'Mum says Uncle Neil has asked you to team up with him in Pakistan, but that you've refused.'

'Yeah. It's not something I would ever consider.'

'Oh,' Reuben said. 'I'm glad. I hate that man.'

I swing around to face Reuben. 'Why such strong feelings?'

'Don't you know? He abused me. When I was around four years old. It must have been after I had returned from the daycare centre. Mum was somewhere else for a while. He was alone with me in the house. He forced me…' Reuben didn't complete the sentence.

'The swine.' I smack my fist into my hand. 'Who have you told?'

'Not Mum. Only the doctor at the hospital. I thought I had told you some time ago. They have identified this as one of the reasons for where I'm at now.'

Wild thoughts of revenge race through my mind as I struggle to calm my breathing and think coherently.

'Are you going to pursue it through the courts? Bring a

case, I mean?'

'It's my word against his. There's no physical damage. Only psychological. Then there's the personal exposure. It's not worth pursuing.'

'How about telling Mum?'

'No, not in her condition. Perhaps later. It won't change anything. I had thought of writing to Neil, but what's the point? He could use the letter against me.'

'And to think that Mum wants us to pally up to Uncle Neil to inherit his estate...' I talk under my breath, desperately trying to order my scattered thoughts.

'I'll confront the man,' I say. 'You wait. I'll make sure he knows what we feel. I'll also make sure that Claire knows – I'm sure he would have kept this quiet. He will face up to this whether he likes it or not.'

'Will you phone him?'

'No, I'm going back to Pakistan. I've got unfinished business there, and this is just another part of it.'

Chapter 9

I return to Kate's home that night incensed that Neil has wrought such havoc in our family. First taking advantage of Mum's loneliness to adulterate the marriage and to cloud the happiness of the new baby in the home; then to mess up Reuben's life by taking advantage of a child's innocence for self-gratification. My anger is palpable – thoughts of cruel revenge stoking the passion. Should I reveal Neil as a paedophile to his office staff, his church members, publicly on social media?

'Is everything all right?' Kate asks as I walk into her lounge. 'You look upset.'

'No, life sucks,' I say, as I sit in an easy chair. 'Something I heard this afternoon was deeply disturbing. But I can't share it right now.'

Kate slides across the sofa. 'Is it to do with the family?'

'Don't ask,' I say. Immediately, I regret my outburst. 'Sorry, I didn't mean to be so sharp. But I need to process this on my own.'

'OK.' Kate stands and walks briskly to the kitchen. 'There's food here if you want it – it's in the oven.'

'Cheers. But I'm not hungry tonight.'

My phone rings. It's Rachel.

'Yes.'

'You haven't phoned me. What's happening? Don't you think I'd like to know how your mother is? How long have you been back in the UK? A few days? Couldn't you just speak to me for five minutes?'

'Look, Rachel, I've been busy. I was rushed from the airport directly to the hospital. I've hardly had time to re-adjust. I'll be coming to Oxford as soon as Mum is out of hospital in the next day or two. We'll talk then. And thanks for asking. She's doing OK. Now please get off my back.'

I terminate the call. Rachel will be fuming but I am past caring.

The following day, I return to the hospital to find Mum has been transferred to a general ward. When I find her, she looks much brighter, her facial muscles relaxed, with the dark shadows under her eyes less prominent, and her hair recovering its sheen. Mum is reading a magazine – a good sign.

'You're certainly looking better,' I say, as I drag a chair to the bedside.

'Yes, the pain has almost gone now. I'm likely to be discharged tomorrow. Make sure you ring before you come. You can get the phone number from the desk.'

'I'm planning to travel to Oxford this afternoon. I need

to talk with my supervisor about the work that still needs to be done in Pakistan. Kate will be in to see you later today. She'll be visiting when she's not working.'

'Oh, well, it's good to see you. Will you be down here again soon?'

'Yeah, I've got the leave sanctioned for the gardening project at Apple Mead, but I'll have to see if I can still take it. I'm pretty close to the completion of the project I've been working on. I'll phone you.'

I arrive at Oxford, Park End Street, and take a bus to the university laboratory. Denise, the assistant to whom I assigned the grunt work of the research during my absence, greets me warmly. She quickly gets me up to speed with the results of the data analyses and the overall progress. The samples from Australia and Pakistan are still outstanding. Both my research supervisor and Denise know the circumstances under which I left Pakistan and are sympathetic. The question remains whether there is time for me to make these trips or to rely on local clinical supervisors to take and send the samples.

'Jordan has asked to see you,' Denise says. 'He wants to discuss the next steps.'

'Oh, is he in his office now?'

'So, you're back!' Jordan says, standing at the door of the laboratory.

I look at the large, muscular man, wearing a short-sleeved flowery shirt untucked at the waist, and plain blue cotton trousers. His plastic ID holder is caught in a button of the shirt, the lanyard hanging loose on one side.

'Yes. Thanks for sanctioning my return from Pakistan. Mum has been very ill but is better now.'

'Is she still in hospital?' Jordan's concern for family members is genuine – I have grown to admire his keen interest.

'Yes, but they will discharge her soon. She's now on a general ward.'

'Good to hear it. It's a long way back from Pakistan, but family is important. Now, come to my office and we'll discuss things.'

I follow Jordan to a room with papers strewn over the desk, and two mugs of half-drunk coffee acting as paper-weights. The waste bin is full of KFC boxes and wrappings from the fast-food chain. It looks like Jordan has been working all hours.

'So, how is progress tracking with the timeline?' Jordan asks.

I look away momentarily. My return empty-handed from Pakistan is an unfortunate delay. I knew it would give rise to tough decisions – hence this conversation.

'We are still on schedule to publish in August,' I say. 'Denise has been getting results. I'll get back to the statistics now I'm in the UK. The findings have been consistent. As you know, we had hoped to include data from people groups in Australia and Pakistan, as well as...'

'Australia is no problem,' Jordan butts in, twisting a pen in his fingers as he slouches in his chair. 'The university research department is assigning students to collect the samples. There's a good understanding of the methodology.

It's the Pakistan samples that are more of a challenge.'

'I'm prepared to go back,' I say. I try not to appear too keen. But this is the crunch point. I am desperate to return both to see Esther and to confront Neil.

'We need you here now,' Jordan says. 'It's a critical time in the research. The results have to be solid – they will be challenged. There's a lot at stake.'

'I've done the groundwork there. I have a base to return to in Karachi, and someone who will arrange flights.' (I am thinking of Nadeem – he isn't my gofer but seems willing to help, even if I impose on him).

'It's the time spent travelling, time away from your desk. You must be here during this critical time.'

A thought occurs to me. 'I flew in and out of Karachi, as we couldn't find any easy connecting flights to Sydney from Islamabad. This time I can fly direct to Islamabad and then onward to Chitral the same day. I'll arrange it so that I'm up and back to Chitral within a couple of days – three at most. Then I'll head straight back here.'

'What about your mother's health?' Jordan asks. 'Isn't that a concern to you?'

'My aunt lives close to the hospital. She'll be on hand to help. The prognosis seems to be good as long as Mum takes it steadily.'

Jordan brings out some papers which I recognise to be Denise's latest report on progress. He studies the papers intently.

'I'm not prepared to sanction the trip. The cost is not the issue. It's your time. We'll give detailed instructions to the university medical staff on what we need and trust that they do their job well. It shouldn't be too difficult.'

'But I need to go,' I say.

'And why, Dr Grant, do you "need to go"?'

'We need to make sure that the methodology is followed correctly – we can't risk a skewer in the data at this point,' I say. I am aware of the flimsy premise of this argument, but I will try anything. I hope Jordan doesn't detect the dubious motives behind my assertion.

'No, we will have to rely on local people,' Jordan says. 'If you have personal reasons why you want to return to Pakistan, you'd better see to this in your own time, preferably when the research results are published.'

Jordan sits straight in his chair and looks me in the eye, his fidgeting with the pen finished. The discussion is over and any further attempts to coerce will get his back up. I mutter something about concurring with his decision and walk out. I am stewing inside.

'I'm coming over this evening.' Rachel has rung twice during the day. I have been curt in my response. Now she is demanding a tête-à-tête.

'OK, will you need to eat?'

'No, I'll eat and come.'

She arrives at 7:30pm with a straight face, shoulders tense, and eyes blazing with indignation. She looks around the lounge, scanning for evidence of the prior presence of another woman. She regards me quizzically, then collapses into the sofa chair, taking her phone from her handbag to check her messages.

'A drink?' I ask.

'Only water. It's hot these days.'

I wander as casually as possible into the kitchen and pour two glasses of cold water from the fridge.

'How's your mother?' Rachel asks, as I place the glass on the coffee table. She had forgotten to ask when she phoned.

'She's making good progress,' I say. 'As far as I know, she'll be home either today or tomorrow.'

'Good.'

'How's your research going?' I ask. 'Any interesting developments?'

'We won't go into that now.'

'OK.'

'More to the point – what's happening between the two of us?'

Rachel certainly doesn't beat around the bush.

'I need space. The pace of work is increasing – we are publishing the results in the next few months. Mum's been unwell. I've got a lot on my mind.'

'But our relationship isn't on your mind?'

'Yeah, but I need to slow down.'

'So, what do I do?' Rachel asks.

I turn away.

'I think sometimes space is good for a relationship. We can check in with each other. A little distance will probably help us to feel more grateful for each other.'

I almost choke on my insincerity. Why am I playing the coward? Why not end the relationship? I don't want to hurt Rachel, yet I know deep down that by stringing her along the damage would be greater down the line.

'You've met someone else, haven't you?' she says, looking straight at me. My unguarded response gives the game away.

Rachel stands and makes her way to the door. 'I can see myself out.' She closes the door quietly.

I stand in the lounge, with a knot in my stomach and running my hands through my hair.

It takes a few days for me to re-engage with the research – my mind and heart have been elsewhere. Denise has caught me on several occasions burying my head in my hands or staring vacantly into space. She's tip-toed away, embarrassed.

I finally snap out of it and get back up to speed. We are hitting an important and exciting stage when we finish the data crunching and produce compelling results. The adrenaline keeps me going.

The Australian samples are in. The initial analysis confirms our thesis. There are whoops of excitement in the department. This is going to be one hell of a publication.

The Pakistan samples are proving problematic. There has been one attempt at the collection, but the samples came back poorly labelled. Some yielded no results at all. It is an unhelpful setback. Jordan is giving it another try and has attempted to connect with senior researchers who would understand the need to ensure good procedures at the grass-root level. We discuss the timetable for the clinical work.

We are making good progress and are on schedule.

I've been writing frequent emails to Esther and savour every email I receive in return. She is missing me. She tells me all about developments in her work, her family, the situation in the country, and issues at church. We chat over the phone and through the computer as much as we can. I enjoy the dance of her light, undulating voice, and the flick of her hair when the video is on – her slight flirt. I often record our conversations to listen again. I am entranced by this woman.

I am also looking forward to fresh air and manual work during the annual leave I've booked to attack the brambles and weeds taking over Mum's garden. Mum has been managing the light work but has kept off anything heavy. The weather forecast for the week is reasonable.

One evening after talking with Esther, I browse the Pakistani website of a local leading newspaper that publishes in English. An advertisement pops up in the browser. Cheap flights to Islamabad from London Heathrow. I click on the link and enter the dates of my annual leave. The price is better than expected.

I turn away from the computer and stand. Pacing the floor, I reason with myself. Why take the trip now in a hurry rather than waiting until the research results are published? I am desperate to see Esther again. And I want it out with Neil. The most compelling argument is that I could oversee the sample collection. I don't trust that the university in Islamabad will do a better job a second time around.

I sit at the computer and re-check the flight schedule from Islamabad to Chitral. An overnight flight from

Heathrow would arrive in time for me to get through customs and board the domestic flight. I would return to Islamabad the next day and then take a domestic flight to Karachi, returning the day after. I would only be in the country for five days.

I book the flight. I send a text message to Mum saying that I have curtailed the gardening from Monday to Wednesday only, due to an urgent trip overseas.

I make a quick call to Denise. It is 10pm. She is not her usual chatty self.

'You know Jordan's been handling the arrangements with The Institute of Medical Sciences in Islamabad,' Denise says. She yawns. 'I have no idea when they will collect the samples. I think it's soon.'

'Do you know the name of the contact?'

'No. And I think you'd better talk with Jordan. You'll have to make arrangements through him. You can't do this behind his back.'

'OK, I'll come in on Thursday morning.'

My hand is shaking slightly when I finish. I send a quick message to Nadeem and a voice recording to Esther. I try watching TV but can't find anything of interest. I dig out a book and, with the radio playing quietly in the background, immerse myself in the plot.

It is a sultry night with little breeze. I unbutton my shirt as the oppressive air clings to my body. A thunderstorm is on its way. At close to midnight, I prepare for bed, opening the window to improve air circulation. I vaguely remember clambering into bed, but must have dropped off to sleep quickly.

The high-pitched beeps of the smoke detector penetrate my sleep. It takes a few seconds for my brain to realise what is happening. I fling off the solitary sheet and immediately smell the smoke. The street lamp outside the flat complex beams a soft white glow into the room, illuminating the smoke billowing under the bedroom door.

I whip the sheet off the bed and use it as a mask for my face, teasing the door open to see the damage. The corridor to the front door is ablaze. I slam the door shut, doubling up with the retch of coughing. Grabbing my phone from my bedside cabinet, I dash into the ensuite bathroom and call the emergency services. I sit on the floor to be as close to the corridor of fresh air as possible. I hear the fire appliance roar down the road. A neighbour must have seen the flames. I know Trixie from the flat opposite is finding sleep difficult these days at her late stage of pregnancy – perhaps she has been on her night watchman duties. We often joke about the effects of her insomnia in the corridor when we pass on the way out or back into the flats.

The appliance stops outside. A cacophony of noises breaks the stillness of the night – men talking quickly and then a neighbour shouting that I am still inside. The windows vibrate with the low drum of the pump. In a moment, they break down the flat door. I can hear water flooding the corridor. A firefighter wearing an oxygen mask appears in my bedroom. I grab my dressing gown and shoes. Wrapped in a special blanket, I follow the firefighter out through the smouldering corridor to the lift stairwell. A crowd has gathered above and below my floor, and my neighbours are peering around their doors to keep out of the way of the fire crew's operations.

'The ambulance will be here shortly,' the senior fire officer says. 'You've had a lucky escape.'

'Actually, I don't need hospital treatment – just a bit of smoke in the lungs,' I say.

'The paramedics will decide.'

The water pumping stops. Firefighters walk in and out of the flat. I am tempted to steal a look inside but know better than to get in their way. Anyway, I'm not sure I am up to facing the significant damage to the flat and furnishings at so early an hour in the morning.

A female paramedic arrives and escorts me down the steps to the ambulance outside. Her colleague has an arm festooned with tattoos. They are both sympathetic and make sure I am comfortable while they check me over. They start with questions to make sure that carbon monoxide has not got the better of me, and then concentrate on the effects of smoke inhalation. After a thorough examination, they are satisfied that I don't need an overnight stay at hospital and wish me goodnight.

The fire crew is still busy. The senior officer takes me to one side. 'The flat is not habitable. You'll have to find somewhere else to stay. Any neighbours or friends?'

Rachel's flat flashes through my mind, but I quickly dismiss the idea. She would make a fuss and restart moaning about how badly I am treating her.

'Steven, you can kip down on the sofa for the rest of the night,' Trixie's husband, Gavin, says. I mutter my thanks and stumble wearily into their flat.

'Cup of tea before you crash?' Trixie asks in a far too

energetic voice for the early hours.

'No, I'm really tired. I'll just take the sofa, thanks.'

Trixie brings sheets and a pillow. The leather sofa is not particularly comfortable – too taut, like trying to sleep on a horse saddle.

Trixie brings a cup of tea at 9:30am. Gavin has left for work. She sits in an armchair opposite the sofa and eyes me as I prop myself up and take a sip of the tea.

'How did you sleep?'

'I'm not used to the sofa,' I answer diplomatically, 'but I'm grateful to you and Gavin for taking me in.'

'That's what neighbours are for. What would you like for breakfast?'

'Anything – perhaps a few slices of toast with whatever spread you have.'

Trixie leaves and returns five minutes later with a tray of toast and marmalade.

'I can't remember when the new member of the family is due,' I say. 'It must be soon.'

'Yeah, I'm thirty-six weeks – just four more weeks to go, hopefully. It's pretty uncomfortable at this stage.'

'Have you thought of a name?'

'No firm decision yet, but Gavin and I have our favourites. I think we'll decide shortly after birth. We don't know whether it's a boy or girl, so we'll keep our options open.'

Just then, the flat doorbell rings. Trixie struggles to her feet and slowly makes her way to the front door, returning with the fire officer and a police officer. They chat with Trixie as they enter. I recognise the fire officer from several hours earlier – a tall, muscular man with a swarthy face.

The police officer is shorter but stocky, and of more advanced years. He discontinues the conversation and walks over to me. I stand, feeling self-conscious in my dressing gown and slippers.

'Mr Grant: Mr Richards, and I have gone over the scene of the fire in your flat. Mr Richards has clear evidence that the fire was started on purpose – in other words, this was arson. Therefore, this is a criminal investigation.

'I need to ask you some questions. Do you know of anyone who would carry out such an attack? Have you any idea of who could have done this?'

I sit on the sofa. 'Are you sure this was arson? Could it have been electrical or something?'

'We found evidence of flammable material on the carpet inside the flat door. We think someone pushed an incendiary device through the letterbox.'

'So, again, can you think of anyone who would do this?'

I am caught in a dilemma. If I mention the threatening letter posted to the university and the attack in Karachi, the police will insist that I stay put in the UK to help with ongoing enquiries. They could put me under some kind of protection that would curtail my freedom. And even worse, Rachel would probably find out and cause a stir. The local police would never find the culprit. It was a professional job. It was pointless involving the police in a fruitless search. So, against my better judgment, I lie.

I look at the policeman squarely. 'I have no idea why someone would do this. Perhaps they mistook my flat for someone else's. Perhaps it was children up to a prank.'

'You don't look too sure about this, Mr Grant. Let me

remind you it is important you share anything you know. There's an arsonist out there we need to find. And I doubt it would be children. The incendiary device that was used would not be available to children.'

I stare into space, trying to gather my thoughts.

'Perhaps Mr Grant needs time to think,' Trixie speaks up. 'He didn't get to bed until late this morning. We've only just woken up.'

'Have you seen anyone suspicious around Mr Grant's flat, or outside the flats, in recent days?'

Trixie shakes her head.

'I'll be asking all the neighbours. If anything comes to mind, here's the number to call.' The police officer hands Trixie and me cards.

'The flat is a crime scene. If you need to recover belongings, speak to the fire officer who's there – don't try to enter on your own. The fire service is getting a structural engineer to look at the damage to the property and the potential damage to the integrity of the flat complex. It's important that you only enter with a fire officer with you.'

I nod.

'Do you have any questions?' the officer asked.

'No, you've made it clear.'

'Well, we'll be on our way. I need your mobile number so we can get in contact if necessary.'

I ask Trixie for a pen and paper and scribble down the number. The two men make their way to the door, with Trixie following them. She closes the door and walks back to the lounge.

'Another cup of tea?'

'Yes, if it's available.'

'That was some crap you told the police,' Trixie says. 'You don't make a convincing liar. Obviously, there have been things going on. Sorry to be selfish, but make sure it doesn't affect any others of us here in the flats.'

'OK, don't worry. I can assure you that what's "going on" is particularly concerning me and my circumstances. I don't want to share more, but you and Gavin and the other folks in the block will not be affected.'

Trixie tosses her head and marches back to the kitchen.

I try to work on a plan. First, recover my clothes and belongings from the flat. Go to the office first thing on Thursday and convince Denise to contact the university in Islamabad. Collect buccal swabs and swab envelopes. Then, leave for Mum's – at least I would be out of the way. Lie low at Mum's until the flight to Islamabad. When I return from Pakistan, work on making the flat habitable (if the police have finished their futile enquiries at that point).

OK, sniper and arsonist, you're seriously bugging me. You wait until I find you. I'm going to expose you. You'll hurt. The people paying you will hurt big time.

'I'll be leaving to spend time with my mother,' I say. 'We swapped phone numbers some while ago, from what I remember. If I need to know anything, give me a call.'

'Yeah, and you call us if we need to know anything,' Trixie replies. 'It's a good job I couldn't sleep last night. I would have raised the alarm earlier if I had recognised the shady figure out in the stairwell at 2am as an arsonist.'

CHAPTER 10

The flight to Islamabad is incident-free. I've skimped on the ticket price and have flown with a budget airline. The leg space is sufficient for midgets but for my 1.83 metre frame, it's a pain. I limp off the aircraft with a severe cramp in my right leg. The oppressive heat bearing down on me saps my energy.

I board the shuttle bus and wait while other passengers swarm into the vehicle. A white woman with a toddler, obviously of mixed parentage, climbs onto the bus, the child yelling and stamping in protest. The mother yanks his hand and traps the irate youngster between the side of the bus and her body, avoiding eye contact with the other passengers. I wonder whether the child is simply tired or whether there is more to the situation.

After the bus deposits us at the airport terminal, I quicken my pace towards immigration. The queue tails back several metres. I have a thirty-day multi-entry business visa, so I am confident that they will allow me through without too many questions asked. The immigration officer is frank and professional and I'm through.

With no hold baggage to collect, I trundle the cabin bag behind me towards the domestic departure gate, wondering where in the airport complex the PIA ticket office would be to purchase the Chitral ticket.

'Steven!' I hear a man's voice.

'What are you doing here?'

Tahir approaches me. He is also carrying a small holdall.

'I'm accompanying you. Nadeem told me you were returning to Pakistan. After the attack in Karachi, we were both unhappy about your travelling alone to Chitral.'

I feel my heartbeat quicken. 'I'm not a child who needs to be accompanied. I can manage perfectly well on my own. What will you do that I can't do on my own?'

A security guard at an exit gate eyes me suspiciously as I face off Tahir.

'You're too proud for your own good,' Tahir says. 'You admitted the attack in Karachi unsettled you. You won't let friends help you. Is this the way you Englishmen work?'

'I don't know why Nadeem put you up to this, but I don't need help,' I say. 'Then there's the expense. Who's paying your way?'

'It's your family at home that I care about, whatever family you have. What will they think if we send your body back in a wooden box? What impression will that give of Pakistan? We care about our families. And don't worry, I have the money to pay my way. I don't need your money.'

I am about to make a snide remark but stop myself.

Steven, learn. Ease back.

'OK,' I say. 'I'm sorry. Yes, I am stubborn. If you and Nadeem think it best for you to come with me, then OK.'

Tahir smiles. He places his holdall to his side and takes out a cigarette. Within a few minutes, he is puffing away, oblivious to the 'no-smoking' signs in the near vicinity.

'I didn't think you smoked.'

'I don't smoke in Karachi. The wife smells it on my clothes. By the time I get back, there will be no smell.'

I march off towards the PIA office. I book two seats for Chitral. I am relieved that my initial web enquiry from the UK has proved accurate – the flight is not fully booked.

I stride back to where Tahir is waiting and show him the tickets. He looks at them carefully. 'My relatives in Islamabad want to meet you,' Tahir says.

'Fine.'

'We can go now.'

'We're catching a flight.'

'Yes, but we have three hours to wait. My relatives live near the airport.'

'OK, as long as we're back in time for the flight. You will have to make sure of that. I can't miss it.

'How do we get to your relative's home?'

'Taxi.'

We walk towards the road. Tahir starts to bargain with the taxi drivers who approach us. He dismisses the first quickly. Other drivers crowd around. After a short while, Tahir and the driver settle on a fare.

We scoot off after the driver. He is in a hurry to get away.

'So, who is this relative? How is he or she related?'

'My *taaya* – my father's eldest brother. He and the family have been in Islamabad for seven years. He moved here for work.'

'When did you arrange this? You were quick off the mark.'

'Before leaving Karachi. We use our extended family connections when possible.'

After ten minutes in the taxi, we enter an area of housing. The faded sign board reads, 'Satellite Town'.

Why would they adopt the technical description coined by city planners as the definitive name? Stark and unwelcoming, or what?

We drive through blocks of housing and pull up at a modest house, set back from the road. Tahir gets out and pays the driver. I follow him to the house.

Tahir knocks on the door. I hear a young man calling out something to the house occupants. In a moment, Tahir's *taayamma* is at the door to greet us. We take off our shoes and are shown into the lounge. The young man follows us into the room.

'This is Bilal,' Tahir says. 'He is studying in 8th grade at Siddeeq Public School.' Tahir ruffles his cousin's hair.

'How is the study going?'

'Fine.' Bilal answers shyly, looking at the floor as he does so.

After a few moments, the door opens, and I see someone beckoning Bilal. He disappears and then returns with a tray of cold water and glasses. Tahir pours the water.

'Your uncle has a pleasant home here. What work does he do?'

'He is a manager of human resources at Procter and

Gamble. They have a big setup here. He is very busy.'

'And your uncle's wife?'

'She doesn't work outside of the home. Her work is here, looking after my cousins.'

'How many children do they have?'

'Only four. Bilal is the youngest. The others are out working.'

The phone beeps.

'No! My uncle says that Esther has been kidnapped in Karachi on her way back to her home. She had stopped off in the *bazaar* and was taken at gunpoint.'

'Show me,' Tahir says.

I pass the phone to him, my hand shaking with shock.

'How do you know Esther?' I ask as Tahir scans the message.

'Nadeem introduced me to her and her family when I visited the church. I don't know her well.

'Why are you so upset?' Tahir looks at me with a sly expression.

'I've spent a bit more time with Esther than you have,' I say. 'She's a good woman.'

'These things happen in Pakistan. Esther and her family are well-connected. No doubt the kidnappers want money or are seeking political leverage. It will be sorted out.'

'Give me the phone. I'll text my uncle. If I can get Mr Li's number, I can talk to him directly.'

Tahir hands back the phone and watches me as my fingers race to compose a brief message. After several minutes, a reply comes. I have the number.

Bilal walks in with a tray of *chai* and biscuits. He leaves the tray on the coffee table and sits on the sofa.

I call the number. Mr Li answers in a grave voice. He isn't able to give me any further details beyond those I already know. He says that the police are on the case. The identity of the kidnappers is unknown – they have not yet been in contact. Mrs Li and the family are trying to remain calm. Many people at the church are praying for the situation.

I sink into the sofa, numb with shock. Tahir pours the tea and passes it to me. The sweet liquid helps to calm me.

Dig deep. Focus. You've got friends who can help...

'Was there some kind of arrangement going on with you and the Li family?' Tahir asks.

'There was interest,' I say, blushing slightly. 'Nothing more.'

'Don't try to get involved in this. Leave it to the police. Mr Li will be able to get the right people to work on this at a high level. We can pray. Allah is merciful.'

I have no religious conviction. But I agree with the sentiment, at least in principle. But my mind is churning. What is Esther going through? How are the kidnappers treating her? Are they handling her with respect or abusing her? How would this damage her? What effect would this have on the family?

We drink the tea. Tahir leaves to find a taxi to take us back to the airport for the Chitral flight. After fifteen minutes, he returns. I pick up my cabin bag and shouting a 'thanks' for the hospitality towards the kitchen area, follow Tahir out to the awaiting taxi.

In the domestic departure lounge, I watch Tahir walk around the small complex of shops aimlessly, browsing magazines and books. He seems restless. I sit and read to kill time. We have over ninety minutes before the flight departs. I see Tahir looking out at the aircraft docked at the jet bridge of our departure gate. He then strides confidently to the seating area and sits opposite me.

'What do your family think about your joining me on this trip?'

'They are used to my travelling at short notice,' Tahir says. 'In the export business, I often travelled to other cities. They know I can take care of myself.'

'When do you think business will pick up again for you to restart your work?'

'It's uncertain. I visit Munir, the owner. He keeps telling me that things are picking up. But I don't see any sign of it.'

'What will you do if nothing happens?'

'Journalism and then politics. My father has sources in the Jang Media Group. I used to write during my student days.

'I'm wasting my time in the export business. The poor are getting poorer here. Things are better now than they were, but there is still corruption and inequality. Men are chasing after wealth. There is little fear of Allah.'

'Journalism is very different to Head of Logistics in an export business,' I say. Is it a good career move?'

'I want adventure. I want to do something in life, not just earn good money. I want to influence where it matters.'

The flight is straightforward. Again, Tahir seems restless. I wonder if he fears flying. Perhaps the small aircraft is the issue. He seems relieved when the aircraft touches down at Chitral Airport.

We disembark and make our way past baggage reclaim to the exit. Suddenly, my phone rings. The deep male voice of a Pakistani northern tribesman speaks in surprisingly good English.

'What is your name?' the voice asks.

'Mr Grant speaking,' I said, cautiously.

'Mr Grant: We have Esther Li. She is well. We require a sum of US $250,000 for her safe return. You need to contact her family for them to arrange the money. The money will need to be given within a week. Otherwise, Esther will not be returned safely. Further instructions will follow.'

I freeze. Tahir grabs the phone from me.

'Who is this?' he asks. 'How do we know that you have Esther with you?' Tahir switches to speakerphone.

'Here is Esther,' the voice says.

'Steven, do not worry. I'm OK. They treat me well. You must pass on information to my father.'

'Where are you?' I shout into the phone, but the tribesman answers.

'Get this information to the family.' The call then ends abruptly.

'What are you going to do now?' Tahir puts his holdall on the concrete and straightens himself.

'Obviously, call Mr Li with the information. I'll send the phone SIM card to Mr Li. They should be talking directly with him.'

'And yet the kidnappers chose to pass on the message through you,' Tahir says. 'Esther would know her home phone number. So why did she give your number instead?'

'Perhaps the kidnappers thought the police would tap her home phone and her father's mobile, and they insisted on using a different number.'

'See what Mr Li suggests,' Tahir says.

We walk to a quiet area of the Chitral Airport concourse. I phone Mr Li and explain the call I have received. Mr Li is thoughtful. He suggests we wait until he is in contact with his police caseworker. We find a stall selling soft drinks and sip cola. We wait.

Come on, man, get back to us. We haven't got all day.

Mr Li phones back.

'You need to get back to Karachi with that phone. The police want to analyse the call log. They want to be ready for when the kidnappers phone again.'

'I've just arrived in Chitral. I have to get this work done here. What if I send the phone to you by courier? Surely the kidnappers will talk with whoever answers the phone?'

'The police aren't so sure.' Mr Li's voice crackles with tension. 'It may be they want to speak with someone removed from immediate family. That person is you. They want you and the phone back here as soon as possible.'

'How about I go to the police in Chitral?' I ask. 'I can go there now. The police can analyse the phone and give it back to me when they've finished.'

'The police want you and the phone back in Karachi.'

'But I have work to do here. Ask the police if they can work through their station in Chitral – they must have a station here.'

'I'll talk to caseworker and phone back.'

Tahir spits out of the corner of his mouth. He smiles suggestively. 'You are making it difficult for your future father-in-law.'

After five minutes, the phone rings. 'The police say to keep the phone. Install free app that records all incoming calls. Get the kidnappers to agree to talk to family member. Go to the police station on Fort Road. Meet DPO Imran Sultan. He will take the phone from you, analyse it and then return it.'

The taxi roars along the road from the airport into the city. After a few kilometres, a blue and red sign welcomes us to the police station.

Tahir and I walk into the station and ask for DPO Imran Sultan. The police officer on duty directs us to a bench on the veranda. After five minutes, Mr Sultan comes out.

'You have phone for me?' he says.

'I hand him the phone. He looks at it suspiciously. 'Wait.' He walks back into the station.

Half-an-hour passes. Eventually, he comes out and gives the phone back.

'You go back to Karachi?'

'Yes, soon.'

'Do as Karachi police say.' He walks off.

'Well, we might as well get to the clinic at Bumburet. We need to find a vehicle to take us there.'

We walk out of the station compound to the road and find a local shopping complex. Tahir speaks to the storekeeper who phones a friend – a local driver who regularly takes tourists up the valley. After twenty minutes, a jeep arrives. We pile in and the driver heads out of the city towards Ayun village on the Kunar River.

It is a long and slow drive along the N45 national highway. The Kalash Valley Road is spectacular – on the one side a sheer drop into the river, whilst on the other shrubs and foliage protruding from the rocky ground. We turn off on the Bumburet Valley Road and bounce along to Bumburet, enjoying the valley's meadows, maize and wheat fields, and its apple, apricot, and *shinjoor* orchards. We stop off at the Pakistan Tourism Development Corporation building and ask for directions to the clinic.

The jeep can only take us half a kilometre up the track leading to the clinic. We pay the driver and walk. Tahir pauses at a junction where the track splits into two narrow paths.

'I have Dr Irfan's number,' I say.

'That won't be necessary.' Tahir sets off down the wider of the paths. I follow.

We ask directions from a man trying to manoeuvre his motorcycle along a bank of mud that has swept across the path. We walk on and come to a wooden building set on the side of a sparsely wooded hill. Women dressed in black and orange robes topped with embroidered caps and hair in plaits sit on benches outside the clinic. A few men sit on another bench farther from the clinic entrance, their plain *shalwar-kameez* suits in contrast to their womenfolks' garb.

'Is this the clinic?' I ask Tahir. I'm not yet able to read Urdu.

'Yes, the signboard says so.'

I am conscious of the gaze of both men and women as we walk up to the entrance and peer inside. I am tempted to stare back.

The doctor seated at a desk stands and walks towards us.

'*Asalam-a-lequm.*' He shakes my hand vigorously. 'I am Dr Irfan Muhammad.'

'Dr Grant from the UK,' I say. I hope your supervisor at The Pakistan Institute of Medical Sciences in Islamabad has briefed you about the sample collection.'

'Yes, your assistant in the UK has told us you were on your way here. I wasn't certain of the exact day you were arriving.'

'I have the buccal swabs and swab envelopes,' I say. 'Is it possible to start today?'

'No, sorry, it is too late. I need to inform the patients about the testing. We can start when the clinic opens tomorrow.'

I look at Tahir. He shrugs. 'OK. We'll wait until you finish the clinic. I want to discuss the demographics of the people we test.'

Dr Irfan calls a nurse from a separate room. She shows us to a third, small room at the back of the building where we can wait. She then sends a small boy to arrange *chai* and refreshments.

We move out to the balcony and listen to the music of a rivulet gurgling below the building. In the distance, we can see smoke fires from the rustic dwellings. I begin to relax, the stress of the previous days slowly draining from my body. Tahir dozes in his chair.

After two hours, the clinic is closed. I sit with Dr Irfan and go through the details. I am looking for men and women who have as little contact with the outside world as possible. Women who keep to their isolated homes and eat from the land. Men who don't travel far. Young children who have little exposure to life outside the valley. Each sample is to be labelled with gender, age (guestimate if necessary), and a brief description of background as far as is known.

Dr Irfan nods.

'Where are you staying tonight?'

I look at Tahir. 'We have nowhere to stay here. We will need to book in at a lodge.'

'Be my guest where I stay.' Dr Irfan smiles. 'It is very basic. It will be string beds on mud floors. There is food and water to drink.'

'Fine. We'll come with you.'

Dr Irfan secures the clinic building at 6:30pm. We follow him back along the track we climbed earlier to a well-used jeep parked at the side of the road. We clamber aboard and the jeep splutters into life. Dr Irfan jams the gearbox into first gear and takes off, spewing a cloud of dust behind the vehicle.

'Is this your first time in Chitral?'

'Yes, for me.' I let Tahir answer for himself.

'I've been here once before,' Tahir says. 'For work, not with the family.'

We lumber on, throwing dust and dirt behind us as we traverse roads and tracks. After twenty minutes we draw up outside 'Brun Guest House.' It looks extremely rustic – a building hewn from local rock and girded with timber from the area. We climb out of the jeep and follow Dr Irfan into one of the rooms. After the sunlight, I can hardly see the dimensions of the room until my eyes adjust. I make out the stringed bed that Dr Irfan told us about and a solitary desk.

'The water in the clay pot is filtered,' Dr Irfan says, pointing towards a short stand in the corner. 'It should be OK for you to drink. I have a local family cook for me. Their son will be here soon. I'll tell him to increase the portions for tonight. I'll get two more beds into the room.' Dr Irfan makes his way to the bed and relaxes.

I feel claustrophobic. 'I'll sit outside while I wait,' I say and make for a bench I saw when we first arrived, only a few metres from the room entrance.

I would be entranced by the beauty before me, the snow-capped mountains of the Hindu-Kush range, the lush foliage, the babbling streams, yet my mind is on Esther and her situation. Her strained voice echoes through my mind. She gave just basic information – she was well, was being treated well, and needed me to contact her father. What remained unsaid? Was it simply a kidnapping for money or were there other factors? Can the Li family raise this amount of money, or will they negotiate a smaller amount? Will they stay true to their promise when the ransom is delivered?

Tahir joins me on the bench and sees my absent-minded twisting of a blade of grass in my fingers, and the anguished stare out across the valley.

'It's about Esther, isn't it?' he says.

I nod.

'We are used to such things here. It's a game – an expensive game. The family will sort it out.'

I can take little comfort from Tahir's words.

How can this be a 'game'? Don't they take it seriously? Do they take anything seriously here?

CHAPTER 11

Esther

'This room stinks. The bands are tight, cutting my wrists. Why tie me? Where can I run?'

The woman runs past me, ignoring me. She's just the cook. I'm invisible.

'I need my medication. Tell them I need it.'

I ponder. Mama, baba, what do they think now? Jie, what is she doing? How worry affects them?

Office: Damn. Behind schedule. Must file the return. Baba knows. He'll get Emaan to do it. She must do it well. Otherwise, penalty.

Medication. I took it yesterday. Today OK. Tomorrow? How will I feel unwell? When they get medication to me?

These men: The big man. Smart guy. Strong. Educated. Why this? What waste.

I kick the wall. Why anger? About the confinement? No. About my life as it is. I'm Miss Responsible. Miss Loyal. Miss Respectable. What is this emptiness within me?

The Englishman. Handsome but immature. Hurt Mei Mei. Delayed

her education. He never cared...

There is a rap on the metal gate. I hear voices. The smart man enters the room. He strides over to me, grabs a plastic chair from the corner and sprawls across the seat.

'Oho, you look uncomfortable. And unhappy. I don't like to see this.'

He gets up and walks to the back of my chair.

'Hashim! Why did you tie these bands so tightly? Can't you see our guest is uncomfortable?'

The oldest of the three men in the lounge comes running out. He remonstrates in a mixture of Urdu and Punjabi as he makes his way to my corner and unties my wrists. I splay and then flex my fingers, smoothing the deep red indentations in the skin. I wince with the discomfort. Younis looks on, bemused. He leans forward in the chair. His cheek lines sink and eyebrows furrow.

'This is unpleasant. I know. But I want to help you.'

'How? You have not helped me. I need medication. You did not get it to me.'

'We are sourcing it in the *bazaar*. It's coming,' Younis says. 'It's not life-threatening if you don't have it for a while, is it?'

'But I will get ill. I need medication.'

Younis dismisses the point with a flourish of his hand. 'And you will get it. This afternoon my man is collecting it from a pharmacy.'

I relax. 'OK', I say bewildered at this sudden outcome.

'I can help you and the family. I am negotiating. There is something you can bring to the table.'

'Why would I do anything for you? You have brought anguish to my family.'

'It's a minor inconvenience. That's all. Negotiations are going well. You will be back with your family soon enough.'

Younis stands. 'I am not what you think. I come from a respectable family. My family is virtuous. My uncle is Chair of the Department of English Language and Literature at Lahore University. I fear Allah.'

'So, why this?'

Younis sighs. 'You know how things are here. Squabbles in the family. My father had a tract of land that my grandfather gave him in a village. He was preparing to build the family home on it. On the death of my *dada*, my uncle seized the land, saying that as the eldest son, it rightfully belonged to him. There was feuding in the family. It became bad. One night, men came to my home and shot my father.

'I was too young at the time. I saw my mother and sisters with harrowed brows and pinched faces as they scraped together food enough for one meal a day. *Ammi Jan* standing tall and strong, her clothes clean and pure despite the squalor of a home without electricity and gas. My baby sister crying out from hunger as my mother raked the charcoal and embers from the fire pit to cook the watery *daal*. My brother returning to the house from the biscuit factory, exhausted and demoralised from working long shifts to earn for the family.

'I prayed. I pleaded. Then some men came to my house. They saw the plight of the family. They offered me some business. They paid a small amount of cash up-front. I went with them. I earned their trust.

'I know life's uncertainties. I know the risks of this business. I have studied hard to prepare for the future. Do you think I want to stay like this?'

Younis tosses the chair across the room. The men peer around the corner from the lounge. He glowers at them. They retreat to their business.

He glances at his phone. 'I have to leave. We will talk more tomorrow. I will tell the men not to tie you so tightly.'

He smiles endearingly at me. I read his eyes but see no lust. He is determined but respectful. I like that in a man.

Chapter 12

Steven

I find it difficult to sleep. The cotton mattress is comfortable, but the bed sags. The pillow smells. I toss it to one side, but then can feel the rough fibres of the rope digging into my head. I can't convince myself that all will work out well with Esther's kidnapping – something lurking in the back of my mind warns me of difficulties and heartbreak ahead. I toss and turn and only snatch a few hours of sleep in the early hours of the morning.

Dr Irfan wakes me at 7am. He and Tahir are already dressed. I struggle out of bed and wash and shave at the communal washbasins for men. By the time I step back into the room, there is a thick tablecloth spread out on the floor with plates of fried eggs and *parathas* and coarse mugs of steaming tea.

I struggle to sit elegantly – Tahir and Dr Irfan seem to find it a natural posture. We eat in relative silence.

'The boy will clear it up,' Dr Irfan says, as I start to

gather the plates. 'We need to be going. The men and women come early to the clinic.'

'Bring your luggage – you will be back on your way to Islamabad this afternoon.'

The ride back to the clinic is similarly bumpy and rough, but the cool morning air revives my spirits. I hope we can get the samples done quickly. I plan to join the Li family in Karachi and find out first-hand more details about the abduction.

At the clinic, there are already fifteen men, women, and children seated on the benches, waiting for consultations. The nurse we had met the day before is busy organising patient records from an ancient and beaten-up filing cabinet in the corner of the consulting room. Dr Irfan sits at his desk and gets out the stationery he needs for the day, his stethoscope, and other medical instruments. Once everything is in place, he relaxes back in his chair and, drumming his fingers on his desk, looks at us.

'I briefed Nurse Benazir yesterday about the people from whom you want samples. She's sorting out the records now. If I could have the swabs and envelopes.'

I dig out the packets from my cabin bag and leave them on the table. Dr Irfan places them in the middle drawer of the desk.

'I suggest you wait in the same room as yesterday. It's best that no one sees you – it could make the men and women suspicious and reluctant to co-operate.'

Nurse Benazir shows us to the room. We make our way to the balcony and sit. The excited and anxious murmur of voices floats through to the balcony as the clinic opens and

Dr Irfan starts his consultations.

Two hours pass. Tea and biscuits arrive.

I am deep into my book – I have prepared for lengthy periods of waiting. Tahir appears to be dozing. I can still hear voices in the background and the occasional shout from the benches in the courtyard.

A Kalash young boy suddenly appears below the balcony, staring up at me. I smile and point back towards the front of the building. His eyes are riveted on me – as though I am an alien from outer space. After a minute or so I ignore him and carry on reading.

I feel a slight tremor, and then everything starts to move. The mugs clatter on the balcony floor. There is a roar from the direction of the benches. Tahir wakes, leaps up, and scrambles down the steps to the ground beyond the building. 'Quick,' he shouts.

What the heck. I follow as the building starts to sway like a drunken sailor on the high seas. I can hardly negotiate the steps due to the movement. I hear screams and the sound of buildings crashing to the ground. I look across the valley and see columns of dust rising into the air.

We step several metres away from the building. It is difficult to stand with the ground gyrating to the dance of tectonic plates hundreds of kilometres beneath the surface. Trees sway as though a reaper is cutting through a swathe of corn in a field. It is like an apocalyptic horror film.

After what must have been three minutes, the swaying subsides. I hear weeping in the distance. Dr Irfan and the nurse come round to the side of the building we are standing opposite. They are visibly relieved when they see us standing unharmed.

'Is anyone injured from the clinic?'

'No. We all got out of the building quickly,' Dr Irfan says.

'And the building itself?'

'I need to look. But we will stay outside for a while just in case there are after-shocks.'

Tahir and I follow Dr Irfan and Nurse Benazir around to the front of the clinic. It is deserted. The patients have all left for their homes. There is rubbish strewn in the courtyard. Some of the benches are overturned.

There is little serious damage in the clinic consulting room, but pieces of paper are lying on the floor. Everywhere around me, I can hear distant cries and shrieks.

I look down the track that leads to the road. I can see branches and loose boulders blocking the pathway.

A sudden jolt, then the shaking begins again. The four of us stumble further away from the building and instinctively fall to our knees. The cries and shouts in the distance increase in intensity. Then the tremors stop.

'Do you have regular earthquakes here?' I ask, crouching on the ground.

'In 2015, there was a severe earthquake. It's just the area.' Dr Irfan's nonchalant expression does little to encourage us.

We slowly get to our feet. A frightened clinic boy appears. Dr Irfan tries to comfort him and sends him back to his family. He then walks towards the clinic and cautiously enters. Nurse Benazir follows. Tahir and I stand outside at some distance. Chill, Steven. You're not on your own.

'It's OK,' Dr Irfan calls. We join him in the consulting room where he and the nurse are picking up medical records from the floor.

'This clinic was constructed by an NGO. They had a specialist construction engineer who made sure it was earthquake-proof, unlike the local homes. We have to pack up and close the building quickly. There will be many who need help.'

'Do you have the swab envelopes?' I ask.

'Yes, they're here. But I'm not sure how and when you will be leaving. Rubble will have blocked the roads.'

I stuff the envelopes into my cabin bag that lies relatively undisturbed on the floor where I left it, except that it is coated with heavy, brown dust.

Dr Irfan dismisses Nurse Benazir. She walks off quickly towards her lodgings. He then puts together an emergency relief package of medicines, bandages, and water flasks. He is barring the windows when two women approach, howling. He listens to their story and then calls us.

'They need help. Their menfolk are trapped in the rubble of their home.'

The women set off. They are sturdy, hardy folk, used to the terrain. They pick their way along the tracks like nimble goats. We have difficulty keeping up.

We dodge tree branches, small landslides, and rubble to arrive at a dwelling set into the side of a hill. Half of the wood-and-mud house is lying at the foot of the track. The other half lies collapsed farther up, timber and stones in a heap. The women cry out in anguish and wail. A goat runs down the hill, bleating as it goes.

Dr Irfan, Tahir, and I scale the hill as quickly as possible and start calling out. We hear a faint cry from within the rubble. 'Quick,' Tahir calls. 'Over here.'

We start lifting stones, wood, and dirt, throwing the objects to the side of the site. We avoid causing further movement in the rubble in case something falls on the survivor. We are playing a giant and grim game of 'pick-up sticks' against time.

Eventually, the bloodied head of the survivor comes into view – covered in dirt and with matted hair. The man's face is twisted in agony.

We increase our pace and clear the man's body of the remaining objects that are pinning him to the spot. Then Dr Irfan examines him.

'Broken leg, abrasions to the head and concussion,' he says under his breath. 'Nothing too serious. Help me get him out.'

We ease the man sideways out of the way of the remaining debris. Dr Irfan encourages him to stand on his good leg with the two of us taking the weight from his broken leg. He winces with the pain but hobbles over to a boulder to sit.

One of the women runs up, ecstatic with joy and relief, while the other continues her low howling. The man looks up at her dolefully. Dr Irfan gives him painkillers and water to drink. 'We'd better look for the other man – I'll attend to this fellow properly later on.'

I get as close as possible to the ruins to listen for any signs of life. The woman stands close to the rubble and indicates where she thinks her husband was when the earthquake struck. She is distraught, weeping uncontrollably.

Tahir and I carefully clear the area while Dr Irfan speaks to the woman. We pull on a large piece of wood, shaped from a single branch. I feel a twinge in my back as we lift it away to the side. I gently straighten my back and loosen up my muscles. Tahir looks on. He seems amused by this foreigner who is unused to heavy lifting.

'Look, there!' I can see the edge of some clothing. We increase our pace in clearing the area. Slowly, the body of a man comes into view. This man has not been so fortunate. His skull is broken – blood oozing from the indentation, turning the matted wood and bark that lies next to the figure a dark red. I turn away quickly, breathing deeply and concentrating on what beauty of the surroundings remains to stop myself from retching. Meanwhile, Tahir and Dr Irfan extricate the corpse from the rubble. The woman's howling becomes more intense. She beats her chest in agony of the loss. The other woman comes close to hold her, but she refuses to be comforted.

A man arrives, hobbling and bleeding. He speaks to Dr Irfan in urgent tones and gestures to another part of the hillside less than a kilometre from where we are standing.

'This man needs our help. His wife is missing. Their house has collapsed.' Dr Irfan speaks quickly to the surviving man with the broken leg. The newcomer shifts uneasily – he seems desperate to be off. As soon as Dr Irfan is ready, we leave, following the man as he scales the hillside, willing his broken body forward.

We come to a scene similar to the one we have left

behind, only that the building has stood on a level clearing, rather than clinging to the side of a hill. A young man is frantically clearing rubble while a young woman, probably his sister, is shouting at him.

The woman stands aside as we arrive. The men exchange a few words – the barest of information. Then we start pulling, twisting, and extracting wood and stones from the site.

Other men converge on the scene and join us. The pace increases – it becomes a frenzied excavation; the men throwing wood and stones indiscriminately onto the perimeter of the site. Tahir shouts and the men stop. The men restart at a slower and more cautious speed.

'Watch out!' I look up surprised to hear English. Out of the corner of my eye, I see the wall behind me beginning to fall in my direction. I jump and roll forward. I feel the jolt of the earth as the heavy stones fall behind me and dust stings my face. I stop in a heap a distance from where I was standing. Tahir rushes over to me.

'Are you OK?'

'Yeah, I think so. How did that wall collapse?'

The men have stopped their digging temporarily but get back to work. Tahir and I cautiously make our way to the rear of the collapsed wall. There is no one there – no indication of why the wall collapsed on top of me. It was a stable wall when we arrived, apparently unaffected by the tremors of the earthquake.

'Someone isn't happy that you are here,' Tahir says. 'You do need to get out of here. It's not…'

One of the men begins crying out excitedly. The other

men join him. He can see a hand. Dr Irfan rushes to the area. The men carefully pick away at the rubble above the figure, revealing more and more of the dirt-stained woman.

The woman is unconscious but is still alive. The men, directed by Dr Irfan, carefully lift her clear of the site. They crowd around as Dr Irfan examines her. He speaks to the husband. His face lightens. He turns to us.

'She's suffering from concussion, but I think that's all. I'll check when she comes around. She's had a lucky escape.'

The husband, son, and daughter crowd around the woman whilst the other men make their way back to their properties. Tahir and I sit on a hill nearby to plan. The green vista before us, trees, fauna, and flora, belies the pain felt within the floors of these valleys as families excavate for the wounded and dead.

Should we stay? Can we just walk away from such suffering? I sound Tahir out.

'We don't have any equipment. We're no more use than the menfolk who have survived and who will be excavating the rubble themselves. There's no point in staying. We need to get you to safety quickly.'

'OK, but how do we get back? We can't walk.'

'We'd better try to find a jeep and see what parts of the road are passable,' Tahir says.

We shout a brief farewell to Dr Irfan, who is attending to another earthquake victim, and go to retrieve our luggage where we have placed it, at the steps of the broken-down building.

'They're gone. Someone's taken them.'

'What?' Tahir asks.

I search through the small pile of clothes and other belongings I packed. The swab envelopes are missing. Someone has snatched them while we were working.

'Have you got your passport and money?' Tahir asks.

'Yes, of course I have. You think I'm stupid enough to store that in my baggage?'

I sit, crumpled with defeat, smoothing my greasy hair as I come to terms with this loss. Tahir stands, looking on helplessly.

'Look, I know it's why we came, but we have to get back now. They will have to take samples when the clinic restarts and send them to you in the UK.'

'But there's no time. We have to conclude the research. This data would have been extremely useful to us, even pivotal in our conclusion.'

'Come on, get up – we have to get going. We need to get to Chitral by nightfall.'

Tahir sets off, disgruntled. I stand and follow. We retrace our steps back to the clinic, from where we can get our bearings to the road. I hear the hum of a helicopter engine in the distance. The Pakistan government is drafting in the army to begin the search for survivors. Soon search and rescue responders from around the world with their specialist rescue dogs will be on the move. Survivors will need water, food, shelter, and medical treatment. The logistics of getting all of that up to this remote area will be mind-blowing.

I think of Dr Irfan back on the hillside, trying to treat

the injured. How far would the small number of medical supplies in his briefcase stretch? How many would he see bleed to death or die unnecessarily from their injuries because of the absence of supplies? How long would it be before medics could join him on the hillside?

I feel a pang of hunger but keep quiet. Getting to Chitral is the priority. We have water from Dr Irfan's clinic.

Eventually, we arrive at the road. It is quiet. We walk in the direction of the town. A few men hurry past. A motorcyclist rides by with farming implements strapped to the back of his saddle. He has no intention of stopping.

I hear sounds of men shouting. We round a corner to see a gang of labourers trying to move boulders and rubble from the road with rough spades and thick sticks as makeshift crowbars. One of the men seems to be taking charge. They look up at us as we approach, but then return to the labouring. We walk to the side and climb over the rubble that is already there, taking care not to cause further slippage onto the road, or else incur the men's wrath.

The phone rings. Surprised, I whip it out of my pocket.

'Mr Grant. One day has passed. The ransom is US $250,000. The family will need to arrange this money. You will be in contact with the family?'

'The family requests you to speak to them directly.' I recount the response I have prepared in my mind. 'I cannot be a go-between.'

'I will only speak with you,' the tribesman answers. 'You will pass on the messages to the family.'

'But the family requests you to speak to them directly. I am not in a position to pass on messages.'

'No, I will not speak to them. You will speak to them.'

'Is Esther Li safe? She is my dear friend. She is well-loved and respected by…'

I don't have time to finish my rehearsed statement. Esther's voice comes on the phone.

'Steven. I am good. Tell my parents they look after me. They give me all I need, even fish,… the fish is quite *tanda*. They…'

The phone is snatched from Esther.

'Six days. I will give you instructions about how the money is to be paid. You will pass on these instructions.' The call ends.

I sit down at the side of the road and phone Esther's family. They have heard about the earthquake from the TV news. They have tried phoning but all the lines are engaged. Mr Li hears the repeated ultimatum from the captors in silence. I can hear Mrs Li talking and asking questions in the background as he conveys my message. The discussion changes from English to Mandarin. Obviously, he is taking a break from the office while he and the family process the kidnapping situation. I assure him I will send the audio recording of the conversation to the police as soon as I have a good enough signal.

When the phone call finishes, I stand and set off again with Tahir towards Chitral.

'I knew they would be working on it…' Tahir says. 'The police will know how to force negotiation. They will use their networks to source the kidnapper's contact number. They won't be paying US $250,000.'

I mull over Esther's words in my mind. She seems

deliberate in her words. They were treating her well, but why mention the fish? I remember the potent smell of fish when I first visited the family at their home. No doubt Chinese families enjoy fish. Perhaps it was comforting for her to eat fish – at least it provides her with some protein.

We walk on, down the road. I glance at my watch. It is 4pm. We haven't made much progress. We come across further gangs of men removing boulders from the road. At this point, the side of the road has slipped down into the valley, leaving a very narrow section that any vehicle will need to cross carefully. I take a photo with my phone. The men do not seem bothered.

Footsore and weary, we struggle on. The earthquake has damaged fewer buildings in this area. People are attending to normal business, but without traffic on the road. The sun begins to descend in the sky. We have counted on making it to Chitral for the night. I feel hungry and sore. My back and Achilles' tendons ache. I hope that Tahir will come up with a plan.

I hear an engine in the background. A jeep comes around the corner – a lone man at the wheel. We flag it down enthusiastically.

Tahir begins an urgent negotiation with the driver. I learn later that he was from Chitral. His extended family owns a guest house in the valley, and he was concerned about seeing the damage to the guest house. Tahir tells him that the road ahead was impassable, so it is best to return to Chitral and try travelling when the road is repaired. He seems reluctant to believe our story. Tahir asks for my phone and shows him the photo I have taken. The man shakes his head slowly in disbelief.

The jeep turns around and we climb in.

'What fare did you negotiate?' I ask.

'Five thousand rupees. It's far too much. But we have to get to Chitral. We probably won't make it tonight. The driver says the road is partially blocked in two places ahead, so it is slow going. But he has a friend with whom we can stay the night. We'll continue in the morning.'

I am relieved to rest my aching limbs but hit my arm against one of the safety bars when the suspension throws us into the air – the driver is taking the boulders and rubble too quickly. Tahir speaks to him roughly. He argues back and then drives at a slower pace, but with a scowl on his face.

We come to one of the partial roadblocks that the driver has mentioned. The army has arrived and is using heavy machinery to remove the rubble. We negotiate a path through the rocky landscape. *Bang*. The jeep hits a rock on one of the front axles. The driver gets out, cursing in his local dialect. Taking a look underneath the vehicle, he jumps back in behind the wheel and reverses, choosing a different path to clear the landslide.

It is 6pm when the driver slows and pulls into a side alley from the main road. The alley, with local mud and stone houses on either side, becomes progressively narrower as we drive on. Eventually, we arrive at a large building where the road veers to the right. The driver turns into a track off the road and shouts instructions to Tahir. He then goes off. Shortly afterwards, he returns and directs us to the back of the building where two-stringed beds are waiting. We drop our luggage next to the beds and relax, grateful for a place to spend the night. Within a few minutes, a boy comes with two metal glasses of water.

'I don't suppose the water will be filtered?' I ask Tahir.

He looks away, seemingly unconcerned about such details. He seems tired and distracted.

The driver joins us after a while, with a young man from the household. Tahir chats with them. He later tells me they were asking about the earthquake as we had experienced it, deep in the valley.

After an hour, food arrives – some kind of lentil curry. At least it is hot. Then the host and driver walk off towards the building, leaving Tahir and me on our own. Night is falling, and the temperature is dropping slowly. I pull one of the rough blankets up around me in case the temperature drops further. The conversation with the tribesman and the few words spoken by Esther reverberate in my mind. I am anxious but powerless to help.

'I still wonder why Esther spoke about the cold fish,' I say.

Tahir looks up. 'Why "cold" fish?'

'You remember – she said the fish was *"Thanda"*. That means "cold" in Urdu, doesn't it?'

Tahir swings around and sits up. He stares across at me. 'Yes, but it sounded to me like *"Tanda"* – there's a difference. Esther's been here far too long to make that mistake. She's proficient in Urdu.'

'So, was she trying to tell us something? Perhaps she knows roughly her location and was giving us a clue.'

'Pass your phone over.' Tahir taps the screen to access the

call recorder app I have installed and listens to the conversation.

'Why would they feed her fish unless they're near a plentiful supply? But they wouldn't be down south – the accent gives the tribesman away. They wouldn't risk the south – it's more difficult to buy off locals to keep quiet. They must be in the north, near a stretch of water where there are fish. Perhaps Tanda Lake, Kohat.'

'Where's that?'

'It's south of Peshawar – a good eight-or-nine hour drive from here. But don't get ideas – we're not going there. This is something for the police. You need to get somewhere safe.'

I stay quiet. Lying back on the thin mattress, I think about what Esther is experiencing. Is she bound by ropes or chains? Is she allowed to exercise? What will her mental state be after this ordeal? Will her family be over-protective? Will this impact the development of our relationship?

I awake to the sound of running water and the clatter of pots and pans as the womenfolk of the house begin their chores of bathing and preparing breakfast. I look at my watch – it is only 5:55am. Already I can feel the heat of the sun's rays on my body. I get up and make my way to the primitive washroom. It stinks. I use the plastic jug-like container to throw water down the hole, but it makes no difference to the foul odour. I avoid looking at the encrusted scum floating in the hole and am glad to exit the hut as quickly as possible to wash and shave in the equally rudimentary bathing hut. I give the plastic-surrounded mirror on the wooden shelf a clean before use.

When I return to the bed, Tahir is stirring. Sitting up on the bed, he grunts an acknowledgement when he sees me and then takes off towards the toilet.

Shortly afterwards, breakfast arrives. Curried omelette with *paratha*. Then tea to wash the grease down.

'What time are we leaving?' I ask Tahir. 'Did the driver mention anything?'

'No, except that it will be early.'

The boy comes to clear the crockery. I stand up and wander from the house towards what looks like an orchard fifty metres away. I find myself among apricot trees.

The lower branches have been picked clean, but I can see the fruit on the higher branches. The trees are straggly – radical pruning would have produced better specimens. The area shows signs of neglect, with rocks and stones heaped indiscriminately. A chukar partridge runs quickly under the bough of a tree towards the rear of the orchard.

'Steven!'

Tahir is shouting after me. I make my way back to the house.

'Our driver is ready to leave now.'

We climb back into the jeep and hang on as it reverses out of the track onto the road, taking off in the direction of Chitral town.

We know we have missed our reserved flights to Islamabad. I accompany Tahir to the PIA desk to enquire about rebooking. I am unsurprised when the booking clerk announces in rudimentary English that nothing is available for a week.

'We'll have to try the coach,' Tahir says. 'The taxi driver will know where the coach leaves from.'

The taxi whisks us off to the Ataliq Bus terminal. Tahir makes further enquiries. The bus will be leaving at 8pm – an overnight journey. We have several hours to kill.

'How about buses to Peshawar?' I ask.

Tahir stares at me as though I am out of my mind.

'You're going back to the UK. Why Peshawar? There's no point going after Esther's abductors. When is your flight to the UK?'

'That's just it. I've already missed it. It was booked for yesterday late afternoon. The earthquake and the additional stay overnight put paid to my catching that flight. I want to find out about buses to Peshawar. Otherwise, my trip to Pakistan has been completely fruitless.

Tahir becomes angry. He takes hold of my shoulder and shakes me. A bearded young man sucking the edge of a scarf looks on.

'I thought as much. Some romantic, idiotic notion of rescuing your sweetheart. You need to get back to your work. I need to take this phone back to Karachi. Have you sent the voice recording to the number?'

'Yes, I did that as soon as I had a good enough signal. But I still want to find out about buses to Peshawar.'

I make my way back to the desk and enquire. The bus to Peshawar leaves at the same time as the Islamabad coach.

'We have to stay together,' Tahir says, raising his voice in desperation. 'I can turn the phone off during the flight to Karachi, but not on the long journey by bus to Islamabad.

If the abductors try to phone, they need to speak with you.'

'So come with me to Peshawar.'

'No. It's a waste of time and money.'

'Well, let's think about it. We have nine hours to wait. What are we going to do to pass the time? I read somewhere that there's a fort we could visit. Is it worth looking at?'

Tahir shrugs. 'If that's what you want to do. We could take a taxi there.'

We set off towards Chitral Fort. I notice that even in the town there is slight damage from the earthquake. Reports say that the epicentre was in the mountain area.

We are back at 7:30pm. The coach leaves at 8:20pm. A heated argument strains our relationship. We are on the coach to Peshawar.

CHAPTER 13

I sit near the window during the journey. It is an overnight service, yet I feel more assured of our safety by having sight of the edge of the road, where the light from oncoming vehicles' headlamps illuminates the highway. I know this is a purely psychological comfort blanket – only the driver can save us from plummeting off the road into the valleys below. Thank God it is summer – I would refuse to take the journey in winter when snow lies on the ground. Tahir is in an aisle seat ahead. When I last spoke to him, he was fuming at my insistence on taking the trip to Peshawar and then on to Kohat. I look in his direction from time to time. He is snoozing off and on. I am jealous of his ability to sleep at the drop of a hat.

We arrive at Bilal Travel, Peshawar, at 5:15am. We find a local restaurant and order tea and *paratha*.

'How long will it take us to get to Tanda Lake?'

'It's not far. Less than an hour. But I'm not sure what we

do when we arrive. What are we looking for?'

'We can ask around. See if anyone has witnessed unusual visitors to the area.'

'But which area? Esther could be anywhere. She could be here in Peshawar. She could be hidden away in any number of locations. It's like – what is the proverb? Looking for "a pin in hay"?'

'Needle in a haystack,' I say. 'At least we can try. The kidnappers will phone again. Esther may give further clues.'

Tahir returns to his eating. He is hunched over the plate and looks dishevelled, with his creased shirt untucked from his trousers. He's not trimmed his facial hair, as is his habit. We are both jaded.

Tahir leaves the bench for the *bazaar* and returns with a taxi to take us to Tanda Lake. We quickly get onto the Peshawar ring road and then the N55 highway to Kohat. The taxi driver keeps looking over his shoulder at me in the back seat and speaking broken English. I largely ignore him while Tahir repeatedly curses him for taking his eyes off the road.

We arrive on the outskirts of the dam. The driver takes us along the Tanda Dam Road to the tourist area and pulls up sharply on the rough stone track, sending dust into the air. The restaurant is busy with many tourists walking and lounging in the shade they can find. We get out and walk to the lake. The driver secures his vehicle and makes his way to the tea booth.

'There were houses we passed on the way here,' I say.

Tahir kicks at a stone. 'Yes, but which house if any of these houses? This is a hopeless trip. It's not possible to help

Esther. Why can't you understand? We have to leave this to the police and their sources. If...'

Tahir's angry retort is interrupted by my phone ringtone.

'Yes?' I answer cautiously.

'Mr Grant. The money is to be paid in four days – US $200,000. It will be given in cash to the administrator of Salman Rasheed Faizan School, Peshawar Cantonment, Mr Sadiq Khan, by midnight on June 29th. There will be no attempt to restrict the delivery or onward passage of the money. Otherwise, Miss Li will lose her life. You are to pass on these instructions to the family.'

'Is Esther OK?' I ask. 'Can I talk to her?' The line goes dead.

I call Mr Li and explain the telephone message. Mr Li is cautiously optimistic.

'Yes, the police have found channel of negotiation. The ransom demand comes down. We get the money ready. Send the recording as soon as you can.'

I send the recording.

Tahir and I walk along the edge of the lake'. I skim stones into the water as I think through the kidnapper's demands.

'How can the kidnappers retrieve the money from a school?' I ask. 'The police will demand that the administrator hands over the money as soon as they release Esther.'

'The kidnappers will threaten attacks on the school and the children if they do that,' Tahir says. 'It's a well-established school with children of important people. No one will risk attacks on the school or children for US $200,000.'

'But how will they get the money out of the school? Surely, they could search everyone entering and leaving?'

'Search the children also? No, they wouldn't do that, for fear of reprisals.'

'At least we know the kidnappers are somewhere in this region, asking for the money to be deposited at a Peshawar school.'

I stop as we come to a bough of a tree overhanging the water. A short distance out in the lake, there is what looks like a small animal thrashing around in the water.

'It's a boy,' Tahir says. He eases off his sandals and, passing his phone to me, rushes into the water.

I look out to where the water is disturbed. The ripples are breaking onto the shore, but the epicentre is now quiet. A body is floating in the water – like a submerged log.

Tahir reaches the boy and thrusting his head above the water, begins to swim back to the shore, dragging the limp body behind him. The boy looks to be around seven years old. He's naked apart from cotton briefs.

I help Tahir lift the floppy figure from the water. Tahir carries him to a part of the shore that is clear of stones and places him on the ground, face down. He begins to pump his upper back. Then, when the boy finishes a fit of coughing, puts him in the recovery position.

Meanwhile, a crowd gathers.

Tahir speaks roughly to the onlookers, presumably to keep their distance, as one or two withdraw from crowding him. There is an excited babble that I can't understand.

'Stand back,' an approaching man says. He introduces himself to Tahir as a doctor taking a picnic with his family.

He kneels by the boy and examines him.

'Looks like a snake bite caused the boy to become unconscious,' the man says. 'Could be a *Kala Nag*. Probably bitten as he entered the water by the tree over there. He needs to get to a hospital quickly. I will take him in my car.'

The man scoops the boy into his arms and carries him up towards the car park. He turns to us.

'You had better come with me.'

Tahir joins the man and I follow, trudging along the stone shore.

'Why on earth do we need to go to the hospital as well?' I ask.

'A safeguard – just in case the family accuses the doctor of somehow harming the boy. We can back up his story. The police are always ready to accuse…'

A woman and three children join the doctor as we make our way to the car park. He speaks quickly to them in Pushto. They nod and follow him to the car – a red Suzuki saloon with faded paintwork. The doctor lies the boy on the back seat and Tahir gets in beside him. The doctor gestures for me to get in the front seat. In a moment we are off. The woman and children walk away.

'Was that your family?' I ask.

'Yes, they will continue with the picnic until I return.'

We remain silent while the doctor drives quickly back along the Indus Highway to Peshawar. We stop at Kohat Toll Plaza. The doctor fishes in his pocket for rupee notes and then, in a few moments, we continue our journey through the Friendship Tunnel.

'Which hospital are we going to?' I ask as we approach Peshawar.

'Lady Reading,' the doctor says. 'I have dealings with this hospital. I know some of the consultants.'

'Sorry, we don't know your name.'

'Rehman Khan. I live in Peshawar and work in a clinic.'

We pull into the car park at the hospital. Dr Khan picks up the boy and quickly makes his way to the Accident and Emergency admittance. We follow closely.

Dr Khan places the limp figure on a hospital bed and briefs the triage nurse. After a few minutes, a hospital doctor comes to the bed and greets Dr Khan warmly. He examines the boy while they chat.

'We stick out like a sore thumb,' I say. Tahir looks searchingly at me. 'It's an expression, meaning we look as though we don't belong here.'

Nurses and doctors hurry from one bed to another. We keep close to the wall to keep out of people's way. I feel uncomfortable with the noise level – patients moaning, calling out, and vomiting. I catch the stench of vomit and to steel myself to avoid retching.

'How will the boy's parents find out where he is?'

'He looks like a local boy,' Tahir says. 'Dr Khan's family will tell people at the restaurant. News travels quickly here.'

Dr Khan comes over to where we are standing.

'The boy's condition is stabilising. They have cleaned the wound and given him a painkiller. We do not know which snake it was, but his body seems to be dealing with the venom. They will monitor his heart and breathing for 24 hours.

'I need to get back to my family. You will stay with the boy until his family arrives?'

'Yeah, I suppose,' I say.

We walk over to the bed. Tahir finds two plastic chairs around an unoccupied bed nearby and lifts them over to our area.

'I need to use the washroom,' I say, and get up to look for signs to the toilets. I feel conspicuous as a Caucasian amidst a sea of brown faces, particularly as I have no reason to be in the hospital apart from hanging around with a patient who we know little about. I make my way through the corridors, anxious to return to Tahir as soon as I answer the call of nature.

'Where have they gone?' I ask a passing nurse on my return, finding the area vacant where the bed has been.

'The porters moved them to a ward, sir. Through there.' The nurse points down a corridor.

I walk briskly, barging into a preoccupied young man on his way out of the building who hasn't seen my approach. I catch up with Tahir and the bed with the tiny figure lying on it, hooked up to various monitoring devices. I follow the party into a ward. The porter parks the bed by the wall and the nurse fusses around, making sure all is in place.

'I'll look around for some more chairs,' Tahir says, sneaking off down the ward as I stand. I peer down at the boyish face. After two minutes, he returns, and we sit for our long vigil.

'I could do with a drink,' I say. Tahir stands and flexes his legs.

'I'll find some bottled water. Or a soft drink?'

'Water's fine. Buy a large bottle if you can.'

Tahir has just left the ward when I see the nurse crowded by a man and two young men. She nods towards the bed and the party makes their way over to where I am sitting. Instinctively, I rise from the chair. The man seems taken aback to find a foreigner sitting at the bedside.

'*Asalam-a-lequm*,' I say, trying to pre-empt any awkwardness.

The man replies in Pushto and carries on speaking, shaking my hand warmly. His grip is vice-like. He soon realises that I understand nothing of what he has been saying. His sons gather around the bed to examine their youngest sibling's condition.

'My father was saying he is thankful for your rescuing his son,' one of the young men says. 'Our villagers heard how you pulled him out of the water.'

'Well, it wasn't me – it was my friend. He'll be back soon.'

The father bends over the bed. His son continues to talk.

'The nurse said a snake bit Humayun. Did you see the snake?'

'No, it could be that Humayun was bitten while he was getting into the water. When we came across him, he was already struggling to keep afloat.'

Humayun begins to stir. He looks up and smiles when he sees his brothers. His face clouds with fear when his father's shadow falls across the bed.

I hear footsteps. Tahir approaches cautiously, carrying a large plastic bottle of water. The father extends the same greetings and handshake. Tahir stands next to me a short distance from the bed.

The brothers start to talk with Humayun. The father speaks to him with what sounds like an angry voice – little wonder he is fearful of his father's presence in the ward.

After fifteen minutes, the father beckons Tahir and me to the bedside and again, starts sharing his profuse gratitude for our help. The son interprets – Tahir is not a Pushto speaker.

'My father asks why you and your friend were at the lake. Are you visiting from the UK?'

I look at Tahir, unsure of what to share. He returns my gaze with a non-committal raising of his eyes.

'I had some work to do at a medical clinic in Chitral. I had to leave the area because of the earthquake. A friend of mine has gone missing and my friend Tahir and I are looking for her in this area.'

Tahir looks away. I can tell from the tensing of his shoulders and the scowl that I have said too much.

OK, but we have to get leads. We have to take the risk.

The father looks thoughtful as his son interprets. He speaks quickly – his son has difficulty relaying the message.

'How has your friend gone missing? How do you know she is in this area?'

Tahir turns his back on me and walks away. I know the risk I am taking, but I also know the sense of indebtedness that comes when a life is rescued, and how this could be repaid.

'She was kidnapped,' I say. 'From Karachi.' I explain the story. The son interprets while the father studies my face, occasionally interjecting with a question.

'We can find out,' the son says. 'If there have been any visitors in the area with a Chinese woman, we will tell you. We are a well-connected family. Our family members live in different parts of the area. How do we contact you? Which hotel are you staying at?'

'We've not arranged hotel accommodation yet,' I say, looking towards Tahir. 'We'll find somewhere in the area.'

'No, you must come and stay with us,' the son says. 'My father insists. We have space.'

Again, I look across at Tahir. He seems to be warming to the family and gives a slight nod.

'Thanks. How do we get to your home?'

'Abdul will stay with his brother here at the hospital. The rest of us will return home in our jeep. You can come with us.'

The father speaks again to Humayun. The boy nods feebly. Then he straightens up and walks towards the exit. The other boys except one follow him. The son who has been interpreting gestures for us to join them. Then the father stops at the nurse's desk and talks with her in Pushto, whilst the boys crowd around. Tahir and I stand a distance off.

'What is the risk if we go with this family?' I whisper.

'It's difficult to tell. If the tribesmen who kidnapped Esther are from the same tribe, then we could be in trouble. They certainly would not betray their own people. If they are from a different tribe, then we are safe. The family is indebted to us and their honour code requires them to offer hospitality.'

The family finishes talking with the nurse and heads

towards the car park. We trail along like sheep following the shepherd, not knowing whether we are walking into trouble or will find our host to be an invaluable resource in locating the kidnapped girl.

'This is extremely good.' The succulent, melt-in-the-mouth lamb dish is a welcome change to the oily hotel food we have been eating on the way.

We are sitting on a crude wooden bench, eating from plates to our side. The family, and it seems the whole immediate community, are seated on the ground in the courtyard of the family home, with a very large cloth weighed down by dishes of vegetable, chicken, and lamb tandoori cuisine. We enjoyed *Patthar Kebab* as starters. My stomach is aching from the onslaught of rich food.

'It is an honour for them to be entertaining a Western guest,' says Tahir, quietly, so that the others don't hear. Many of the guests steal glances at us and several of the small children run over to the bench, stop, stare, and then run back to their places or to another part of the courtyard.

'Do you enjoy the food?' The son who interpreted is standing with his back to the crackling fire where the food has been cooked.

'Yes, it's great. It's not as spicy as some of the Pakistani food I've tasted.'

'There are other dishes you must try. Come, we will serve you some more dishes.'

I still have half a plateful of food but can't resist trying more of this distinctive cuisine.

The community meal goes on for two hours. Then, as

the sun dips in the sky, people depart, leaving the women of the house to gather the crockery and wash the enormous cooking pots. One of the sons brings out stringed beds for us and sets them down in a corner of the courtyard. We stroll over to the beds, take our sandals off, and relax. I can hear the buzz of mosquitos as the sun sinks further in the sky.

'I don't suppose they would have mosquito nets?' I ask Tahir.

'I doubt they have thought of that. Use your repellent and keep under the blanket.'

The son who interpreted comes over to us.

'Abdul says that Humayun is doing well. He is hoping to come home after the doctor sees him in the morning.

'My father has asked the community to find out if there have been unusual visitors in the area. We will do all we can to help you find this woman.'

I doze into mid-morning. I am tired. There is nothing to get up for. I pull the scratchy blanket up over my face and listen to voices, the clanging of metal objects presumably in the preparation of breakfast, and other sounds. I glance out from the blanket at Tahir's bed. He must be already awake and active. Eventually, I pull the blanket off and look at my watch. It's 9am. I swing around and find my sandals. I need a good wash and shave.

They serve breakfast to the two of us on the benches. Tahir tells me he has been for a walk. He looks more like his usual self and has shaved.

Suddenly, there is a roar from the household. Standing

at the gate is Humayun with his brother, Abdul. The older woman, presumably his mother, rushes to greet him, followed by his sisters. The boys look up and smile.

Humayun comes in and sits on a stringed bed across the courtyard from where our beds are laid. The family gathers around. After ten minutes, our interpreter friend comes across to us.

'We received a report this morning from a cousin who lives between here and the lake. A neighbour of one of our tribesmen has seen a foreign woman being taken into a house belonging to men from the city.'

'It could be anyone,' Tahir says. 'What did the woman look like?'

'The neighbour said she looked Chinese, but she couldn't be sure.'

'Can we go and take a look?' I ask.

'No, your arrival would be reported. It is best if you stay here. My father will send Humayun with a phone to take a photo. A local boy wandering around will not cause suspicion. He will bring the phone back here and show you whatever photos he has taken of the woman.'

'How long will this take?'

'It is not far away. I will drive him near to the area and wait for him. The neighbour will take him in and then find an opportunity to photograph the woman. We should be back by late afternoon. You stay here and rest.'

'OK.'

The young man leaves and joins Humayun.

'So, what should we do while we are waiting?'

Tahir shrugs. 'It is probably best for you to stay here –

we don't want to give anyone more opportunity to target you.'

I groan. I feel lethargic. I've eaten too much and need to exercise. I pace the courtyard and then get back to the bed.

Humayun and his brother return early evening. He shows me the photo he's taken from the neighbour's house. The image is not clear, but it is definitely not Esther. I return to my bed and sit, wondering what the next step is. Tahir sits on his bed.

'We're running out of time,' I say. 'The family will have to pay the ransom. At least the kidnappers will return Esther safely.'

'Yes, this is a waste of time. I told you. You need to get back to the UK. Forget Esther. You don't belong here.'

Charming. I'll be the judge of that...

There is a rap on the gate. One of the sons lets a scraggly young man into the courtyard. He limps to a bed and sits, exhausted from his walk. The son fetches a metal tumbler of water. I hear an excited discussion. Then our interpreter comes over to where we are sitting.

'Asadullah, our cousin, owns a shop in a quarter not far from here. His son says that there have been strange men arriving and leaving a small house near the shop. He saw a Chinese-looking woman with them. Humayun will go with the boy to take a look.'

'OK. We'll wait here.'

The two boys set off, Asadullah's son limping out through the gate.'

'Why the limp?' I ask Tahir.

'Probably polio. It's still around in Pakistan. There is suspicion about the vaccine. Some families refuse to let their children be vaccinated. Families like these would not have access to therapy for their children. It is easier to ignore the problem.'

As we are talking, tea arrives with metal tumblers of water. I sit back on the bed and sip the sweet, hot liquid – the goat milk giving it a distinctive, tangy taste. I take in my surroundings. I see kites circling in the sky, high above us, rising on the hot air currents, looking down from hundreds of feet to view their next meal. In the distance, on a hillside, goats make their way along a track, stopping to graze on stubble and anything edible in their path.

Finishing the tea, I must have dozed as Tahir shakes me on the shoulder. I look up to see the boys at the bed and Tahir peering at a phone screen.

'It seems to be her,' Tahir says.

I take the phone and look hard at the screen. Humayun has obviously approached the house – he's taken the photo through a window. It's blurred and dark, but I can make out Esther's delicate features. My mind goes to our first meeting. I remember her dainty hands and relaxed but confident poise. She looks tense and uncomfortable in the image before me.

'So, we go to the police.'

'Isn't that risky?'

'No. The Pakistan police have successfully rescued numerous kidnapped victims. They even rescued the son of a former Prime Minister several years ago. This kind of thing used to happen much more. They have experience and the means,' Tahir said.

'But are the abductees safe if there is a raid?'

Tahir looks at me sternly. 'This gang will be armed. The police are armed. There is always a risk. As I said, the police will know how to go in. Phone Mr Li. He can tell the police caseworker in Karachi. Then they will contact the police here. You must leave it up to them.'

The phone rings several times. Mr Li answers without salutation. 'Yes, speak...' I tell him what we had found out.

'Why are you in Peshawar?' Mr Li asks. 'I thought you return to the UK.'

'Esther gave a clue to her whereabouts when the kidnappers allowed her to speak. I'm surprised the police didn't pick up on this. Anyway, Tahir and I have traced where she is being kept. We need to go to the police.'

'We not tell the police this,' Mr Li says. 'It's too dangerous. Esther will be harmed. We have already negotiated with the kidnappers. We pay the ransom.'

'But paying ransoms only encourages criminals to continue to kidnap people,' I say, exasperated at the family's timid response. 'They will be free to kidnap again. If the police catch them, they'll be stopped.'

'Only if they don't have sources in high places. Anyway, it is too risky.'

'Esther could be free by tomorrow. As it is, you will pay the ransom and have to wait for her safe delivery.'

'That is part of negotiations,' Mr Li says. 'It is all being arranged. Please keep out of this.'

'But I care for Esther – I'm only trying to help. Like you, I want to see her returned safely, but not at the expense of criminals getting money to fund their activities.'

'No. I understand your desire to help, but we not need your assistance. It is all arranged. Please continue to forward recordings from the kidnappers. When you leave the country, you send the phone with Tahir to Karachi. That is all. Goodbye.'

I terminate the call. I am stunned. 'Where is the fight in this man? How can they give in so easily?'

'Mr Li is a pragmatist,' Tahir says. 'They want Esther returned with the minimum of risk and publicity.'

'I'm not standing around seeing criminals get away with this. If Mr Li won't involve the police, I'll get Esther.'

Tahir curses. I am surprised he knows the expletives he comes out with.

'You would be a fool to engage with these criminals. They will be armed. They will either shoot you or add you to their list of abductees. Do not be stupid. The family has said they want you to stay out of it. Keep away.'

Our hosts have gathered around to hear our heated exchange. Some seem to understand that the family has acquiesced to the situation – perhaps they understand more English than they speak. The womenfolk stand at the periphery, largely unconcerned with the issue.

'I cannot walk away now,' I say. 'I cannot let criminals get away scot-free.'

Chapter 14

I look out the gate into the alleyway next to our host's home. In the lengthening shadows, I can make out the form of a stray dog, scratching the side of its body with one paw while tottering against the wall. It has a massive, blood-stained wound gouged out of the top of its head. It has been in a fight and has come off badly. The dog looks up and, seeing me, slinks off in the other direction.

'We are only going for a recce… you understand?' Tahir is following me with a grave reluctance. I appreciate his loyalty.

'Yeah. I know where you stand.'

Humayun skips ahead of us, oblivious to the tension. We turn the corner at the far end of the alley. The shop-keeper from the small corner shop calls out. Humayun responds with a spiel of guttural sounds and, turning round to check we are following, continues walking.

After several minutes, we reach the main road.

Humayun guides us to a bus stop. The car is not available this evening.

'Should I pay for a taxi?' I ask. There are no buses in sight.

'It is probably best to go by local transport – we can mix with the crowds. We will not have a taxi driver blabbing about a foreigner he picked up with two local passengers.'

After fifteen minutes, a beaten-up bus slows to the side of the road, passengers hanging out of the door. Humayun starts towards it, then looks at us and thinks better of it. To my relief, he lets the bus go on its way. After ten minutes, another bus arrives, looking equally worn, with jagged rusty metal visible under the steps of the door. This time the entrance is clear. Humayun signals to the driver and hops onto the back steps. We follow.

There is only one spare seat. Tahir indicates he expects me to take it. I don't argue. The nylon fabric is worn to a glean and has holes in it. My fellow passenger sitting by the window is a stocky man with a full beard and moustache. He turns to look and stares at me.

The bus transmission grumbles to a start and a boy quickly approaches, obviously collecting the fare. Tahir glances at me to warn me against paying and retrieves rupee notes from his pocket.

The bus lumbers on, stopping every half kilometre or so. I look out of the window beyond the passengers sitting adjacent to me, to avoid the stare of the ignorant traveller. House passes after house, interspersed with small, rustic shops of various kinds, the occasional petrol pump, and roads leading to who-knows-where.

Suddenly, Humayun rises from his seat. Tahir walks, head bowed low to avoid the low ceiling, towards the exit. I follow. The bus slows and we jump off. Two passengers also dismount at the same time. They stride off in one direction while we stop at the side of the road for instructions from Humayun.

'We are going through the back streets to his cousin's home,' Tahir says, nodding his chin towards the boy. 'The cousin will take us to the tribesman's house near where they sighted Esther. Just try to remain inconspicuous.'

Humayun takes up the pace and we follow.

We come to a clearing where there is rubbish strewn about – I make out plastic bags, old tyres, and offal. Two buffalo nose their way through the rubbish, looking for anything edible. There are several street dogs, like the one I saw outside the house, competing for scraps of food. Humayun stops, fear in his eyes. There are no side alleyways to disappear down to circumvent passing the dogs. He looks back, as if considering whether to retrace his steps. Then he bends down and picks up concrete rubble. He mutters something to Tahir.

'Pick up whatever you can find to ward off the dogs,' Tahir says. He too is afraid, backing towards the wall as he walks.

The dogs look up at us, distracted from their rooting in the rubbish. Their mangy ears twitch as they listen. Tahir shouts and one runs towards the buffalo. The others decide to follow. We inch past and then walk hastily to the next intersection.

'Why are people so frightened of dogs here?'

'You've seen the state of these animals. Many carry rabies. They bite children. There are thousands of dog-bite cases across the country each year. These dogs need to be got rid of,' Tahir says, disgust registering on his face. 'Dogs are dirty and impure. A friend of mine, Razak, stumbled across a dog on his way to the mosque in Liaquatabad. The dog nipped him through his clothing. He couldn't worship as he was unclean. Thankfully, he didn't get ill from the bite. Usually, the council puts poison down to kill these pests, but they soon breed.'

'So, dogs are not man's best friend here,' I say with a wry smile. 'If the council put down poison in the UK, the police would prosecute them. Society doesn't accept culling by poison.'

'Yeah, but the West spends too much on their pets. People should give food to the hungry instead.'

Humayun slows as we approach a house on a corner. He climbs the concrete steps and raps on the metal gate. After a few minutes, an older boy appears.

'*Asalam-a-lequm*.' That is the only part of the conversation I understand. The rest is an animated exchange in the distinct gravel-in-the-mouth sound of Pushto.

I start towards the steps, but the boy from the house closes the gate behind him and steps down to meet us. He speaks to Tahir in broken Urdu.

'This boy is taking us to our friend's house,' Tahir says, in a whisper. 'He will take us a back way.'

We trudge on, past similar-looking houses of various kinds – some small, fragile-looking buildings of mud and wood, and others of bare block. A solid concrete edifice sticks out from one of the dwellings, with rusty pipes forming a frame that supports a corrugated iron roof. Smaller pipes run horizontally across under the roof, from which meat hooks dangle. Several of the hooks have fatty meat hanging from them, flies being the only interested consumers at this time of day. A man sits nearby on a low stool, a meat knife ready between his toes. He looks up at us nonchalantly.

After five minutes, we arrive at another house, this time at the rear of the building. The boy knocks on the gate. An elderly man with grey flecks in his beard and a pronounced stoop comes to welcome us. He looks up and down the street and then ushers us into the house. Immediately, he takes us to a flight of coarse concrete steps. We climb round a corner, and the man slides back the bolt of another gate. We emerge on the house roof, with a low wall between us and a sheer drop to the dusty street below. Tahir pulls me behind a dilapidated water boiler. The man speaks with both the boy and Humayun, using his chin to point towards a house across the street. We can see into the courtyard.

'That is the place where they are keeping Esther,' Tahir says. 'The man says there are three men there. They come out and sit in the courtyard. Sometimes, they talk on their mobile phones. They all have weapons.'

'Did he mention if Esther comes out into the courtyard?'

Tahir speaks with the man. He replies, again jerking his head to indicate the place over the road.

'No, they do not allow Esther in the courtyard. She stays inside.'

We stay in our position watching the house. No one emerges.

'Are there back gates to these houses?' I ask. Tahir speaks with the man. He shrugs. It seems that most houses have back gates, but some don't.

The sun disappears behind the sea of mud and stone buildings, sending its dying shafts of light between the byways and alleyways of the western vista before us. I shudder as the cool of early evening hits its mark.

'I'm taking a look at the back of the building,' I say. Tahir glances at me.

'You had better go with the boy. Take a *chardar* to wrap around your head and shoulders. Just be very careful. These men will kill.'

A different attitude now? Eh? The adrenaline is kicking in.

Tahir speaks to the man. He descends the steps and then returns with a thin blanket. Tahir shows me how to wear it. Then I follow the boy back down the steps and out into the street.

The boy is very nervy. I find myself affected by his disquiet and have to take deep breaths to relax. I try to take in my surroundings and to focus on unusual objects that catch my attention – a shop sign with the English word 'elektriks' and the frame of an old bicycle tossed to one side by a wall, the handlebars rusty and bent. I imagine the former rider of the bike disappearing under a car driven mercilessly quickly down the road and being fished out from under the car with numerous broken bones, the bike tossed aside as an insignificant loss of an injured owner.

The boy nudges me out of my distraction. We come into

a long street, and he points towards the back of a house a hundred metres in the distance. I stand there wondering how to approach it. One of the men would be covering the rear of the property and would be certain to spot me. The boy senses my hesitation and squats on the ground, looking at me dolefully.

Out of the corner of my eye, I see movement. I swing around to see a young, shabbily dressed man pushing a cart with cheap plastic toys – guns in packets hanging down the sides, cars and trucks, crudely made aircraft, packets of marbles, and colourful boxes of various kinds. I use my chin to point to the man. The boy looks at me enquiringly, then understands. He races over to the man and stops him. The babble of conversation rises in pitch. I walk over to them. The volume decreases. I am comforted that we are out of view of the occupants of the house ahead.

The cart pusher seems reluctant to part with his tool of trade, even for five minutes. I search in my trousers for a five hundred rupee note and flash it before him. His attitude changes. The boy continues in further discussion. I later understand what the acceptable arrangement was to be – my young companion would stay with the man as a guarantor while I push the cart.

The boy gestures I should take over the cart and the man moves away. He and the boy cut down an alley to walk in parallel with me behind a row of buildings. No doubt the man would be ready to pursue his treasure if I try to scarper with the cart.

The cart is light to push, though it does veer to the left slightly. I trundle along at a slow pace, keeping my eyes firmly set before me as I approach the rear of the house. After I have passed the edge of the building, I draw the cart to a stop and busy myself with shifting some of the toys, making sure that the rear of the building is in my line of vision. From this position, I assess the accessibility of the building from the back. There is a small wooden gate. It looks as though it is in use, but the kidnappers would have secured it.

I sense my cover is in danger of being investigated, so I quickly start back at the rear of the cart and push it onwards down the street, half expecting a shot to ring out. Thankfully, all remains quiet. I turn the cart to the right into an alleyway to be met by the relieved proprietor and the boy. There is an excited babble and then the cart vendor takes off, without any further acknowledgement or interest.

Tahir comes around the corner. He walks over to a narrow passageway between two shops and gestures for me and the boy to follow. 'Why are you still here? We have been waiting for you to get back.'

'There is a gate. It looks relatively easy to get through, even if it is locked. I have an idea. Stay here. If you hear a commotion and a loud whistle, break down the gate and get Esther out. I'll join you as soon as possible at this spot. You do know which back gate?'

'Yes, I can work that out.' Tahir scowls. Despite all appearances, it is obvious he is enjoying the quest to rescue Esther.

'OK, ask the boy to come with me to buy some meat.'

Tahir looks incredulous that I am thinking about buying

food items at this time, but speaks to the boy, who looks equally bewildered. I take off down the street, the boy racing by my side to keep up.

I surprise myself by successfully retracing my steps towards the house of Humayun's cousin. As I do so, we pass the butcher's shop.

It is getting dark. I assume the butcher has taken the meat into the house. I go to the gate and tap loudly. After a few moments, the man comes out, still wearing his dirty *shalwar-kameez* suit. I take out a five hundred rupee note and look at the boy to interpret.

The boy hesitates, but then speaks in an even tone. The man looks at me, goes inside, and brings out pieces of meat, still on the hooks, with rudimentary scales in one hand. He hangs up the meat and sets out the scales. I notice one of the weights is a stone wrapped in some kind of cloth and secured by black rubber bands.

I point at what looks like the cheapest cut of meat and hand over the money. He weighs it out and looks up at me. I take two more notes and place them by his side, indicating that I require more meat from the same source. He returns to carving off the fatty flesh until again the scales balance. I nod my approval, and he gathers the meat in the scales pan, ready to cut out the fat. I shake my head and point to several blue plastic bags he has brought out with the scales. The man speaks with the boy. He can't offer any explanation, so the shopkeeper shrugs and puts the meat in a bag, shaking fat from his hand onto the concrete beside him.

I take the meat and head off down the street. Humayun's

cousin comes with me but then draws back as we near the area where we met the dogs. He climbs the steps of a building just off the street and refuses to go any further.

The dogs are still there. I can see the gleam in their eyes amidst the blackness of the rubbish heap. They are sitting close to each other, heads in paws. They catch the scent of the meat. They stand up and, catching sight of their intended supper, start walking towards me. The walk turns into a run.

I run as fast as I can down the street towards the house where Esther is being kept. The dogs follow in hot pursuit – probably seven of them. For stray dogs, they are quick, but I am a practiced runner. The lead dogs are snapping at my heels. I sense other dogs join the party in pursuit of an easy meal.

I am hot, sweaty, and frightened. If I stumble, the dogs will be onto me. I could be bitten and become the next rabies death statistic. I feel my muscles complain – a hot sting. I haven't run this quickly for a long time.

At last, I catch sight of the house. I will myself towards the front gate, straining as if to cross a finishing line. Barely stopping, I toss the bag of meat over the wall into the courtyard, then bang on the gate as loudly as possible. Within a moment, I shoot across the street and jump up the steps of a house.

The dogs have caught up with me. I feel the warm, rough fur against my legs but mercifully no bite. I trip over one warm body: The animal yelps and slinks away. The scavengers are confused that I no longer have their meal. One has followed me across the street, snarling. The others wait by the gate, smelling the flesh from a distance.

The gate opens slightly. A tribesman peers out – pistol hidden behind his back. In a moment, the dogs rush in, barking loudly. I hear what I imagine are swear words in Pushto and loud shouting. A shot rings out and there is a loud 'yelp'. One of the dogs is down. The others intensify their growling.

With the dogs out of the way, I run back across the street to the gate and peer into the courtyard. The two men who were in the house have appeared, weapons in hand. I imagine their consternation at a bag of meat landing in their courtyard, and the gate hanging wide open. A man inches towards the gate but draws back when a rogue dog takes after him.

I put my fingers into my mouth and whistle as loudly as I can. The men are suspicious – one brandishes his pistol and braves the dogs to approach the gate. I run back along the street towards the narrow alleyway I have agreed with Tahir as a meeting point.

Tahir later tells me what had happened at the rear of the property.

When he heard the dogs and the men shouting, he got ready by the back gate. At the sound of our agreed signal, he charged the wooden structure and burst into a rear room. Picking himself up, he quickly stumbled into the room where Esther was being held. He cut her ropes with his penknife and whisked her out. Esther was in a daze, so he had to drag her to safety.

I arrive to see Tahir forcibly silencing Esther with his hand over her mouth. 'Quick, we need to get out of here.'

Humayun's cousin appears. Seeing Esther with us, his eyes widen in fear. He quickly leads us out of our hiding place down the road. He is running as fast as his legs will carry him. We march behind, quick-step, to keep up, Esther struggling to keep on her feet. Eventually, we arrive at the boy's home we visited earlier. Humayun gives an urgent rap on the gate. As soon as the gate opens, we pile in.

The narrow passage is lit by a dim bulb hanging from a loose wire on the wall. They show us into a rear room with mattresses on the floor. We sit, grateful for the opportunity to recover our breath. Various members of the household glance round the wooden door at us as they pass in the passage – the boy snatching conversation with them. After a while, metal tumblers of water appear.

'How you know where I was?' Esther says, her wits beginning to return to her.

'Local families helped us,' I say. 'We struck lucky when we rescued a local boy from the lake. The family was indebted to help us. It took some time, but their network of relatives identified the house.

'Are you OK?' I am concerned. Esther appears to be dazed.

'Yes… confused, that is all.'

'Do you want to phone your family?' I say, wrestling the phone from my pocket.

'OK.'

I hear a faint knock on the gate. Another brother of the family returns with Humayun. He looks agitated and speaks rapidly to Tahir.

'We need to move further away,' Tahir says. 'The men may have contacts in this area. They will come looking. We need to move now.'

'Yes, I am safe. The men got me out…' Esther was mid-sentence when Humayun's cousin appears in the doorway and speaks excitedly.

'Sorry, end the call now,' Tahir says. He gets up from the mattress. 'It's time to leave. The boy has spotted the men at the end of the street.'

Esther passes the phone back to me. Within a moment, the phone rings. I turn the phone off as a precaution – I can't risk it ringing while we are outside.

Esther stands, still weak from her ordeal. She is pale and languid. I rise to my feet and hold her. I want an embrace but know it would be very unwise in the present company.

The boy quickly shows us to the back gate of the house. We tumble out into the dark yard, Humayun racing off in the direction of the main road. We follow as best we can in the darkness.

Tahir catches up with Humayun and speaks with him. He slows to where Esther and I are shuffling along, Esther still finding it difficult to walk. I look into her eyes to encourage her, but she looks away.

'We will not go to the bus stop,' Tahir says. 'They may have men watching. We will cut through the back streets to much farther along the main road towards the city. We will try to find a taxi in the back streets.'

Tahir must have heard the sound first. He glances at the side of the street, looking for cover. Spotting an old Datsun taxi parked outside a house ahead, he pushes us towards it.

We crouch behind the black form and stay still as the motorbike races past us. The pillion rider holds something to his side – probably a firearm. We guess Humayun has taken shelter ahead. We hear the motorbike continue its journey up the street. Humayun is safe.

After a few minutes, we join Humayun in the street. He and Tahir speak.

'We need to keep off the roads to the front of the houses. They could be back.'

Esther groans. She doesn't look well.

'OK, let's go.'

Humayun leads us through the *guli* to much narrower paths. It is difficult to see the way in the dark. For once, I am glad of light pollution from Peshawar that augments the dim luminescence of the heavenly bodies.

'We need to get Esther to a hospital,' I say, as I try to keep her fatigued body from collapsing in a heap.

'Yes, but first we need the protection of the police. Not the local police. Anyone can bribe them. We need to get to the station in Peshawar.'

'What about phoning Esther's father in Karachi? He could contact the station in Peshawar.'

'No. Bad idea. We need to keep on the move.' Tahir is adamant.

We stumble on through narrow passages. Esther becomes more and more agitated. She collapses onto a step.

'We can't go on,' I say. 'Esther can't bear it.'

Humayun calls out to Tahir. I can make out a few of the words in his broken Urdu – something about 'relative'.

'Humayun has a *chaacha* living nearby. We could go there.'

I put Esther over my shoulder in a firefighter's lift and stumble on towards the dark form of Humayun waiting at a back gate several metres ahead. My foot slips into a narrow groove. I feel liquid – probably a toilet runaway. The smell disgusts me. Tahir sees me struggling and comes to help me to the spot Humayun is indicating.

'He says we should stay here. Humayun will go round the front of the house and get his uncle to open the gate.'

After five minutes, the gate opens. We are ushered into another home, similar to the house we left an hour ago.

A man, presumably the uncle, leads us to a small room with mattresses on the floor. Looking at the rough furniture and the decorative *shalwar-kameez* suits hanging loosely from the ledges, I gather this is the women's bedroom. The man points to a spot. I carefully lower Esther onto the mattress.

We join our host next door, sitting on our mattresses. I prop my back against the flaking plaster on the wall and close my eyes. I feel bone tired. I drink down the water and pick at the lentil curry and rice another cousin of Humayun has brought to the room. I desperately need to sleep.

'It's OK,' Tahir says. 'Family members are taking turns to keep watch out the front during the night. We can rest here.'

Tahir stretches himself out on his mattress. I stay put, too tired to move. But we have done it. We have got Esther out. We only have to get to the police.

Chapter 15

Shafts of sunlight piercing through the ragged curtains hanging at the windows disturb my sleep. I toss and turn, but find the mattress uncomfortable. The body odour in the room is unbearable. I struggle to my feet and creep out. The other men are still asleep. I look for steps to the roof – I want some fresh air and time to think.

From the roof, all seems calm. Men are walking down the street, *chardars* wrapped around the lower half of their faces. I cannot understand why men need these light scarves in the heat. A motorcyclist with milk churns fixed to the rear of his bike passes below, weaving between the pedestrians, reminding me of the incident last night.

I hear a commotion downstairs – women are calling out. I rush down the steps. Tahir is outside the room where we laid Esther. The women are talking inside.

'Esther is not here,' he says. 'She has gone.'

A wave of burning panic sweeps through my body. The

next moment, my skin is clammy and my legs are weak. I prop myself up against the wall to brace myself.

Why?

Tahir curses. 'Where has she gone?'

He runs to the front of the house, opens the gate, and walks down the street, looking for any sign of the missing woman. I hesitate. There is no point in looking down the back alley – I have been scanning the comings and goings from the rooftop. I run out to join Tahir.

'Perhaps she's suffering from some sort of Stockholm Syndrome. She was weak last night. She can't have got too far.'

We keep to the side of the road and walk two kilometres towards the house from which we had rescued Esther.

The road becomes busier with men and women beginning their daily activities. Even at this time of the morning, I can feel the waxing strength of the sun's electromagnetic energy.

'I think they have picked her up,' Tahir says. 'We had better get back to the house, get our belongings, and leave. There is nothing we can do now.'

I am at a loss for words. I know Tahir is right. Nonetheless, it all seems wrong, a miserable end to our attempts to free Esther. I feel angry and defeated.

We amble back to the house. Tahir speaks to the host. We start to collect our few personal items.

Suddenly there is a loud hammering on the front metal gate. Humayun's cousin bolts up some steps and looks through a window. He tells us there are two armed tribesmen outside.

We rush to the rear gate. I peer through the crack between the top of the gate and the wall. Two men are watching the gate from the *guli*, one has a pistol.

'We are trapped,' Tahir says. He draws me aside to the small lounge while our host starts to engage the men in conversation.

'There is no point in trying to hold out here,' Tahir says. 'They know we are here. If they start shooting the gate down, someone will get hurt. Our best hope is to go out the front. They are less likely to shoot on the main street with people watching. If we go with them, they will probably leave the family here alone.'

The shouting between our host and the tribesmen becomes more heated. I can't understand what is being said, but the level of vehemence in the exchange scares me. I don't want to be the cause of injury or death to any of the family members. I walk to the gate, nudge our host to one side, and then unbolting it, walk out to the street, hands on my head. As I look back, I see Tahir behind me.

The tribesman who seems to be in charge waves a pistol to direct us into the back of the jeep. His colleague covers us with his firearm while the leader gets into the front of the jeep to drive.

We set off with a trail of dust billowing out behind us. The few onlookers who have been staring in our direction during the incident are encouraged to get back to their business by glares from the tribesman and the waving of his pistol in the air.

We keep quiet. A blanket of despair descends on me. This doesn't look good.

The tribesman heads off in the same direction from which we had come the previous evening. After several kilometres, I realise he isn't taking us back to the same house. The buildings in this neighbourhood look different – larger, with extensive ground surrounding the property plots.

We pull up at an expensive-looking property. A guard emerges from a concrete enclosure, looks at the driver, and opens the gate. We drive up to a veranda at the front of the property. The man sitting with us gestures for us to get out. We follow the men towards the front door, another guard standing to attention as we approach.

It takes a moment for my eyes to adjust to the dim interior after the bright sunlight of the early morning. I can make out two or three men and two women, plus someone in a wheelchair. Esther is there.

They show us to a low couch. A guard stands close by.

One of the men approaches and sits adjacent to us. He is clean-shaven, expensively dressed, and exudes an air of sophistication. He takes out a cigarette packet and starts to smoke, eyeing both of us with intelligent interest.

'Dr Grant and his friend Tahir. We've been waiting a while to see you. It's been difficult to get your attention. You've finally decided to pay us a visit.

'The guys here have some things they need to say. But it's a courtesy to let the guests speak first. So, over to you, Dr Grant. Would you start by telling us the progress you've made in your research project? After all, it's because of your research you're here in this country.'

I look askance at our host. How does he know about my

research and how much does he know? What's his interest in it?

'It's going reasonably well,' I say.

The man laughs. 'Is that all you can say about it? After all this work? How about telling us about the intended publication of the findings? From what I understand, you intend to publish soon.'

I try to remain calm but can feel my heart knocking inside my chest. I look away to distract myself.

'OK, as you seem reluctant to speak about your work, allow me to inform those of us assembled here about your research.

'You have had a longstanding interest in the topic of plastic absorption in the human body, dating from when you were employed in the laboratories of the BPF Plastics and Flexible Packaging Group. There you were monitoring how certain plastics, if absorbed by the body over a length of time, could become carcinogens. You read widely as part of your work and came across accounts of serious mutations that could not be traced to the use of one kind of plastic. You, as the gallant English knight in shining armour, felt the need to investigate further, suspecting that some plastic food receptacle and bottling companies were withholding information that could be very damaging to them if disclosed. So, you left the laboratories of BPF Plastics and convinced a professor at Oxford University to allow you to take up a self-funded research project, probing deeper into the plastic compounds that could do lasting damage to DNA and that would result in infertility and abnormalities in humans through successive generations. It was useful that you inherited a large sum from the estate of your great aunt to pay for this private research. It came at just the right time. Is that right?'

The man blows a puff of cigarette smoke into the air and looks at me enquiringly. Tahir shifts on the couch. I look back weakly.

'Good'.

'Your research involved identifying irregularities between samples that were recognised as 'safe' plastics and unexpected occurrences of DNA modification in the populations where the food packaging was used. You tried to find out if some companies were not telling the whole truth about what was in their plastics. You were suspicious about one company, Cranford Plastics, when you traced which bottling companies they provided their products to, and the incidence of unexplained birth abnormalities in the larger population of that country.

'So, you got in contact with scores of medical professionals all around the world and collected data. Wow, you collected a lot of data. To contrast the deviation of the statistical results, you have also been on a quest to get data from remote tribes that have had little or no exposure to plastics from any kind of food packaging. And the conclusion of your research to this point is quite worrying. Is that true, Dr Grant?'

I remain quiet. I am thinking about who has provided this information. Who is the 'mole' at the laboratory? Who have they paid off? Is it Rachel? I quickly dismiss the idea. I have no proof. It could be anyone with any number of motives.

'Are you going to tell us what you have concluded, Dr Grant? We might as well hear an accurate summary of the results, rather than my version. Don't worry about disclosure issues – we all promise to keep mum.

Our host stands.

'OK, well, it will have to be my version. You have identified a chemical compound that has been a factor in the mutations causing birth defects. You have traced this compound to a small number of companies, including Cranford Plastics. When you publish your research, there will be full investigations. A lot of heads may roll. Share prices will plummet. Many people will get very upset.'

'No, that's not true. We haven't got to that point. We're still doing data analysis.'

'It's a pity you didn't heed the various warnings my friends and I sent you over the past several weeks. We have been concerned about your wellbeing. There's a lot in the media about "wellbeing" and "wellness" in your country. Is that right?

'If you had taken the warnings seriously, you wouldn't be in this place now. The future of your wellbeing is in grave jeopardy. There is nothing more I or my friends here can do to save you.

'Wait. But you said it would only be a warning.' The woman in the wheelchair swivels around hastily and stares at Younis. You said you would warn him and then release him. Esther, you can't go back on this. You promised.'

Esther glares at me and then turns to Rita.

'Things are changed. I am not in charge here. There's another agenda.'

Younis smiles benignly at the squabbling sisters. 'But before we dismiss you, these two young ladies would like to speak with you.'

'You remember Rita?' Esther asks. 'She is my sister. She came to visit me recently in Karachi. She remember you. She remember the prank that caused her lot of pain and disrupted her studies – trauma that she didn't need. She tell me you never apologised to her or owned up to fixing her wheelchair. You never tried to find out how she was doing. Obviously, the wellbeing of my sister is none of your concern. You just want to stay out of trouble and get on in life. My sister suffering as result of your foolishness does not occur to you.'

I stand. 'I'm sorry,' I say. 'I didn't know Rita was your sister.'

'So, you are concerned, now you know she is my sibling? Concerned about what? That our relationship will be affected? That I will no longer want to marry you? Obviously, you have no concern for this person as human being. The pain she still experience resulting from the break. The real possibility of arthritis in later years.'

'I was young and easily influenced in those days,' I say. 'I deeply regretted what happened. I swore to myself that I would never do anything like that again. I should have tried to find out about Rita. College life was busy… it must have slipped my mind.'

'That is poor comfort to my sister,' Esther says.

Rita lowers her gaze. 'I've forgiven you, Steven. It was very painful and upsetting at the time, but I knew other students egged you on. I was very disappointed that you didn't follow up on how the surgery went – if you remember, I needed a pin in the bone. You could have done more.'

'I'm sorry. That's all I can say. I'm sorry.

'So, is this kidnapping just a scheme to lure me to those who want me out of the way?'

Esther smiles. Smug, conceited. 'No. These men kidnapped me for ransom in Karachi. Younis then told me he and his men planned to lure you into a trap. Rita was already in Karachi. She told me you were the student who fixed her wheelchair. So, I did deal with Younis. Rita stay with me here and reduce the ransom demand in exchange for your life. Younis agreed.

'Rita walked into trap. I wanted to confront you with your poor treatment of my family for many days. It works well for my family. Your research harm them.'

'How?'

'My family has shares in the food packaging business run by your uncle.'

'What?'

None of this makes sense. I try to get my head around the web of vested interests. Neil? Mr Li and the family?

'I'm sorry, Steven,' Rita calls out. 'I didn't know it would work out like this.'

Esther exchanges glances with our host. He smiles.

My mind races. How has Esther stooped so low to connive with her kidnappers after so few days of captivity? I've read of emotional bonding between captor and victim in extreme circumstances but have never thought it real. I shudder, a sense of cold sweeping over me at the thought of Esther's possible moral compromise as part of the arrangement. I feel sickened.

'I have decided on a fitting treatment for you before they execute you,' Esther says. 'My sister suffered the pain of broken arm. You have never experienced such pain, I do not think? It is a pity to miss out on such an experience: I have arranged for the men to break your arm one hour before your execution, just like Rita's break.'

'No, that's callous,' Rita calls out. 'I don't want that – it won't make things any easier for me. You said you would let him go!'

'It is what Younis and I have decided,' Esther says. 'Steven has pain-free life while you suffer. He should suffer before he dies.'

The clean-shaven tribesman smiles at Esther approvingly, but says nothing.

'Steven, I'm so sorry. I didn't know these men were planning to harm you. I would never have agreed to come had I known this.'

Rita sinks back into her chair in defeat. Esther tuts dismissively.

'It's time to get on with things,' Younis says, raising an eyebrow at a henchman standing in the doorway. The man picks up an iron rod and approaches me.

Rita screams. Younis feigns disappointment.

'You had better take the young man outside to avoid upsetting our lady guest,' Younis says.

Two tribesmen grasp me firmly, twisting my arm around my back, and march me towards the entrance. Tahir rises, but Younis motions with his pistol for Tahir to stay put.

I am shaking. I tense my body and dig in my heels. The men have to drag me along.

'Not keen on the medicine?' Younis says, mocking my resistance.

As we approach the door Tahir springs to his feet and bolts towards the men, kneeing one in the groin, and punching the other. I hear a shot ring out and see Tahir fall to the ground. I seize the chance and pelt out of the door, turning towards the area to the back of the house. Younis calls out to the security guard at the front gate. He joins in the chase as a bullet hits the wall to my side. I quickly turn the corner and spot a breeze-block enclosure for the water pump against the rear wall. I take a good run at it and vault over the wall. Further shots ring out but I take off at an adrenaline-fueled pace. I can hear shouting behind me. I don't look back.

The housing in this quarter of the city is less dense with large plots of open land. I dodge between the open spaces, trying to find my way towards a more congested area. I can hear the jeep in the distance behind me. I want to go to ground as quickly as possible.

I see a parade of shops ahead of me. I run across the road and into a side street. I jump into a deep trench running down the *guli* and crawl into a recess at the far end of the trench.

It isn't long before I hear voices above me. I follow the sound of footsteps on the tarmac down the *guli*. It stops at the trench. I back into the recess as far as I can. A man's shadow falls across the opening as he peers into the darkness. He stands there for fifteen seconds and then makes off back up the road. I gently breathe a sigh of relief.

I rehearse the events of the last few hours in my mind. How can I have been so wrong about Esther? Why did Tahir so willingly give his life for me? How will I be able to face telling Nadeem and Tahir's family?

Man, you're in a deep mess. How did I get to this point?

I wake from a fitful doze and manoeuvre my arm into a shaft of light from a solitary fluorescent tube fixed to the back of a house adjacent to the trench. It is 4am – time to move. I find footholds in the jagged wall and climb out of my hideout, looking up and down the street for any of Younis' men left on watch. The street is quiet. A rat, disturbed by the noise of my boots on the tarmac, shoots past me into a pile of wooden crates. My heart races. I creep to the corner of a building and stretch myself against the stone wall, breathing deeply and quietening my body.

I walk down the side street and then curse. It is a dead end. I retrace my steps up the street and gingerly peer around the corner of the shop. In the distance, I can make out a tribesman on my side of the road, dozing on a wooden chair, pistol in hand. I creep back to where a narrow connecting lane runs at the back of the shops and stumble to the end, turning right to emerge behind the sleeping sentry.

I strike the man on the head with a rock I found in the lane, and as he slumps forward, snatch the pistol from him. Thrusting the gun behind my belt, I walk off briskly, in the direction of the city.

I take as many turns as possible to bury myself deep in

the *bazaar*, stumbling on to cover as many kilometres as possible. I am desperately weary. I pass stray dogs, scavenging among the rubbish piled on empty plots. They keep a wide berth, eyeing me suspiciously.

I hear a vehicle approaching from a distance. I hurry to a *guli* and hide until it speeds past.

'Why…?' I spin around to see a figure lying underneath a cart at the side of the *guli*, looking up at me. It is the man whose cart we borrowed the previous day. I withdraw my hand from the pistol grip and attempt a smile. Fingering in my back pocket for a hundred rupee note, I give it to him and gesture that I want to lie near his cart. He shrugs. I collapse onto the ground between a wheel and the wall and fall asleep within seconds.

I wake with the sound of movement. It is light. Looking up, I see that the toy vendor is removing the sheets he uses on the top of the cart to secure the articles from theft. He eyes me suspiciously. I stand and help him. Then I gesture that we should have breakfast together. He looks bemused but goes to the rear of the cart and pushes it out of the *guli* into the main street, then to a wider street that veers off at forty-five degrees. There is a labourers' café at the intersection. I follow. He leaves the cart and sits on a rough stool. He smiles when I sit opposite.

A boy brings the tea and *paratha*. I scoff down the fried bread greedily and gesture for more. The toy vendor looks pleased to indulge in a second serving, and pours the tea into the saucer, examining me warily as he sips the hot liquid from the saucer brim. All around there are muted conversations in Pushto, a language I can't understand. Are any of the men talking about me? I notice one labourer a few tables away fumbling with his cheap mobile phone. I decide it is time to leave and give a fifty rupee note to a young man behind the café counter as I step down into the road.

Farther down the street, I come across a shopkeeper hanging his second-hand clothing articles on a wire fence. I notice a Chitrali cap dangling on a makeshift peg and check the fit. I choose the most suitable pair of trousers and two shirts that look in decent condition and are my size. I flit to an adjacent stall and buy underwear and shaving equipment. A cart vendor with plastic household articles walks past. I splash out on a small, cheap mirror. I look at myself. My shirt is creased and dirty, my hair matted and my chin full of stubble. My face is smeared with dirt and my eyes are bloodshot. I could be a typical Peshawar equivalent of a rough sleeper.

Would I be safe in the hands of the police in Peshawar? There was no telling either way. Younis could have contacts in the local constabulary. It would be easy for a rogue policeman to whisk me off, out of the way of the other police, to the tribesman's den. I decide to get to the capital city of Islamabad, navigating the bus hub in Peshawar.

I stumble out of the *bazaar* onto a major street and find men and women at the side of the road waiting for a bus. A bus pulls up. 'Peshawar?' I ask the most educated-looking man in the crowd. He looks at me nonchalantly. I wait. Two more buses come. The man gives the same stare back as if I was asking if a bus runs on four wheels. When the third larger bus arrives, he indicates with a jerk of the chin that this is Peshawar bound. But no smile.

I pull myself up into the wagon and find a seat as far from the window as possible. The conductor makes his way towards me.

'Gulbahar, Peshawar.' I delve into my pocket for small notes and hand over one hundred rupees. The boy hesitates – I imagine he was deciding whether to give me the change. He quickly passes on to the other passengers.

Within two hours, we arrive at Gulbahar. I try to remember the layout of the roads and buildings to find the Daewoo bus terminal. My mind is dazed from the ordeal of the last twenty-four hours: Esther's betrayal, Tahir's demise and my knocking a man unconscious. I worry I killed the man. As I battle my anxious thoughts, I realise this is unlikely. But I will never know.

Finally, I come across buildings that I vaguely recognise and find the booking office. I also find what appears to be one of Younis' henchmen stationed to look out for me. He is standing opposite the office, chewing pan, with henna-dyed hair and beard. I dart out of his sight and wait.

I walk back along the service road, away from the depot. A taxi slows as it hits the line of traffic queuing into the departure area.

'Excuse me,' I say to the man on the passenger side whose window was wound down to let in the air. 'Could you do me a favour? Could you buy a ticket to Islamabad for me and bring it to me here?' I hold out a thousand rupee note.

There's no response. I can hear horns and the bustle of traffic. The smell of diesel fumes nearly chokes my irritated nasal passages. I stare up at the corridor of blackness where the fumes hang in the air.

The man hesitates and then smiles. 'My dear, can't you buy the ticket yourself? The office is only round the corner?'

His wife looks at him anxiously. The children in the back of the taxi grow quiet.

'I don't know the language,' I say. 'I don't feel comfortable trying to buy the ticket. If you could buy the ticket and bring it to me, it would help me. You can keep the change. It will be your good deed to help a foreigner. I am sure Allah would be pleased.'

The wife looks away. Her husband thinks for a few moments.

'Yes – if you need me to do this, I will buy the ticket. Stay here. I will not have time to come looking for you. I will bring you the change. What is the name?'

'Smith,' I answer. 'Don Smith'.

The man takes the rupee note, and the taxi surges forward, to edge behind the car in front.

I wait at the side of the road, trying to look inconspicuous. After fifteen minutes, my friend arrives, ticket in hand. 'You will have to come quickly,' he says, as he hands me the ticket and change. 'The coach leaves in five minutes.'

I grin a 'thank you' and make off towards the depot, hanging back as he strides into the distance.

Five minutes later, the coach turns out of the terminal into the service lane. I am waiting. I jump out in front and wave frantically. The vehicle comes to a halt and an armed guard opens the door, pointing his AK-47 in a menacing gesture.

'I'm so sorry,' I say, in an affected English accent. 'I have a ticket but didn't get to the coach in time. Would you mind if I came on board?'

The guard looks at the driver. He stands aside. I climb the steps into the vehicle.

I am tense. Is one of Younis' thugs sitting somewhere close? I scan the faces of the passengers. I make eye contact with the man who helped me with the ticket purchase. One of his children is sitting by his side with the older child next to his wife behind him. He glances at me with a puzzled expression and then looks away. The other passengers, whose features I could see, seem to be genuine.

The coach pulls into the Islamabad terminal. I have rehearsed my next steps during the journey: I will get a taxi to the British High Commission. I will explain my situation and request a High Commission officer to accompany me to the police station.

I leave the coach and hurry towards the parked taxis. Islamabad feels more familiar to me – a safer place in the sea of uncertainty and fear. Yet I am ill at ease. I am bereft. This trip has been a disaster. I have lost hope of a relationship, a friend in Tahir, and the samples that were collected at the Bumburet clinic. I stop in my tracks and curse out loud. How can I return to the UK empty-handed?

I approach a taxi. 'Airport.' The man nods, leaves his fellow taxi drivers with whom he was chatting, and climbs behind the wheel. I get in. I am not going to the Consulate – at least not in Islamabad. I am going back to Chitral. I can redeem the trip, at least in part.

Chapter 16

I arrive at the clinic late in the afternoon, a day later, after crashing out on a seat in the airport and sleeping solidly despite the ambient noise. My unkempt appearance and body odour kept people away. I feel relatively refreshed.

The aftermath of the earthquake is still evident. Large stones and boulders lie in heaps on the side of the roads. Homes are still in a state of disrepair, with rubble piled up at the side. In some areas, I see tents providing shelter to those whose homes have toppled. Larger tents and marques are populated with army personnel, or in some cases, doctors and nurses treating abrasions, broken bones, or diseases. Food and water are in short supply.

'*Asalam-a-lequm.*' I greet Dr Irfan as I ignore the attempted restraint by Nurse Benazir and stride into his office. He looks up from the desk and eyes me with a puzzled expression.

'*Wa-a-lequm-asalam*. I hope you are well?'

'OK.'

'Where is your friend, Tahir?'

'He's no longer with me,' is all I can say. I look away.

'Oh, I see. Please take a seat.' I pull the chair a distance from the desk, aware of my unsanitary state.

Dr Irfan calls the boy to get me water and to prepare tea.

'Life is still chaotic here after the earthquake,' Dr Irfan continues. 'They have cleared the main roads. The relief teams have arrived. Yet there is still much suffering.

'I have been busy here. Many of my patients with injuries from the earthquake could be treated at the camps. But they refuse to go. They trust me. I have to be forceful sometimes.

'Where have you been since you and your friend left?'

I mumble an explanation. I have been to Kohat to visit Tanda Lake and have met some interesting people. I stayed with someone near Peshawar. Tahir and I have parted company. I will be leaving for Karachi soon.

'It seems you have had an interesting trip,' Dr Irfan says.

'Could I use your bathroom to wash?'

'Yes, do,' Dr Irfan replies. 'You know where it is.'

I pick up the cheap rucksack I bought in the *bazaar* the previous day with my toiletries and change of clothes. Thirty minutes later I emerge feeling more myself, clean-shaven, and relatively sweet-smelling. I make my way back into Dr Irfan's consulting room. He has just dismissed a patient.

'I left my old clothes in a bag at the back of the clinic. If anyone wants to wash them, they can keep them. I won't be here long enough to wait for laundry to dry.'

I sit in the chair. The boy brings the tea and some cheap biscuits. Dr Irfan relaxes to enjoy the refreshments.

'I need more samples,' I say. 'As you know, someone stole the previous samples.'

'Yes, that was unfortunate. I can arrange for samples to be taken.'

'Thanks. I need them today.'

The expression on Dr Irfan's face changes. 'That won't be possible. Do you see how many people are waiting outside? We need to prepare. Nurse Benazir will not be ready.'

'Do you have more buccal swabs and swab envelopes?'

'Why, yes, I'm sure we do. But we need to prepare.'

'I can't stay here,' I say. 'I must leave today. I must take the samples with me.'

'Sorry, Dr Grant, but as I have just said, I am not in a position to work on this today.'

I finger the pistol. I'll have to threaten. But I stop with the pistol still in the belt. What will this do to me? How can I treat someone this way?

I collapse back in the chair and curse. Dr Irfan stares.

The dam bursts. I recount the events of the last few days and the urgency of the sample collection, ignoring apprehension about passing on dangerous information to a near stranger. I can't stop. It is therapeutic, but it leaves me with bile in my mouth and fear of Dr Irfan's reaction.

Dr Irfan adjusts his position in his chair. He pauses.

'Nurse Benazir' he calls. The nurse comes into the consulting room.

'Select patients for sampling as we did last week. You will remember the criteria? Get each patient's permission. You will find the buccal swabs and envelopes in the store cupboard. Dr Grant requires that we do this before the close of the clinic today.'

Nurse Benazir looks confused but nods. She leaves the room. Dr Irfan opens patient notes on his desk and starts reading them.

After two hours, Dr Irfan is dozing in his chair. I'm fidgeting, trying to resist the temptation to scratch insect bites that pepper the back of my legs. Nurse Benazir enters the consulting room from the small room where she has taken the samples. Dr Irfan jolts awake as she places the envelopes and a summary of patient biographical data on his desk.

'Should I send the next patient in?' the nurse asks.

Dr Irfan looks at his watch. 'Yes, give me ten minutes. We will have to work late this evening to see the most urgent cases. I need to travel to Islamabad tomorrow. My cousin is getting married.' The woman leaves the room.

Dr Irfan reads through the biographical summary and inspects the envelopes.

'It is all here. Take it.'

I take the envelopes and hand-written sheets and shake Dr Irfan's hand. He smiles.

'Good luck.'

Outside the clinic, I look for somewhere to dump the gun. On the way to the jeep stop, I find what I want – a small area of water that looks permanent. I glance around to see if anyone is looking and then hurl the gun as far as I can into the murky depths.

If only I could toss my troubles with the firearm...

The overnight journey back to Islamabad is long, tiring, but uneventful. I have plenty of time to muse over my disclosure at the clinic. Was it wise or unwise? I give myself the benefit of the doubt. I move on. That's what I always do.

I arrive in time for the late morning flight to Karachi. I buy a ticket from the Pakistan International Airlines booth and make my way towards security. I feel less conspicuous having washed and changed at the clinic. I place my rucksack on the conveyor belt and wait. My bag is not searched and I am allowed through to the departure lounge.

The plane touches down at the Jinnah International Airport, Karachi, in mid-afternoon. I stride out of the arrivals gate into the throng of individuals and families gathered to receive weary passengers. I know no one will be there to greet me.

A taxi driver approaches. I blurt out the name of Pastor Nadeem's *busti* and watch for a response. I know the lie of the land – it isn't so far from the airport.

'One thousand rupees.'

I revert to my crass Urdu to communicate that a thousand rupees may be the tourist rate, but not the rate I am willing to pay. We eventually settle on six hundred. Even though this is exorbitant, money is the least of my worries.

I stop the taxi in a lay-by outside the *busti*. I have little luggage to carry and want to find my way to Nadeem's house, relying on landmarks I memorised previously. After taking wrong paths that lead to dead-ends, I finally arrive at his house. I pause. It is not going to be easy.

Nadeem's eldest son opens the steel gate. He recognises me and cordially invites me in. He tells me that Nadeem is out, but I can wait for him to return home if I want. He directs me to the small lounge and leaves to get drinking water.

Nadeem's wife greets me coyly from the safety of the door. She asks how I am and then retreats into the kitchen. Thankfully, she doesn't ask about Tahir. I settle back to wait, grateful for the cool air current provided by the overhead fan.

After an hour, Nadeem returns. I can tell he knows part of what has happened, probably from the Li family. He is in a serious frame of mind.

'How much do you know about what happened in Kohat?' I ask straight out, sipping the tea nervously. Nadeem stands by the window and looks out onto the street.

'There have been many rumours. The Li family won't say much. They paid a ransom, but no one knows how much. None of us saw Esther when she returned home. Her sister left for the UK. It seems the family is in crisis, but I don't know all the details.

'Rita came to see me before she left. She was very upset. She had something on her conscience and needed to talk. She told me what happened, how they lured you and Tahir into a trap. She told me how Tahir was shot.'

Nadeem stops at this point. I can tell from the tilt of his head and sag of his shoulders that he is struggling emotionally.

'How have Tahir's wife and siblings taken it?'

'They are very angry… at you for involving Tahir. And

at Esther for orchestrating it. They have registered an FIR against Esther. She is now on the run with the gang member.'

'Oh.' I put my cup down and sit gazing at the brown-stained coffee table in front of me. 'I knew I would get the blame. But I didn't invite Tahir to come with me. He more-or-less forced himself into the situation. He met me at Islamabad airport and insisted on coming.'

'Yes, that was my doing.' Nadeem sighs. 'I didn't agree with your proposed attempt to rescue Esther, but I was concerned that you would be in danger without knowing the language and culture. Tahir picked up on this and insisted on meeting you. He was always one for adventure.'

'Have they recovered his body?'

'Yes, the gang left it in a place and phoned the police. They brought it down to Karachi. The funeral has already taken place.'

'That was quick.

'How come Rita was allowed to leave?' I ask.

'She gave statements to the police and managed to convince them that she wasn't involved, though when she spoke with me it seemed that she had gone along with the plan, even just to confront you about something you had done many years ago. Mr Li managed to pull some strings to get her off, and she left as quickly as possible.

'You know that you will need to report to the police? They need a statement from you.'

'I thought as much.'

'Should I visit Tahir's wife and family to explain and to apologise?'

Nadeem turns and sits in the wicker chair opposite me.

'No; on balance I think it is best not to visit. I explained the situation, and that I was partly to blame for Tahir's misadventure. It will not help for you to visit them at this point.'

'I could write from England.'

'No, that won't help.'

I sit contemplating the mess. I shudder when Esther's image flashes across my mind – not the sweet, coy Esther I knew, but a calculating schemer, intent on seeing me suffer for an indiscretion in my youth. I curse under my breath.

'Do you think Esther will see sense and separate herself from this gang?'

'No. She's involved. Her parents are distraught. But stay away.'

'When should I go to the police?'

'I will shower. Then we can go. You leave your things here. You are welcome to stay here until you fly back to the UK.'

The Central Police Office at I.I. Chundrigar Road is a dated concrete-and-glass structure with criss-cross bars on the windows and radio masts on the roof. Nadeem seems to know where to go, so I follow. We have to wait for an hour until the case officer finds interviewing officers who have a good grasp of English. He briefs them on the case.

The interview lasts two hours: It is painful to recount the course of events that led to Esther's betrayal of both Tahir and me, and to Tahir's death. By the end of the interview, I am tired, melancholic, and homesick. The roar of traffic on the busy road, the heat and the dust do nothing to quell the sense of dejection and gloom.

'I will take you to a hotel for refreshments,' Nadeem says. 'The Beach Luxury Hotel is nearby.' He flags down a taxi and we take off down the road.

In the hotel over a light meal, Nadeem initiates the conversation. He works skilfully as a pastor, talking through the experiences of the past seventy-two hours that have taken their emotional and mental toll. We explore every incident that has left me numb with grief and pain. We talk about Esther – her loss to her family, the local and church community, as well as my personal loss. I am frank with Nadeem about my intentions. He knows them already. He intimates that I am immature. I do not know about Chinese culture. I am not part of Esther's life or the life of her family or community in any meaningful way. It would have taken a long time to build that bond between us that was essential for a stable marriage.

'Is it the right time for you to marry?' Nadeem asks. I muse over the question for some time before answering.

'Yes, I know what I want in life. In the past several years, life has been about exposing a certain plastic company for endangering humankind by wilful negligence, and waking up the world to the long-term effects of plastic use. My research is coming to an end but I have good connections in Oxford. I've already put out feelers for the future. There are more research opportunities out there – perhaps another mission I will feel strongly about. I've had a lot of adventure in my life – as a single. I'd like to find someone who will join me in a less-than-conventional life in the UK or elsewhere.'

Nadeem looks at me hard, his eyes burrowing into mine. 'Well, do not rush the matter. Ask the advice of friends and family before getting too serious. Marriage involves families and is lived out in the wider community. It seems that too many Westerners forget this. Emotions are far too flimsy upon which to build a sound foundation that will last through the difficulties life brings.'

Nadeem's phone rings. 'Sorry, this is the ringtone I reserve for Mrs Nadeem – it must be urgent.'

I can hear the vague refrain of rapid Urdu speech. Nadeem listens intently, his eyebrows rising as the voice becomes louder. He stops the caller from continuing, muttering something into the phone. He puts the phone on the table and looks up at me.

'Your mother has been trying to contact you. It appears she is very worried. It's something about your brother. My wife couldn't understand the details. Your mother asks you to phone her as soon as possible. I suggest we return to my house. You can use a calling card to phone through to the UK.'

'I'll get the bill,' I say. Nadeem looks at me as though I were a child in his Sunday school. I walk to the entrance while he makes his way to the till counter.

Chapter 17

I slam the door, then remember that it is still early in the morning. The taxi driver looks around.

Why is Reuben coming to Pakistan at this point? Why do I have to be further delayed in getting back to my research? Couldn't anyone stop him?

I pleaded with Mum. My job is already on the line. I travelled to Pakistan without permission from my department, against the advice of my supervisor. The research is reaching a crucial point and I have further samples that needed analysing. If Reuben is so intent on seeing Uncle Neil, he can handle whatever the meeting throws up on his own. But Mum pleaded and cajoled. It's my duty to be there for Reuben. He has had a hard time. He was only discharged a week ago. His mental health is still fragile. How would he cope with the noise, pollution, and stress of an Asian megacity?

More to the point is how he will fare confronting Neil.

Is this some stupid idea of a psychiatrist? Or has Reuben himself decided that he needs to have it out with his uncle? Whichever it is, Reuben will find himself facing an ogre. If he isn't protected, this confrontation will quickly undo whatever healing has taken place.

I think back to when I, seething with anger, purposed to confront Uncle Neil myself. He had done serious damage to our family. He had no remorse. I could expose him. I could work to make his life miserable. I could give him some of his own medicine. How would he like to face fear and shame, similar to that which Reuben had struggled with? How would he recover from a sense of being violated, or of the damaged self-esteem from being abused?

I wince when I remember the plots about which I had fantasised – to get a handle on the man and to squeeze him dry. They were mostly impractical, criminal, and, in some cases, immoral. They kept me up at night. The anger burned into my bones. I had relinquished it several weeks before.

Anger is cancer. It was for my own wellbeing that I shelved revenge. But forgiveness has never been on the radar. It would take a saint to forgive that man.

I will dissuade Reuben from meeting him. He can stay the night and then we can travel back to the UK on the same flight. Yet I know that this won't happen. Like me, Reuben has inherited my father's obstinacy. Once he has decided on a course of action, he will charge ahead, whatever damage he does to himself or others. I am worried.

The taxi driver swings the cab from one lane to another,

presumably seeking the path of least resistance. Several other drivers blare their horns as he forces himself through. I pay the negotiated fare and slam the rear door shut, hurrying to the arrival monitors. My brother's flight has just landed.

I join the crowd of friends and relatives waiting by the barriers. I wait twenty minutes. There is no sign of Reuben. I nurture a vain hope that he has thought twice about the trip and has not boarded the flight in London the previous day.

A figure appears in the doorway of the arrivals area and looks anxiously into the crowd. My heart falls – it is Reuben. He hasn't changed from when we met at the hospital – his face gaunt, the leather jacket hunched at the shoulders where he has lost weight, and his trousers too long in the leg and frayed at the hem. His face lights up when he sees me and he heads across in my direction, knocking the metal barrier with his suitcase.

'I didn't know if you would get Mum's message,' Reuben says. 'It's hot here.' Reuben unzips and removes his jacket.

'You'd better come with me. A Pakistani friend, Nadeem, has agreed to accommodate you until we leave. It's basic, but the welcome is genuine.'

I try to smile as I speak. I try to analyse what I feel: Is it pity, compassion, or some brotherly affection? I am surprised at how calm I am. The anger has dissipated.

'How was the flight?'

'Not bad. It was a quick transfer in Dubai. But I made it. And so did my luggage.'

We brush past the taxi drivers touting for business. I

have arranged with the taxi driver who brought me to the airport to drive us back to the house. He approaches from the side. Reuben flinches.

'This is our man, Reuben. Put the suitcase in the boot. He'll take us to where we're staying.'

Whatever medication Reuben is still on, if any, it isn't enough to dampen his nervy response to the chaotic driving. He sits with his back pressed hard against the front seat, fingering his seat belt – his eyes darting from one side to another like a frightened sparrow. Occasionally, his right foot stamps against the floor as he anticipates an impending collision.

'Mum told me why you've come,' I say. 'I can't pretend that it is anything but inconvenient for me. Obviously, you have your reasons. But we'll have to sort this out quickly. I'm booked on a return flight to London Heathrow tomorrow.'

'Well, is that so?' Reuben says. 'I'm sorry that I'm an "inconvenience". I could have done this on my own, you know. You didn't need to put yourself out for me. Anyway, I heard from Mum that you've inconvenienced lots of people recently.'

I quell the rising anger. 'You know what I mean, Reuben. I've been delayed here in this country from returning to the UK for several days. I have to get back to my research in Oxford with samples I've taken. Years of work hang in the balance if I'm not there to oversee the report writing. You know that. Anyway, I can't understand why you need to confront Neil now.'

'I have my reasons. It's part of processing the past that

still affects me.'

'Did a medical professional suggest you do this?' I ask.

'No, not in so many words. But I knew I had to confront the man.'

'You know what his reaction will be, don't you?'

'Yes, I'm pretty convinced how he will react. Anger, denial, threats, perhaps mocking – nothing would surprise me. I just have to say what I need to say. I can't change his reaction.'

'Are you planning to take anyone else with you?' I am concerned. Reuben still seems young and vulnerable. There is also the threat of physical violence, depending on the meeting venue.

'I want to be on my own when I confront him. Just like I was on my own when he abused me. But this time I will stand up to him. I'll give as good as I get.'

'And if he gets violent?'

'I'll take that risk. I'm no longer a child. I'm not much smaller than him and I'm considerably younger. I can defend myself.'

'Does he know you are coming?'

'Yeah, as far as I know, Mum phoned him. Mum didn't want me to come. Knowing that she couldn't put me off, I'm sure she's tried to convince Neil to be reasonable.'

The taxi stops outside Nadeem's house. 'We're here. Just a few house rules,' I say. 'Shoes off inside the house. Don't fancy Nadeem's wife. Keep your eyes down when addressing women. For the rest, follow me.'

'What the…' Reuben kicks the tyre of the taxi as he gets out. He glares at me. I suspect he doesn't like big brother telling him what to do. This is going to be a tough ride.

Nadeem's son comes to the door and welcomes us in. Reuben enters cautiously. I can tell the simplicity and shabby furniture and fittings shocks him. I forgot to assure him that the house and food were clean.

Nadeem is the perfect gentleman. He receives Reuben graciously, offering tea, biscuits, and a listening ear. I can see Reuben beginning to relax as Nadeem puts him at ease. Reuben has had practically no experience of relating to people of other cultures. His overseas travel has been limited to Spain and Malta for holidays. I am happy that his first experience of relating to a Pakistani national is comfortable.

The day draws on. We both have a siesta and wake at 4pm. Nadeem's wife makes tea. Nadeem has been working at a makeshift desk. He joins us, leaving an onyx paper-weight to secure the papers he's been working on from flying around the room with the force of the fan downdraft.

A small wall lizard scurries across the wall and darts behind a cupboard. It fascinates Reuben.

The conversation turns to the reason for Reuben's visit. Reuben shifts uneasily in his seat.

'When are you planning to visit your uncle?' Nadeem asks. I see Nadeem watching Reuben's face closely.

'Well, as soon as possible. My brother here says he plans to be off soon. We could go this evening.'

I butt in. 'We'd have to make sure he's there. Do you feel up to it if he's available and willing to meet?'

'Yeah, the adrenaline is doing me fine. I'd rather get the

business sorted out sooner than later. Do you have his number? I'll ring.'

'Do you mind if we use your phone?' I ask Nadeem.

Nadeem nods.

'I'll phone,' Reuben says, snatching the scrap of paper with the number out of my hand. I would have put him in his place, but don't want to make a scene in front of Nadeem.

I watch Reuben's face closely. This isn't going to be easy. The call starts. Reuben is terse as he speaks. Then his tone changes.

'Oh… I'm sorry. We haven't heard…' Reuben was silent as the speaker on the end of the phone droned on. Reuben's expression softens. He is concentrating hard on what the person is saying. After a few minutes, he puts the phone down gently. I can see Reuben shaking ever so slightly.

'That was Claire. Neil went missing yesterday during an office outing to Paradise Point. He was in the sea with some of the other men. Claire said that he swam out from the beach and then seemed to be swept away by a current. He disappeared. As yet they have not recovered a body.

'How did Claire seem?' I ask.

'Very upset. She was struggling to speak.'

Nadeem stands. 'Do you want to go there?'

I think for a moment. 'Yes,' I think we should.'

'Claire said we needn't visit,' Reuben says. 'But it seems that she could do with support.'

'I'll find a taxi.' Nadeem picks up his wallet and heads out of the door.

I knock gently on the metal gate of the flat. A Pakistani woman comes and slides the bolt back – someone I recognise as a colleague from Neil's office. She is young and pretty but wears a serious expression. Reuben gawks at her. I curse under my breath and give him a gentle kick on the leg. She looks away and walks into the lounge.

Claire turns as we enter. She is sitting in a wicker chair with a box of handkerchiefs next to her, eyes red from weeping. When she sees us, she stands.

'You needn't have come,' she says.

'We wanted to express our condolences. Whatever has happened in the past, none of us would have wanted this.'

Claire sits and gestures for us to sit as well. Nadeem takes a seat near the door. The colleague reappears from the kitchen with a tray of water and glasses.

'When did this happen?'

'Yesterday afternoon,' Claire says. 'It was a day's outing. We arrived at the beach hut in the morning. We had snacks for lunch and then some of the men went swimming. Neil went with them.'

Claire grabs more tissues and wipes her eyes.

'Did any of the men see Neil when he was in trouble?' I ask.

'No. He drifted from the other men. He didn't call out. He just disappeared. I can't understand...why he didn't call for help.'

'Perhaps he thought he could make it back to the shore OK,' Reuben says. 'Was he a strong swimmer?'

'No. That's the strange thing. Generally, he doesn't swim far.'

'Has anyone looked to check if he's clinging onto rocks somewhere?'

Claire looks at me, teary-eyed. 'The local fishermen in the area say they looked. The police from the local station went and scouted around. No one found any sign of a person or body.'

Claire plucks another tissue from the box and dries her eyes. We stop the questions.

'Will you have tea?'

'No, we won't stop,' I say. I look over to where Reuben is sitting. He stares back at me. This is unexpected. None of us know the territory.

'Neil was a bugger at times,' Claire says. 'He didn't treat you well.'

I look away. Yeah, 'bugger' is an understatement. But this is not the time to call anyone to account.

We rise to leave. 'I'll call in tomorrow,' Nadeem says. I have forgotten Nadeem knows my uncle and Claire from church. Nadeem is not a spectator. He has genuine, pastoral concern.

'Thank you, Pastor. Say a prayer for me.'

Back at Nadeem's home, Reuben and I get ready for an early night. Reuben wants to crash early due to his long flight. I'm not averse to an early night after a demanding day. We lie on our low beds, with the sound of traffic, dogs barking, and filmy music in the background.

'How does this affect your processing of the past?' I ask Reuben, as we reflect on the situation. 'You wanted to have it out with him – now that's impossible. Where does that leave you?'

'I'm kind of numb,' Reuben says. 'I'll never be able to tell him the consequences of his actions. I'll never know if there was the smallest amount of remorse. I'll never be able to confront him as a man and redeem my manliness. There's no closure. It's hard. Part of me finds comfort in knowing that he suffered before he died. It's not good, is it?'

'No, but then I also wonder if he really is dead,' I say.

'What, you can't be serious?' Reuben sits up in his bed.

'There's no body. He would know that swimming in the sea during this season is dangerous. He allowed himself to get separated from the others. I wonder if it's a put-up job. Has he schemed to walk out on Claire and life in Karachi? Or was it suicide?'

'Suicide wouldn't make sense,' Reuben says. 'Our Uncle Neil doesn't seem to be of the suicidal type.'

'Do you think your refusal to have anything to do with him and the thought of my coming to confront him about the past could have tipped him over the brink?' Reuben asks.

'It's unlikely. Claire didn't mention that he was melancholic or anything like that. It seems that the beach party was going as expected until he got into the sea.'

'But how would he make a new life for himself?'

'A forged passport with a new name. Money to get across the Arabian Sea to the Gulf States and then an onward flight to who-knows-where. I expect if you pay enough money, you can get a pretty good forged passport in this country.'

'But how would he carry the passport and money on

him when he swam?'

'Perhaps he delivered it to a local person to keep previous to the event and a fisherman's launch picked him up. I don't know. It's all conjecture. But it seems out of character – Uncle Neil being swept away into oblivion.'

The next morning, we are finishing breakfast when the telephone rings. 'It's Claire,' Nadeem says.

I ask her how she is.

'I couldn't sleep last night. I had some news…I don't know what it means,' Claire says. After an awkward pause, she continues. 'A Baloch friend of one of Neil's office colleagues said he saw a foreigner in a village – an older man. He wanted us to know.'

'Have you told the police?'

'No. It could be anyone. But it could also be Neil.'

'Is someone from the office going to investigate?' I ask.

'Yes, Pervaiz said he would go. Would you go with him as family? I've no right to ask you after how we've treated you, but it would mean a lot to me.'

'My return flight to London Heathrow is tonight. We have to work on getting Reuben on the flight. We don't have much time.'

'I'll send the office boy with Pervaiz to collect Reuben's passport. He'll sort out the flight booking. You go with Pervaiz. He's leaving now. He and the boy will come to Nadeem's house – he knows Nadeem.'

'OK, but Reuben will come as well. He would be kicking his heels here. Anyway, he'd want to come.'

'Does Pervaiz know we have limited time?' I ask.

'Yes, it's a distance from the city, but you'll be back for the flight.'

Pervaiz turns up in an old Toyota saloon. Like many of the vehicles on the Karachi roads, it is hardly road-worthy. We travel in silence through the city and port areas into industrial zones, and then on bumpy roads to the remote beaches serviced by Mauripur Road.

'Razak said he would meet us at the crossroads ahead,' Pervaiz says. He slows the car as we approach. A man walks towards the vehicle from a tea shop. Pervaiz winds down the window.

'*Asalam-a-lequm.*' The man grins. He is roughly dressed with a moustache and a close-cropped beard. He and Pervaiz have a long exchange of greetings. I can't make out any of the words.

Razak clambers into the back seat. Reuben shifts farther across. I can smell body odour and fish.

'Razak is taking us to the village where there have been reports of this foreigner,' Pervaiz says. 'He will get out before we drive into the village. He does not want to be seen with us.'

'OK. How do you know him?' I look across at Razak who is fumbling with a packet of betel nut.

'His uncle lives in our area of the city,' Pervaiz says. 'I've had dealings with him over many years. He's brought me out here several times.'

The car slows to a stop as we approach a built-up area. Razak gets out and we drive to a tea shop near the village centre.

'You stay here,' Pervaiz says.

Pervaiz works his contacts in the shop, speaking first to the shop owner at the rough desk near the boiling cauldrons of dark brown tea, and then meeting other men in the shop. After twenty minutes, he is back with us.

'I have the location of where the man was spotted,' he says. 'We will go and see.'

We leave the road and drive down a track of sand and soil, with the occasional *sarmi* weed protruding from the dirt. As we go farther away from the tarmacked road, the track becomes less defined. A quarter of a kilometre further on, we stop. Pervaiz gets out and approaches one of three rudimentary buildings. A small boy by the edge of the complex runs into the largest dwelling. After a short while, a tall, stocky man appears.

I can't hear the conversation, but I can tell from the man's facial expression and body language that he isn't welcoming. Their voices rise. Pervaiz goes to enter the building but the man resists. He gestures wildly with his hands.

Cool it. There must be another way...

A crowd gathers – people seem to come from nowhere. After a while, a distinguished-looking man appears. He strides through the crowd and starts talking with the homeowner. The voices gradually quieten.

Pervaiz walks back to the car and beckons us to follow him. We fall in behind him and walk through the crowd. I feel eyes burrowing into me.

'I think he's here,' Pervaiz says. We stop on the threshold of the house. I am trembling.

The homeowner reluctantly allows us into the building.

I scan the room ahead of us. At the back, I make out a rough wooden door. The host indicates the door with the lifting of his chin. Pervaiz goes ahead. I follow with Reuben behind me.

As I peer inside, I see Neil lying on a rope-woven bed. He is dressed in smart, casual trousers and a loose-fitting T-shirt. He sits up as we enter. He scowls at us.

'Sir, are you OK? The office people have been worried.'

Neil ignores Pervaiz's question.

'So, what happened?' I sit on the corner of Neil's bed. He stares at me.

'What d'you think?'

'Were you swept out by currents?'

Neil looks away. 'No. It was pre-arranged... I wanted a new life. I thought it would work.'

'But why? What about Claire? The office?'

'There's nothing for me here.' Neil sighs. 'I wanted out. I would be in Dubai by now, heading for Australia. I nearly drowned before the boat got to me.'

'So, you would have left Claire thinking you had drowned?' I ask.

'She would have had the payout from the life assurance cover.'

'But not knowing what had really happened...

'So, are you still intent on leaving?'

Neil whips out a pistol from behind his pillow and points it at us.

'You've interfered. Things can't be the same.'

We back off slowly. 'You can't shoot all of us,' I say. 'You'd never get away with it.'

'I know,' Neil says. He suddenly turns the gun on himself.

'No, don't do that, Uncle,' Reuben says. 'You would leave behind grief.'

'What grief?' Neil smirks. 'A son who wants nothing to do with me? A nephew who claims I abused him? A business that will collapse as soon as your research is published leaving me in a quagmire of debt?'

'What?'

'You naïve bastard! Don't you know what business I run?'

'Import/export of some kind. I was never really interested.'

'Yeah, I told you it was organic chemicals. But it's mostly raw plastic for the food bottling industry. That's our major revenue earner.'

'So, you kept this quiet all this time?' I ask, incredulously.

'Of course: You would have never come if I told you the truth. You and your witch-hunt for bad plastics.'

'There's another way,' I say, quickly. 'We could talk through the issues. There's professional help out there. We can work on things as an extended family. Don't take your life.'

'There's nothing to live for now,' Neil says. 'It's over – curtains.' He points the weapon at his temple and pulls the trigger.

Reuben runs from the room. I stay a few moments to see if we can save Neil, but seeing the blood spurt in spasmodic surges onto the pillow, I also exit quickly followed by Pervaiz.

I find Reuben outside. He is pale and shaking. I put my hand on his shoulder.

'It couldn't be helped. It was Neil's decision. We tried to save him.'

'Let him sit in the car,' Pervaiz says. The crowd that has gathered at the sound of the gunshot clears as I help Reuben to the backseat. He sits with his head between his knees.

'What do we do now?' I ask Pervaiz.

'Get on the flight tonight,' he says. 'Your brother is not well. You must get out of the country.'

'But what about Claire?'

'This didn't happen. We didn't find your uncle here. She will not know.'

'But that's a lie. What about the body? How will you dispose of it?

'The fishermen will dump it at sea, weighed down by a rock. It will not be washed up.'

'You can't be serious,' I say. 'How will we live with this lie? How will you live with it in the office?'

'The alternative is that we report it. The police will come. They will charge someone with murder. We will tell them that it was suicide. They will want statements. They will want bribes. After many days, they will settle it. It will cause a lot of tension for us and our families. It will be expensive. It's cheaper to pay the fishermen to dump the body. We can pay the crowd to keep quiet.'

Reuben begins to sob, his body convulsing uncontrollably. He vomits onto the car floor.

'Get in the car,' Pervaiz says. 'I will speak with the house owner and the village leader. I will be quick.'

After ten minutes, Pervaiz settles into the driving seat and pulls the car door shut. The crowd has dispersed. We drive off.

Another nightmare mess. What's left? When will this run of disaster stop?

Chapter 18

Pervaiz drops us outside Nadeem's home and drives off. Reuben still looks white but manages to stand, propping himself up against the neighbour's breeze-block wall.

'Before we go in,' I say, 'we need to get things clear. I'm not going to lie to Nadeem. I'm not going to tell him either. He'll know that something's happened. He's wise enough not to ask.'

As soon as Reuben is in the house, he heads for the room we have been using. I sit in the lounge. Nadeem turns from his desk and walks to the wicker chairs. His son brings me a glass of water. I drink and sit back on the cotton cushion.

'That was not easy,' I say, looking up into Nadeem's face. He studies me.

'Is there any news for Claire?' he asks.

'Only news that I will share with her once I arrive back in the UK.'

Nadeem begins another question but then thinks better

of it. 'We will eat early this evening so that you can leave on time for the airport.'

I smile. 'Reuben may not have much of an appetite, but thanks for seeing to this.'

I feel embarrassed, explaining to the airport security guards that my brother is not feeling well. They eye him suspiciously. His vacant expression, death-like pallor and general lethargy are concerning. I help him heave his suitcase onto the luggage scanning machine conveyor belt. The security staff choose to search his case, even though the X-ray would not have revealed any suspicious objects. He answers their questions half-heartedly.

On the plane, he immediately nestles his head into the seat headrest and dozes. He misses the safety video. When the flight attendant comes round with the food, he passes on that, but takes a small bottle of vodka and gulps it. He gets another bottle of spirit from the back of the plane where the flight attendants are sorting their meal trolleys before we touch down in Dubai.

At Dubai, he lurches down the passenger boarding bridge towards the transit lounge and then collapses into the first seat we come across.

'I'm sorry,' he says. 'I don't feel well.'

'Well, I'm not surprised,' I say. 'Drinking two bottles of spirit on an empty stomach. That's a stupid thing to do.'

I smell the liquor on his breath. It repulses me.

'We have to keep going,' I say. 'We only have a short while to get through security and to the other gate. You'll have to wait until the long flight to rest properly.'

Reuben groans, then vomits. 'I can't go on,' he says. 'I need rest.'

'We've got to go. Otherwise, we'll miss the next plane.'

'I don't care,' Reuben says. 'I'll be sick again if I move.'

I see a shadow out of the corner of my eye and look up to see an attractive woman standing in front of us, peering down at Reuben.

'He doesn't look well,' she says. 'I'll help you get him somewhere more comfortable. It doesn't look like your friend can travel today.'

'No, he's going on the flight,' I say, but as I look up, the woman has disappeared.

'You're causing a scene,' I say to Reuben. My voice is rising. The stench of the vomit catches the back of my throat. I look around for an airport staff worker to clean it up, but can't see anyone. Reuben stays rooted in the seat.

Bro, pull yourself together. Co-operate.

After ten minutes, the woman returns, this time with a member of the airport staff.

'Is your friend ill?' the staff member asks, in a deep guttural accent. The woman winces as she catches a whiff of the vomit.

'He witnessed something unpleasant in Karachi,' I say. 'He also drank on an empty stomach. He'll be OK. He's my brother.'

'He won't be allowed to board the aircraft if he is ill,' the woman says. 'I will call the on-duty doctor.'

'I just need rest,' Reuben cries out. 'I'm not sick. I don't need to see a doctor.'

'I asked at the desk of the hotel here at the airport. There are rooms available,' the pretty woman says.

'Let's do that. I can't go on today.'

The airport official goes off to get a buggy to take us to the hotel booking desk near Terminal 1. The attractive woman stays. I try to place her accent. She sounds like a sophisticated Londoner. She has a deep tan and wears bright lipstick. Her figure is extremely shapely.

'Why are you helping us?' I ask.

'I'm a fellow passenger. I like to help others – it's what being human is about. We must never ignore people who are in need.'

She smiles at me and places her hand on my shoulder. I feel a surge of warmth through my body. I move away.

'Won't you miss your connecting flight?' I ask.

'No, my flight is not until tomorrow. I have time. I'm staying at the hotel myself this evening.'

The airport buggy draws up alongside us. The airport official steps off. I help Reuben into the buggy seat, followed by our hand luggage. The buggy takes off and I follow, racing to keep up.

'Thanks for your help, but we're OK now,' I say to the woman. She is striding to keep up with me.

'Where are you from?' the woman asks. 'I'm from Hornchurch, Essex. The name is Ann Marie.'

'Steven, from Oxford.'

'Perhaps we will meet later?' Ann Marie says. I look around. She has dropped her pace and stands beaming at me as I continue in the wake of the beeping buggy.

After a long trek through the airport terminal, I see the buggy stop inside a wide entrance to a hotel lobby. The driver is helping Reuben out of the buggy and into an opulent sofa. I approach the hotel desk and enquire about a room. The suited man explains that ordinarily rooms are pre-booked. Then the buggy driver approaches and speaks in Arabic while the suited man listens intently.

'So, you require a room urgency, due to the man's ill health,' he says, as a matter of fact rather than a question.

'Yes, it appears so.'

'I only have a deluxe room available. The price will be in pound sterling, two hundred and twenty, sixteen.'

I curse under my breath. The hotel room and the charge for changing the flight will dig into my reserves. This is an unexpected setback.

'OK, I'll have to take it.'

The man asks for our passports and then goes through a series of questions. Once he completes the formalities, a smartly dressed porter shows us to the room. Reuben collapses onto the bed without taking his shoes off. I sit in one of the comfortable chairs and close my eyes, luxuriating in the coolness of the air conditioning.

After twenty minutes, Reuben takes a shower. I leave for the Emirates counter to see what they can do about our missed flight.

I return later and settle down for the rest of the day. Reuben is sleeping soundly. I have no intention of visiting the malls. I turn on the TV and flick through the channels to see what is available. I am spoilt for choice and settle for a documentary.

At 8pm I hear a knock on the door. I open it to find Ann Marie standing there. She smiles alluringly. Her clothing is downright provocative – barely modest enough for the hotel corridor. If it were not for the long dressing gown, hotel security would arrest immediately. She has made up her face to the extreme with mascara, skin cream, and heavy lipstick. Her long chestnut hair hangs loose beyond her shoulders.

'Hi, I'm lonely this evening. Could I spend some time with you?' She smiles and takes a step towards the room.

'No. That won't be possible,' I say, quickly. 'My brother's sleeping. I'm not available.'

'Oh, I'm sure you wouldn't mind if I come in to chat,' she says. 'We'll do our business quietly. We won't wake your brother.' Ann Marie smiles as she forces her way into the room.

I walk straight out to find a hotel member of staff. As I walk up the corridor, I hear Ann Marie from behind me.

'OK, I'm leaving. Don't bother the hotel management. But I won't be sleeping. I'm in room 104. Do come to visit a lonely woman and keep her warm.'

I turn round to see Ann Marie heading up the corridor.

I shudder as I enter my room and close the door firmly behind me. I glue myself to the TV screen as a distraction. I will myself to stay away from that woman, even though Reuben is hardly company, snoring as he lies sprawled on top of the bed, his hair unkempt and clothes scattered around the room.

The next morning, I wake Reuben in plenty of time for the flight. He is ravenously hungry for breakfast and heads for the restaurant. I content myself with a cup of coffee in the room. I don't want to meet Ann Marie.

Reuben returns to the room in good time. He seems to have kept to tea and coffee for liquid refreshment. The colour has returned to his cheeks. The lethargy has gone, though he still looks tired.

At the check-out, Ann Marie stands behind us and pursues us to the gate. I keep my distance.

The flight to London is uneventful. I can't rest. I eat whatever is served and peer out of the window. I am eager to get back to Oxford, but nervous about what I will find. Facing Jordan is my biggest bugbear. I have badly overstayed in Pakistan. Denise complained that the research momentum has slowed and told me that Jordan was incensed. I had been called 'irresponsible', whilst other derogatory language concerning my behaviour my colleagues had banded about was considerably worse.

Reuben has a seat behind me. He seems more settled and from what I can see when I glance around, has only consumed one bottle of spirit during the flight.

Ann Marie walks past and gives a prolonged stare, followed by a nonchalant break of gaze and a little smile. I look away. Whatever her intentions, I'm not playing ball.

At London Heathrow baggage reclaim, Reuben and I wait for my suitcase to appear on the carousel. Heathrow is my least favourite airport. It always seems worn and tired after the polished sophistication of Dubai and other Middle Eastern hubs. The smell of stale curry and fish and chips evokes memories of my childhood around the back of the pub near where we lived – walking home after playing with friends or in the fields, and yearning for the warmth of family and food.

'Are you OK, madam?' I look up to see a man questioning a woman five metres down the belt. She appears to be doubled-up in pain.

'It's that woman who helped us,' Reuben says. 'Something's wrong.'

Reuben walks to where she is standing. I hear fragments of the conversation about a sprain. After a few moments, Reuben appears towing her suitcase behind him, with Ann Marie following.

'Your brother came to my rescue,' Ann Marie says. 'I have trouble with my back. It plays up after long flights.'

'You need a porter,' I say. 'I'll get one for you.'

'I can handle this,' Reuben says. 'The case isn't heavy.'

'Stay here.' I shoot across to the side of the luggage reclaim hall and find a porter. He accompanies me back to where I left Reuben and Ann Marie.

'Here you are. The porter can handle your case.'

'But I don't need a porter,' Ann Marie says. 'I don't have the money to pay him. Your brother is managing fine.'

'Sorry, Reuben isn't available to take your case. The porter will take it.'

Ann Marie glares at me. 'If your brother won't take it, I'll just have to leave it here.' She suddenly walks away from the belt and towards immigration. Reuben takes off to follow.

I reach forward and catch Reuben by the shoulder. 'Don't,' I say. 'You don't know what's in that case. It could be a setup.' I put the suitcase back on the carousel.

As we walk through the Green Channel, a customs

officer stops us. He asks to see my passport and then for me to open my suitcase. He rummages around in the case, watching my expression and body language. He then goes through my and Reuben's hand luggage.

A colleague approaches, beckons him to one side, and talks with him. He then returns to us.

'What is your relationship with an English national called "Ann Marie"? We saw you talking with her in baggage reclaim.'

'Is that the woman's name who wanted help with her baggage?' I ask. 'None, whatsoever. She tried to trap me in Dubai. I resisted. She tried to get my brother here to bring her case through customs, saying that she had sprained her back. I went to get a porter. She was suspicious. I don't know what she was up to, but we kept clear of it.'

'Where did you begin your journey today?' the officer asks.

I explain the circumstances of my trip and then how my brother joined me to visit his uncle in Karachi, showing my official university ID.

He tells us to stay where we are and goes off to speak to colleagues. In the end, an airport police officer returns with him.

'We've analysed the footage of the CCTV and have spoken with the porter. We are satisfied that you had nothing to do with this woman. We may need to contact you in the future. We found drugs in this woman's suitcase. We are trying to trace her.'

Reuben's face turns grey.

'You are free to leave. We have your address. You haven't

changed address since the passports were issued?'

I think of my flat fire. As far as I know, the flat is habitable. I'm not going to say more than I have to.

'No, I'm still at the same address.' I force a smile.

'OK, be careful,' the police officer says.

'Sure.' We exit the airport into the night.

Reuben and I stay a night at Aunt Kate's house. Then Reuben goes back to London and I return to Oxford.

'You're back!' Trixie says. She is waddling down the steps, holding onto the railing as I heave the suitcase towards my flat.

'Yeah. It was an eventful trip. I'll tell you about it someday.'

The new flat door looks good. Inside, I feel the smooth plasterwork. The paintwork is in good condition. I enjoy the smell of the new carpet. The replacement furniture looks fine. The place is in better shape than I anticipated. Trixie has done a great job of supervising the work in my absence. As she said, she had nothing much to fill her days with while waiting for the delivery.

My phone rings.

'You're back!' Denise says. 'I hadn't heard from you for a few days. I presumed you were back in the UK.'

'Yeah,' I say. 'I was waiting until my brother was on the train before getting in contact. He's doing much better than when I last spoke to you. Have you worked on the samples I sent you?'

'Yes. I've been working all hours of the day and night to analyse and assimilate the data. It all points in one direction.

'But Jordan is still upset about your prolonged absence from the lab. You'd better get in here quickly. You have a lot of explaining to do.'

'Did you mention the difficulties I explained to you? I was not to know these things would happen.'

I imagine Denise rolling her eyes. 'Yeah, but Jordan said not to go there in the first place. He's questioning your commitment to the research. As you know, we're behind schedule. He's refused to make decisions that were yours only to make.'

'I'll be there by 3pm – I promise. It'll work out.'

I ease into the laboratory, making sure that I keep out of Jordan's sight. I want to catch up with Denise first. I find her hovering at her desk, ready to take a tea break. She smiles with relief when she sees me. Her long brown hair looks frizzy, and she has bags under her eyes. I wonder how she has been looking after herself. This research is important to her.

She forgets about her tea break and sits at the desk to show me the latest reports on the laptop. It takes an hour to look at all the statistics and check the arguments. The conclusion is there to see. She is buzzing with excitement.

'Denise, you're a gem,' I say. 'When the work is published, I'll take you out for a meal.'

'I should hope so,' she says. 'I'll need a holiday, never mind a good meal. Some of this statistical work has been beyond me. I've had to get Graham's input. He's been really helpful.'

'I see I owe him a pint.'

'Dr Grant. I need to speak with you.'

I look around to see Jordan standing at the door. He is staring at me and frowning. He leads off down the corridor and I follow into his office.

I close the door behind me. I don't even have time to sit before the volcano erupts. 'What? Why? Who? Didn't you think? What are you going to do about it?' Jordan is almost shouting. I try to reverse the rate of decibel increase by talking softly and deliberately.

It is an uncomfortable thirty minutes. I leave with Jordan swigging from his plastic water bottle and wagging his finger at me. I've promised to be one hundred per cent committed until the research project is properly signed off, and to start that very afternoon. I would need to work over the weekend if necessary.

'That was not pretty,' Denise says as I take my place at my computer and try to focus.

'He has his reasons.'

For the next ten days, I live and breathe research. I type, consult, revise, and compare. I send Denise home at 8pm each night. When she spills her coffee due to her shaking hand, I force her to leave at 5pm. I work until midnight, go home for a kip, and then return by 7am the following morning. The unwashed mugs are strewn around the desk perimeter, concealing brown stains where I have forgotten to use a coaster. There is a latent smell of burgers and chips and other fast food, delivered at regular intervals by students on bicycles.

In the end, I press the send button on an email and casually walk down the corridor to Jordan's office.

He looks up at me. 'This is the final manuscript? Are you sure?'

'Yes, I made the corrections you suggested. I had the final feedback from Dr Johannes Denner. I've included all the other revisions.'

Jordan sits back in his swivel chair and looks me squarely in the face. 'You know this is going to be plastered over the internet once it gets out? There will be denials. They will challenge your findings. There could even be threats. I hope you're ready for this.'

I prop myself up at the door frame, my body desperate for rest. I can hardly keep his face in focus. 'I need to get some shut-eye,' I say, and make my way to the bus stop.

I spend the following week working with the editorial team of The Lancet. After initial inertia, the pace quickens. Within three weeks, my research is published.

It causes an almighty stir. As Jordan predicted, it is in every nook and cranny of the web. Online and print papers carry headlines decrying the negligence of the food packaging industry over recent years in allowing such harmful substances in the manufacture. There are discussions and rebuffs. Some call for a ban on plastic altogether to paper-based packaging. A spokesman from the British Plastics Federation puts out a statement. Scaremongers write of gross impotence in the Western world, leading to the collapse of Western civilisation. One man reportedly commits suicide through worry that his children will be infertile after his wife conceives only through IVF treatment. He had a history of mental illness.

I lie low to avoid the press. They are relentless in trying to find me. The BBC interviews me by video. I refuse point blank to appear in person.

The university beefs up security at the laboratories. This is hardly necessary – reporters only want photos. The office receives numerous calls from the press. They also receive a call from a lawyer representing Cranford Plastics wanting to talk to me. Ruby, the secretary, records the call and sends it to me.

The message is terse. Cranford Plastics is initiating proceedings against me for damages. I am unfazed. I checked with the best legal brain I could find in international law that the findings in my research could not be construed as targeting any particular company. The fact that despite warnings, Cranford Plastics had knowingly continued production of packaging that used rogue compounds is undeniable negligence in my book.

Their shares plummet. Their company heads for liquidation.

I think of the business in Karachi. How is the Li family affected by all of this? Claire is back in the UK. Someone else will be picking up the pieces at the office.

My personal story appears in the press. The details are hazy, but enough to paint me in many forms – an ecology activist, a soothsayer, an eccentric philanthropist. I am happy that my share of my late great aunt's estate has been used well. I have no intention of self-promotion.

Three weeks after the phone call from Cranford Plastics, I have a surprise visit from the police. They find me at Aunt

Kate's house. They lose no time in explaining the reason for their visit. Three men, now all in their early twenties, allege I abused them when I was a scout leader in my late teens. They were at a camp in the West Country. They say I cornered them, one by one, in the camp shower block, and committed indecent acts.

The police invite me for an interview at the local station. I hastily contact a lawyer's office.

I meet the lawyer outside the police station on the morning of the interview. He is cheerful and friendly, but professional. We report to the reception, and after a ten-minute wait, a policeman shows us into a room with a police sergeant and officer.

The sergeant explains the accusations in detail. I categorically deny each one. I remember the camp. Yes, I was a leader at the camp. Yes, potentially I could have cornered the boys in the shower block. I point out that like all organisations that work with children, even in those days, they had put precautions in place to make such contact difficult.

The police explain the next steps. The several months ahead of me are going to be difficult. Collecting evidence will take time. Once the police have all the statements, the Crown Prosecution Service will decide whether there is a case.

I speak with the lawyer outside the police building. He reiterates I should contact my former scout leaders and get character witnesses. He will be available as the case develops.

I return to my aunt's home fuming about this attempt at

character assassination. The case will undoubtedly fail. But it is unnerving to know that someone out there is vindictive enough to put me through the mental discomfort of having to prove my innocence.

You've kicked the hornet's nest, you can't complain if you're stung.

I fidget. I can't settle to any task in the house so I go for a walk. I take my phone and call Rachel.

'What are you doing later on?' I ask.

'I'm working late – we have a rush job. I won't be free this evening.'

'Look, I know I haven't been in touch very much in recent weeks, but we could at least meet. How about a stroll towards Sandford Lock for old times' sake?'

'I'll be working until 6:30pm. I'll be tired. I don't want to go out this evening.'

'Well, I could call round to your flat. I won't stay long. I'd just like to see you again.'

Rachel is hesitant.

'I'll come at 8pm. We can talk.'

'We usually argue,' Rachel says. 'Come if you want. But don't stay too long. I've got other things to do tonight.'

Chapter 19

I arrive ten minutes late. Rachel lets me in, looking up and down the corridor – presumably to see if anyone has seen me. I am intrigued.

She offers me a mug of tea and goes off to the kitchen. I follow her.

'Don't follow me around,' she says. 'I'll bring the drinks to the lounge.'

I back out of the kitchen like a dog told to return to its basket and find a chair that is free of hairbrushes and headbands.

Rachel gives me my tea and sinks into the sofa opposite. She cups her hands around the steaming mug of hot chocolate and looks grimly at me.

'Well?' Rachel says.

'It was a difficult time in Pakistan. In fact, a disaster. You were right about the danger. A lot happened in a short time. I'm glad to be back.'

‘Obviously, you’ve finished your research,’ Rachel says. ‘The findings have certainly caused a stir. When did you first have suspicions that there were dangerous plastics out there?’

I explain the history of my interest in the safety of plastic food packaging, starting with my first work as an analyst in the laboratories of the BPF Plastics and Flexible Packaging Group. I leave out some detail. I see Rachel’s interest waning as I talk.

‘And what’s new for you these days?’ I ask.

‘Oh, nothing much,’ Rachel says. ‘In May, while you were in Pakistan, I spent some time on the south coast with my brother. I don’t see him very often. We did a lot of hiking. It was very busy down there – lots of people. Next time I’ll go in a quieter season.

‘So, what’s next for you? More research? Lecturing? You’ve become quite famous.’ Rachel manages a slight smile.

‘I’m not sure. I’m taking time out. To think. The last two years have taken a lot out of me. I could take up another research post. But perhaps there’s something else out there for me.

‘I know my actions haven’t helped,’ I say, cutting to the chase. ‘But I want to know if there is any chance we can rebuild what we once experienced.’

Rachel looks at me studiously. There is a knock on the door.

‘Are you expecting anyone?’ I ask.

She shakes her head. Uncurling her legs from beneath her, she finds her slippers and makes for the door.

I hear muffled voices. One of which I recognise as my brother's, Reuben. I quickly make my way to the door.

'Reuben, whatever brings you here?'

A man says 'goodbye' to Reuben and continues down the steps.

Reuben looks at Rachel. There is silent communication between them. I grow suspicious. The three of us stand there at the front door. Finally, Rachel speaks up.

'Come in, Reuben.'

We all make our way to the lounge. I take my seat again, eyeing Reuben warily. Reuben falters but then takes a seat next to Rachel on the sofa. Rachel holds his hand.

'What's this?'

Rachel begins to speak but Reuben interjects.

'Rachel and I are in a relationship,' he says. 'After you left for Pakistan, Rachel phoned me. She was upset. We spoke. I was concerned for her, so I came to Oxford to see her. We got along well. We started having feelings for each other. We are different and there is an age gap, but there's chemistry. We're seeing where this goes...'

Rachel looks at Reuben lovingly. He looks into her face and smiles. He puts his arm over her shoulder.

I struggle to make sense of it. Their relationship comes across as mother and son, not as lovers. Is Rachel taking advantage of Reuben as a vulnerable adult?

'Were you the one who suggested to Reuben to face off his uncle Neil about the past?' I ask, staring at Rachel in unbelief.

'I didn't suggest it. Reuben shared he wanted to clear up his past. Together, we thought it was the best thing to do.'

I could feel the anger rising in my chest but I keep a lid on it, choking back the venom that so easily could poison our relationship for years.

'I'm surprised,' I say. Rachel and Reuben look at me cautiously. No-one moves.

Rachel lets go of Reuben's hand. 'Steven, what we had was precious,' Rachel says. 'I thought it was right. I thought it would work. But I couldn't cope with the uncertainty… if you would be safe, when you would be back. I screwed myself up with guilt over my possessiveness – I knew it throttled you. Then I realised I'm not the woman you need. You need someone else, Steven. You need a free spirit, someone who can work with your lifestyle.

'As Reuben said, he helped me at a dark time. It was then I could see our relationship wouldn't work. It's best this way, it really is.'

Rachel grasps Reuben's hand again and settles back into the chair.

'I'll go now,' I say. Rachel smiles weakly. Reuben looks away. 'I can let myself out.'

I take a long walk. I feel hurt, yet I know that I, in turn have hurt Rachel. I try to look at the situation objectively, yet there is a gnawing void in my heart that will not listen to reason. I will need to speak to Reuben about the relationship. I doubt Rachel has any ulterior motive, but they need to assess how they relate.

I head for the Turf. Thankfully, no one is there who knows me. I order a pint, sit at a table, and drink. I think again about the allegations that have been made against me. Who's done that? More to the point, do I have any friends left in the world? I drink the dregs of the glass and go to the bar. The rest of the night is a blur.

The following two days, I pull myself together to think through my options. I have to find out who is promoting the abuse claims. The uncertainty is eating away at my soul. My life is on shaky ground. I have to shore up my integrity. The police won't help. I have to get help, even if I have to go to a private investigator.

I scour the internet for a private investigator in Oxford. Having found a number, I pace the floor, trying to decide whether I want to go down this route. My gut feeling is that private investigators are only for the desperate and that it's beneath my dignity to approach such an outfit. I reason with myself – I don't need to commit myself if I feel uncomfortable. There are professional firms out there that meet a legitimate need. After a full ten minutes of indecision, I speak with the receptionist of what looks like the most well-presented and ethical company in Oxford. I am assured – this seems to be a genuine firm that exercises discretion in their enquiries. I make an appointment to visit their office that afternoon.

I walk through the city centre. It is mid-summer. Groups of foreign tourists crowd the pavements, their tour guides jabbering away in their tongue, pointing to the buildings and shops. Locals walk briskly by, the men wearing shorts and the women loose dresses and skirts. A cyclist speeds past me with a fast-food delivery box on a rear pannier.

I enter the reception area of the sandstone building and take a seat. After ten minutes, a junior partner appears and shows me to his small office. I explain the situation. We discuss options. The partner assures me I am not the first person who facing such allegations, has sought their help. After taking the details, he will discuss how to proceed with enquiries with the senior partners, and will then get back to me. I leave their office feeling more optimistic.

The next day I am reading journals on the laptop when a call comes through from the office. A senior lecturer from the University of Warwick has been in touch and wants to discuss my research. Could she meet me in person? The name was Li Chao-xing of the Centre for Mechanochemical Cell Biology.

'Well, I suppose we could meet,' I say. 'It may be more productive to talk over the phone or through the computer first. I can get back to this woman. Did she leave a contact number?'

'No, only an email address,' Ruby says.

'Well, forward the address.'

I hammer out a quick message to Li Chao-xing. A return email comes within two hours. Li Chao-xing is adamant that we should meet in person. She could come any evening and would meet me at a location of my choice. I look at my online diary and suggest an evening the following week. Back comes the reply. 'Could it be sooner?' There is no real reason to delay, so I suggest we meet at 6pm the following evening, at the Thaikhun restaurant, George Street.

The phone rings again. This time, it is the private investigator firm. They have been digging. There is evidence that the alleged victims reported the abuse after receiving money from the USA. The investigator makes it clear that they will not be able to approach the men, but they are trying to find out further details of the funding source.

Thought so. Damn it.

I stand outside the Thaikhun at 6pm. I feel nervous. What is this about? The inside label from the fresh shirt irritates the small of my neck as I look up and down the street for a Chinese-looking woman.

A taxi draws up. The driver puts on his hazard warning lights, gets out, goes to the boot, and hastily lifts out a collapsible wheelchair. He unfolds it next to the passenger door. A woman catches hold of the arm of the chair and manoeuvres into it. She then speeds towards me.

'Hello, Steven.'

'Good evening, Rita.'

As the words leave my lips, I freeze. Intense emotion surges through my body. Fight or flight? I steel myself to remain. Right woman, I'm giving you a brief opportunity to explain, professor or no professor. It had better be good.

She looks up at me. A cautious smile breaks out across her narrow face, accentuating her high cheekbones. Her hair is now straight and luxuriant, neatly trimmed to shoulder length. 'Shall we go in?'

I do not manage a smile but indicate consent with a nod of my head and follow behind the wheelchair.

A waiter quickly spots Rita in the wheelchair and assists

with holding the door open. Rita easily navigates the obstacles to the table I reserved.

I fight off a sense of revulsion. Here is a woman who has been part of a plan to corner me about a past misdemeanour at the risk of my life. What is her motive for meeting me? Is she up to other tricks? I eye her suspiciously as I pick up the menu to order pre-food drinks. Rita only wants water. I order a Magners Cider. The drinks quickly arrive.

'Am I talking to Li Chao-xing?' I ask, looking at her sternly.

'Yes, you are. That's my Chinese name I use for official business at university.'

I continue the conversation coldly but professionally.

'I never knew you were a lecturer. How did you end up at the University of Warwick?'

'After Michael Haw College, I went to the University of Southampton to study bio-medical science,' Rita says. 'I did a Masters and then worked as a research analyst. I worked on my Ph.D at the university of Warwick and stayed there.

'I'm really interested in your research about the effects of plastic absorption – that is genuine.'

As Rita looks down at the menu, I can see the physical likeness to her sister, Esther – the confident poise, the delicacy of her facial features, the petite nose. I shudder.

'But you are not here just to discuss my research,' I say.

Rita puts down the menu card. 'No, I'm here to apologise.' She looks at me intently. 'I'm here to clear my family's name of shame. My sister and I mistreated you. I believe your intentions towards Esther were honourable. I should not have participated in the plan to confront you. Your friend was killed and you barely escaped. I should have put the incident at Michael Haw College behind me. But I really wanted to see you again.' Rita looked at me coyly.

'But you could have arranged to see me without joining Esther in luring us into danger. Your and your sister's scheme led to the death of an innocent man.'

'Yes. But Esther deceived me. When she wrote to me before I left for Pakistan, she mentioned you. I soon realised you were the same Steven Grant that I knew from my college days. She knew about the prank that went wrong and the suffering it caused me. She suggested I go with her to confront you about the incident. I had hoped to see you privately. She didn't speak of the gravity of the meeting.'

'Well, when we met in that house, your demeanour didn't seem too friendly,' I say. 'Why didn't you speak up against what Esther and Younis had planned and try to stop them?'

'I did. They said they would warn you and let you go. She wanted me to confront you with your thoughtlessness. She said once that was done, they would release you. Esther promised.'

'Well, the promise wasn't honoured, was it?'

I'm not sure what to think. My memory of Rita in the house is of someone whose only motive was to get a confession, not of someone desperate to meet for the sake of friendship.

'And what about your parents? Were they part of the scheme to trap me? They lost out when my uncle's business failed. Your father was a director, wasn't he?'

Rita tenses, her brow lowering and her chin set firm as she counters the accusation. 'No, my parents didn't orchestrate the kidnapping or the scheme to get rid of you. They were happy you were getting to know Esther.

'So, pecuniary interest was not a factor in all of this?'

Rita swears. She's really angry now. 'You are insinuating my father had less than honourable motives? I won't listen to such shameful crap. It was a difficult time for my parents. I believe my father's prime intention was to see Esther settled with a good suitor. Your uncle was putting pressure on him to manipulate your interest to get you to back off on the research, but my father was trying to stave him off.'

'OK, let's park that for the moment,' I say, just to move on from the awkward discussion. 'We are at a different point now.'

I rein in the emotions and start further conversation, though the atmosphere remains frosty.

'So, how are your parents doing now?'

'My father and mother have taken Esther's betrayal of the family hard. They are shamed. It has affected their health. My father works long hours. He's found other work to increase his income.

'My mother has not been sleeping well and has anxiety problems. They wanted me to see you, to explain how sorry we are about Esther's mistreatment of you.'

The waiter comes to take the order.

I will myself to exercise chivalry and say quietly, 'The meal is on me. This is my home city and you're a guest.'

Rita looks admiringly at me. We both order.

‘Is there any hope that Esther will return to the family?’

‘I don’t think so,’ Rita says. ‘My parents have done all they can to get through to her. She is fixated on this crook. They left Pakistan some time ago due to the criminal charge against them. We don’t know where they are.’

‘But you plan to stay here in the UK?’

‘Yes, I’ve made a life here. I have friends among the faculty at the university. My flat is kitted out for me. I enjoy the work most of the time.’

‘And you?’

‘I’m thinking about what to do next. I haven’t come to any decisions yet. I’m working through some personal issues. There is time.’

‘Your research publication caused a stir,’ Rita says, changing the subject. ‘It was good science. I’m glad you published, despite the difficulties it caused. It will help to ensure the future of *homo sapiens* on this earth if they can continue to be fertile.’ It was Rita’s turn to experience increased capillary blood flow in the cheeks as she looks at me shyly.

Six months later

Rita and I continue to meet. I’m not sure that it’s ‘dating’. We enjoy professional discussions. I’m warming to her as a person. She is courageous and resourceful. She seems to want emotional involvement. I’m taking it very slowly.

Reuben and Rachel are still close. I was wrong to suspect

Rachel's motives. She has been a power of good to him. He's got a job and is happy. Whether he moves to Oxford or Rachel moves to his location remains to be seen. They've spoken about marriage – Mum is chuffed.

The Public Prosecutor dismissed the case against me. I produced scores of letters testifying to my good character. My scout leaders were especially helpful. I haven't heard anything from the alleged victims.

The private investigators never discovered who had greased the palms of these men to make the accusations in the first place. I have my suspicions.

These days I restrict my international travel. A lot is happening in my life locally. I'm tempted to settle, but I'm wary of the dangers. Life is too short to hunker down. The events in Pakistan piqued my interest in Asia – its culture, customs and languages.

I started communication with Rita's parents. At first, I found it difficult to give Mr Li the benefit of the doubt, but I'm learning to trust him. I have invitations to visit. Rita wants to go soon. I'll apply for annual leave later in the year. China is also on the horizon.

Chapter 20

Rita

We're at Hickory's restaurant, Burton Green. Steven is grumpy. It's a small thing. Whether one of my students, Max, can stay with him for a few days next week. Max is in Oxford for business. But Steven's busy during that time. He's getting used to a new job. He doesn't have time to entertain.

'Entertain? You don't need to entertain,' I tell him. 'Just make your spare room available. Show him where you keep the tea, coffee, cereals, and bread. Point him to a reasonable restaurant for the evening meal. He's not expecting Airbnb.'

Steven sits back in his chair and throws his head back. He picks up his glass and stares into it, then bangs it down on the table in mock anger. A small smile appears. He reaches over and grasps my hand. He admits to over-reacting. Yes, Max can stay.

I took a risk contacting Steven those months ago.

Admittedly, I was sneaky. I crept under the radar. I feared a violent outburst. I just wanted Steven to hear me out. He did. It was hard going. But we got there.

I left the initiative to Steven. I'm not the belle of Warwick academia. He's connected with many of my colleagues and is a frequent visitor. The job he has just started came from one of these contacts with sources in Oxford.

It's not easy going out with a woman in a wheelchair, and a woman of a very different culture. Steven's had to find accessible ramps in venues; rescue me from being trapped by narrow, spring doors, even in the women's toilet; shout at pedestrians absorbed in their phone on a collision course with the wheelchair; deal with blisters on my hand when the battery died, and I had to propel the wheelchair from the car park up a steep ramp to a concert venue.

Steven is in for a surprise. After much deliberation, we have booked a flight to Karachi to see my folks. What he doesn't know is that my parents and I are taking him north, back to Chitral. Tension and loss marred his previous visit. I hope this visit can help him come to terms with the events of the past and rediscover the beauty of this land, its peoples and customs. It will also be a gesture of appreciation to people like Dr Irfan and the Kalash men and women who provided those samples. A dangerous plastic has been taken off the market. The world is a better place.

I hope you have enjoyed reading this novel. Please consider posting a review on amazon.co.uk
by searching for the book by name and then by signing into your Amazon account. This would be most appreciated. Thanks. Paul

Milton Keynes UK
Ingram Content Group UK Ltd.
UKHW041023070923
428145UK00003B/68